LOVE TO
HATE YOU

Damned if I don't
Damned if I know

AS ELIZABETH STEVENS
NEW ADULT/ADULT BOOKS
Grace Grayson Security
Chaos & the Geek
Hawk & the Lady
O Lord & the Queen
Rollie & the Rocker
Tank & the Rebel

Loving the Sykes
Caden
Carter
Luther
Oscar
Ashton

MATURE YA/NEW ADULT BOOKS
the Trouble with Hate is…
Gray's Blade
Being Not Good
Popped
the Art of Breaking Up

Accidentally Perfect Books
Accidentally Perfect
Perfectly Accidental

LOVE TO HATE YOU

ELIZABETH STEVENS WRITING AS

PIPPA LANGHORN

Kinky Siren
An imprint of Sleeping Dragon Books

Love to Hate You
by Pippa Langhorn

Print ISBN: **978-1925928297**
Digital ISBN: 978-1925928280

Cover art by: Izzie Duffield

Worldwide Electronic & Digital Rights
Worldwide English Language Print Rights

To second chances,
In romance. With friends. For genres.

♥

Contents

Author's Note

I've taken a few liberties with the setting of this book. Chester University and its associated Chester University Senior College is, to my knowledge, an utterly fictional scenario. It is based on combining two things; my vague understanding of the US college system, and the school I went to for my final year which was a Year 11 and 12 high school run at one of Adelaide's universities that acted as a bridge between high school and uni. I have set Chester University up so it works for what I wanted to do with the plot and am hoping you can suspend any potential disbelief at the cover and join me on what has been one of my favourite books to date.

Love to Hate You is a standalone new adult, high school/university/college romance. It features (fr)enemies-to-lovers vibes, and an ex's teammate who is also a best friend's little sister. It's full of alphaholes with secret hearts of gold, sassy women who won't take their shit, awesome friendships, sibling rivalry, bed sharing for no purpose other than annoying each other, a Seven Minutes of Heaven self-fulfilling prophecy, and a whole lot of forbidden steam.

As a warning, River suffers from significant childhood trauma and subsequently lives with mental illness. As a coping mechanism, he often acts sarcastic and shallow, and he frequently self-medicates with alcohol and makes some questionable life choices, most of which occur off page but are talked about by the characters. As these things come to light in the course of the novel, there are some frank discussions surrounding it. Given the general tone of the story, I have tried to keep these brief and purely plot-driving/resolving. However, I wanted all readers to be forewarned and forearmed.

There is swearing and drinking within the pages of this book, as well as sexual content. All characters in this story are engaging in legal activity to the best of my knowledge according to the laws governing the state of South Australia at the time of writing.

Please be aware that this story is set in South Australia and therefore is written using Australian English. This will affect the spelling, grammar and syntax you may be used to. It might come across as typos, awkward sentences, poor grammar, or missed/wrong words. In the majority of cases (I won't claim it's infallible, despite all best efforts), this is intentional and just an Aussie way of speaking (it took my US beta readers a bit to get used to). I can't say 'the' Aussie way, since we seem to differ even within the same state. Just think of us as a weird mix of British and US vernacular and colloquialisms, but with our own randomness thrown in. I still hope you enjoy it, though!

♡1♡
Skye

As I hurried across the quad, I checked the time on the great big clock on the Lincoln Building.

"Shit. Five minutes late," I muttered to myself, gripping my books tighter, prepared to run if I had to. And I was going to have to.

All around me was the bustle of Chester University. Students lounging, playing, relaxing, waltzing carefree to their next class or the café or library, enjoying the rare bit of sun at the beginning of Winter or, like me, desperately trying to make it to their next class on time and wishing they hadn't picked subjects that were on the opposite ends of the campus.

Then something hit me in the back of the head, my arms opened so they could catch me if I fell, my books dropped to the pavement, and I managed to catch myself from tumbling forwards. I closed my eyes and tilted my face to the sun to pray for patience.

It was Friday. Just a few more classes until I could pretend that I was going to take a break for the weekend. In my defence, I did have a *small* break planned. I had an actual date and I'd promised my older brother that I'd make an appearance at his party for a few minutes. All that should take me a few hours, then I could get my essay finished.

But to get to that, I had to collect my books off the ground, find a paracetamol or two for my burgeoning headache, and make it through Richard's English Literary Studies lecture and following tute.

I heard familiar laughter as someone jogged up behind me, and I was in even more desperate need of that patience.

"I called 'heads'. Didn't you hear me?" the familiar voice asked.

I picked up my last book and turned to find him checking out where my arse had been moments before. He was in a baggy green tank top and grey track pants with grass-stained trainers. His patented cocky smirk travelled up my body to meet my eyes as he tucked the offending soccer ball under his arm. I kept one eye on it. Just because he was holding it didn't mean it wasn't going to hit me in the head again.

"Gaol-bait," he said with a nod.

"Pond Scum," I replied with a nod of my own, figuring the deployment of one insulting nickname deserved another. "Don't you have classes to get to?"

"Unlike you, mine are optional."

I rolled my eyes. "Yours aren't optional," I reminded him. "You just don't have to be *in* the lecture theatre."

He shrugged. "Same difference. That's what little children get."

Ugh. I wanted to thump him.

Yes, strictly speaking, I was still in high school, and he was at university. Big freaking whoop.

Chester University ran a pre-entry program for Year 11 and 12 students as Chester University Senior College. We lived, half-boarding school/half-college dorm style, in the Chester township about an hour out of Adelaide and took our classes on the university campus. As minors, we were given a very long leash.

However, given that every student who passed through the CUSC doors had to be unreasonably excellent in a chosen field – academia, sports, music, arts – we weren't what our parents considered normal teenagers, and were somehow therefore more trustworthy? Honestly, you'd have thought that parents had forgotten what it was like to be in your late teens. Still, as a student of CUSC, I would have automatic entrance to the course of my choice at Chester University proper. As long as I continued getting a Distinction average or higher.

"Aren't you late?" he asked, his eyes leaving my chest for long enough to look at the Lincoln clock.

"Yeah. No thanks to you. Richard's going to give me hell."

He snorted. "You've got Richard now? Fucking luck, then."

"Why don't you just go and dick over yet another girl?" I snapped at him.

His eyes sparkled nothing good but everything enticing. "Offering?"

I gave him my most withering glare. It had been known to scare even Taylor, my older brother who, as a soccer goalie, was used to throwing himself behind fast-paced balls and hoping he didn't bleed. Unfortunately, my impressive glare didn't have the same effect on said older brother's best friend.

"You're so cute when you're angry," he teased and actually booped me on the nose.

I spluttered and swatted his hand away. "I will *bite* that the next time it comes close enough, River," I warned him, my voice dropping dangerously low.

He took a step towards me. "In my dreams, Gaol-bait." He gnashed his teeth playfully and gave me a wink.

Okay. So what if River Torres was over six foot of taut muscles, unnecessary tattoos, gorgeous pale brown hair, mesmerising chocolate brown eyes, and a mischievously sinful smirk that I'm sure had literally melted the pants off someone at least once? He was a grad-A hole. Arrogant. Conceited. Superior. Condescending. And only one new girl a night was considered pathetic.

Shame then that Taylor had adopted him as his best friend something like seven years earlier and River was, therefore, a permanent and annoying fixture in my life.

"So cute," he chuckled as he shrugged his shoulders and wrinkled his nose, then tossed his ball in the air and turned back to whoever he was playing with.

I paused for just a moment longer. The threat of Richard's apathetic reprimand wasn't even enough to stop me waiting to watch the way River's arse moved under his shorts as he kicked the ball back to the others hovering on the grass. River was a jerk, but his arse was the stuff of legends in the halls of Chester University. So was his cock apparently, but thinking about that was veering into the danger zone.

Putting all of River's anatomy firmly out of my head, I ran to class and tried to slink into the room undetected. I failed.

"Ah, Miss Devereux," Richard drawled.

Let it not be said that the man didn't love to use embarrassment as a form of punishment and deterrent.

"The class was just speculating whether you had been struck immobile by some horrendous ailment," he continued, and my cheeks heated horribly.

Despite my firm belief that I was a strong modern woman, Richard had the unfailing ability to make anyone feel small. River could laugh all he wanted, but I knew for a fact that Richard had almost made him cry once.

"Sorry, Richard," I said as I found a seat at the back and tried to make myself as invisible as possible.

Richard nodded. "Let it be the last time this semester, Miss Devereux. Academia is but a siren call to those who refuse to strive for greatness."

There would be zero point reminding him that I was the top student in his class. A grade I fought hard not only to get but to keep. Richard didn't care that I hadn't been on a third date in my whole life. He didn't care that I had a better relationship with a guy I despised than I did with any of the guys I'd hooked up with in the last two years. None of the lecturers did. As long as we got the grades or won the games, they didn't care how we did it.

And all of us coped in different ways.

I pretended to have a healthy and active dating life.

Taylor lived, ate and breathed soccer, night and day.

My best friend Tansy mainlined coffee and made her way through sport teams.

River was somehow still enrolled despite a near-daily two-bottles-of-whiskey hangover. Or lack thereof.

Chester University was competitive and a cesspool of terrible habits and expectations, but it was the best school in the country and opened doors that very few other places in the world could open.

Richard thankfully took his focus off me and went on with the class. I pulled my laptop out of my bag and my chat with Tansy was the first thing that popped up.

Tansy Ho-Silver-Away
I've just come up with the
best hypothetical!

                    Sky'mDevestated
                    Looking forward to it.
                    I'm going to need it after
                    Pond Scum made me late.

          Tansy Ho-Silver-Away
          Something you need to tell
          me? ;-p
I rolled my eyes.

                    Sky'mDevestated
                    When will you believe I'll
                    never sleep with him?

          Tansy Ho-Silver-Away
          When you're dead.

                    Sky'mDevestated
                    You have a very long wait
                    ahead of you.

          Tansy Ho-Silver-Away
          You hope.

                    Sky'mDevestated
                    Morbid much?

Another message interrupted us.

          Riv.Torn
          Did you get detention?

                    Sky'mDevestated
                    Get out of my DMs.

          Riv.Torn
          Once   I'm   in,   Gaol-bait,
          there's no getting me out.
          sexy winking GIF
How had he managed to find a GIF that looked so much like
him when he winked like that? Ugh.

I ignored any reply from Tansy and closed my chats. The last thing I needed was River getting me in trouble while I was in class. So Tansy had to wait to tell me her hypothetical until we were sitting on our little couch in our apartment that afternoon, catching up before my date.

"Okay, you're doing seven minutes in heaven–" she started.

"How old am I?" I teased, opening one eye.

Tansy smirked. "Shut up. It's my hypothetical. Seven minutes in heaven." She looked at me pointedly and I dutifully closed my eyes again. "Good. Now. It's dark. You're both blindfolded–"

"Oo, kinky," I laughed.

"Shut up and just enjoy. You don't know him. He doesn't know you. He is hands down the best kiss of your life. Toes curling. Stomach fluttering. Clit throbbing. It's the kind of kiss to leave you weak in the knees and begging to know his name. Then, the lights go on and it's…River Torres! What do you do?"

I felt myself smile, then realised who the hell she was talking about and slammed down a frown. I opened my eyes and mouth to protest, but she was grinning like the cat that ate all the cream.

"Aha!" she cried victoriously.

"No," I told her firmly. "No. That's not fair! You can't tell me he was the best kiss of my life then claim it means something when it turns out to be Senor Pond Scum."

"I can, did, and do," she laughed.

I grabbed my tea off the coffee table. "Shut up," I grumbled.

"Just admit you've thought about it once," she begged, as though it would be the first time we'd had a very similar conversation.

I levelled a glare on her. "Of course, I've thought about it. More than once. He's a freaking Adonis. He's sinfully delicious, wickedly cocky, and pushes every single one of my buttons. Good and bad."

"So, remind me why you haven't scaled that man mountain?"

I rolled my eyes. "I'm not about to give him the satisfaction of even guessing he has any effect on me whatsoever."

Which was ridiculous because River and I both knew we had an effect on each other, but denial was a beautiful thing.

She nodded knowingly. "No. Much better that the two of you hate each other."

I nodded in agreement. "Much better."

"The way you two fight, you just know the sex would be off the charts."

I did know that. At least, I suspected it. It wasn't like my life was lacking in good sex, but there was this…vibe between River and I that made me know, with absolute certainty, that any sex we had wouldn't just be great, it would be phenomenal.

"The point is moot," I reminded her.

She rolled her eyes. "Hate sex is better than regular sex."

I looked at her because she knew that wasn't the reason River and I would never be more than enemies without benefits.

Tansy huffed and sat back against the couch. "He's still fucking you over."

That was also not the reason. There were many reasons. Of which the ones she'd mentioned were but two.

I shrugged. "He never fucked me over," I disagreed. "It was mutual."

She rolled her eyes, and I knew any sort of championing my ex was going to get us nowhere. Tansy had never really liked Jax, for no other reason than he wasn't River and it was my best friend's firm belief that River and I were written in the stars. We weren't, and no amount of me reminding her we hated each other was going to change her mind.

"Jackson Gerralt can die in a fire for all I care," she huffed.

I smiled. "He's not that bad."

"He took one look at you and ensured that you'd never have a chance with another player."

"So?" I shrugged. "I'm not the one who wants a whole set before graduation."

Tansy slunk back on our couch and sighed. "And I was so close with the lacrosse team."

"Clearly they don't suffer from the bro code."

Tansy smirked. "Their code doesn't apply as long as you keep it casual."

I smiled at the audacity of this fabulous bitch. "You are incorrigible."

"I just think it's fun to sleep with guys a *little* more physically active than the chess team."

"I take exception to that. It's not all about muscles."

"Yeah? Remind your libido of that next time it's fantasising about River."

Which it would do now. Vividly. "Thanks, Tanz," I said sardonically.

She gave me a cheerful grin. "You're welcome. Now, when's Mr Grand Master 2038 picking you up?"

"About an hour. From the Chasers' Mansion."

"Do you need to…like shower and shit?" she asked, hinting maybe I did need to do just that.

I threw back the rest of my tea and stood up. "I'll see you at the McMansion about nine?" I said and she nodded.

"I'll be there with bells on."

I didn't doubt it. "Just promise you'll be wearing something else as well."

She gave me a grin and shrugged. "I make no such promises."

I snorted and went to get ready for my date. It wasn't all that taxing. I didn't agonise over my outfit. I very nearly didn't shave, but I was a little prickly and didn't like being felt up over my stubble.

The benefit to being what River liked to call 'Miss Future Librarian' was that, when a guy asked me out, I was never looking my best. I *was* in a bra, but more than likely in a slouchy cardigan and my ugg boots. So, who was I trying to impress by dressing up for a date? If they were interested in me enough to ask me out in my natural state, then I wasn't going to waste time on crafting an image that would be impossible to maintain if I did ever get to that third date, or further. I liked dressing up as much as the next person, but I was also very lazy.

Once I was somewhat more presentable than usual, I headed over to my brother's place.

Where Tansy and I lived in what was generously described as a two-bedroom apartment, my brother and the rest of the Chester University Chasers – the multi-trophy-winning soccer team – lived US college frat-style in a McMansion with something like twenty bedrooms. Most of them had their own rooms, their kitchen was massive and had three fridges, and the whole place was designed for fun, frolicking and deflowering.

As I walked up to the front door, it wasn't the first time I wished I could be on the soccer team and live there. But then I wouldn't live with Tansy and that wasn't really what I wanted. Besides, I could live with Tanz *and* be treated like I lived in the Chasers' Mansion anyway. Best of both worlds.

"Mini Dev in the house!" Hank called to the place at large when he opened the door and saw me there.

"Hank." I nodded to him as I walked into the hallway.

Taylor and I were Devereuxs. This led to him being called Devo or Dev in the same way Australians had been shortening people's names for forever. This also made me, in the eyes of the soccer team, Mini Dev or Little Dev. I was apparently the unofficial team mascot and, because of the infamy of the team, I was known the uni over. It had upsides and downsides.

"Hey, what are you doing here?" Taylor asked as he jogged down the stairs.

I followed him into the kitchen. "My date's picking me up from here."

He looked back at me as he started opening a carton of beer and piling them into an esky.

Tansy said Taylor was hot. I was going to have to defer to her opinion on the matter.

Taylor and I both had the same dark blue eyes and dark blond hair that we got from our parents. Like me, he wasn't the tallest person alive, but he was still taller than me. He took more after Dad. I took more after Mum. He was cheeky and a whole butt load of trouble, but I loved him all the same. Without him, I wouldn't have survived the years our parents spent trying to find whatever we could excel in that would secure our place in the hallowed halls of Chester. For him, that was soccer. For me, it was being enough above average in everything without being truly brilliant at anything that I just scraped an offer of admission. Our whole lives, Taylor and I been as close as the almost three years between us allowed.

"Remind me why you're having your date meet you here?" Taylor said as he wrenched open the fridge.

"Oh, has Devo's wittle bitty sister got a date?" River teased as he walked in, and I frowned at him. "How's your head?"

"Fine. Thanks. And like you know what a date even is," I told him, and he stuck his tongue out at me.

"Good. And one can grasp the concept without feeling the

need to experience it."

"Is this the same rule you apply to your manners, or…?" I left the sentence hanging.

"Do not make me put you in your corners," Taylor warned, stepping physically between us.

"She started it," River protested.

"He's older," I argued. "By definition he started it."

"Naw, I couldn't get started without you, Gaol-bait," River said, saccharin sweet with an accompanying wink.

"Oh, my god," Taylor muttered. "I've turned into my parents." Then he levelled a look on both of us in turn. "I don't care who started it, I'm ending it."

River snorted at my brother's attempt at authority. "Yeah, all right, Mr Devereux."

Taylor nodded at him, then looked to me again. "So why is your date meeting you here?"

I pulled myself up onto the bench and sighed. "Because any guy who's brave enough to knock on the doors of the Chasers' Mansion is well worthy of my time."

Taylor scoffed. "I'm not going all big brother intimidation on him."

"That's fine," I told him honestly.

I didn't need Taylor to actually intimidate or threaten any guy who asked me out. His existence – in fact, the existence of the whole soccer team – and the reminder of said existences, was plenty. They were an unavoidable and annoying part of my life and anyone who couldn't deal with that had no place in it.

"If you ask nicely, *I* will," River offered with a heavy sigh, like it was hardship.

"And exactly what do you call 'asking nicely'?" Taylor laughed as he walked out, presumably on his way to do something party-related.

River stepped up between my legs, dripping raw sexuality. He planted his hands on either side of my legs. "You willing to beg for it?" he purred.

Look, I'm not proud of my reaction, but I thought about it. I thought about begging for it. 'It' of course not being him going all big brother on my date but taking me up to his room and showing me what all the fuss was about.

Tansy's hypothetical was all up in my head and my brain was trying very hard to convince me it was actually a memory that we were in desperate need to relive. Right there on the Chasers' kitchen bench if needs be.

Before I did something seriously stupid, I lifted my foot and put it on his chest to push him back, being careful at least not to spear him with my heel. But I was under no delusions; he only moved because he let me push him away.

River's amused half-smirk lit his eyes as his hand went to my ankle. He slid his hand around to the back of my leg and cupped my lower calf. As he slid his hand up my calf, and my leg bent to let him step closer, a shiver ran through me, and my clit throbbed. I cursed the fact that my body gave zero bothers that I hated him. I could at least be comforted in the knowledge that his body was just as traitorous when it came to me.

"Goal-bait," he groaned huskily, almost like a prayer.

I smirked. "Pond Scum?"

"Skye, your gentleman caller is here," Taylor said as he headed back in.

I pushed against River again and he took the obliging steps away from me with a very large dollop of teasing mischief in his eyes. He scrubbed a hand over his chin and turned to my brother.

"Right, let's meet the dweeb," he said, clapping then rubbing his hands together.

Taylor threw a look to me. "Did you actually beg him?"

I rolled my eyes as I pushed off the bench. "Of course not. But what else is he supposed to do while he waits for his harem to turn up?"

Taylor laughed. "Harem. Funny."

"Don't pretend you don't have your own," I said, and he chuckled and dodged as I tried to hit him.

"What? I'm not pretending anything."

Annoying but unsurprisingly, they both followed me to the front door.

Grant, my date, was hovering just inside the door, looking around nervously. I didn't blame him. Like, half the team had assembled to see me off. Gossip spread through that McMansion faster than it had at my old all-girls school.

Hank, Lachy and Whistler were lined up on the stairs.

Frankie D, Robbie, Blake and Tim were leaning against the banister on the first-floor landing.

Forbsy had just walked in from the games room with Ajax.

And Taylor and River were at my back.

"Uh, Skye," Grant said with an uncertain smile.

By comparison, I could see why plenty of people would be confused as to why I was going out with Grant instead of one of the guys in the room.

Eleven of the guys in the room were in tees and tanks that moulded to their muscles. They had tattoos peeking out of their clothes. Those who weren't yet dressed for the party – like River – were in shorts and trackies that left absolutely *nothing* to the imagination in the crotch department. They stood tall, with a butt load of arrogance and self-assured confidence.

Grant was tall and lanky. He wore a dark olive-green button

up shirt with a navy and brown argyle sweater, and pale chinos. His curly hair was the very definition of not styled, still with the fuzz of the newly washed. As we all stood staring at him, he pushed his dark-rimmed glasses further up his nose and blinked quickly.

But none of that was unattractive to me. Sure, he was missing nearly all the rippling contours of the soccer teams' perfect bodies, but there was something very important to be said for geek chic. Nerd cute. And all-around willingness to please in more way than just my pants. Plus, there was a benefit to dating a guy who looked good but didn't spend hours a day on sculpting his body; it meant he paid more attention to mine.

Or, at least, that was what I told myself in aid of resisting the likes of River Torres and anyone remotely like him.

"Grant. Thanks for meeting me here," I told him as I walked over to him.

I shouldn't have, but I totally exaggerated my hips as I walked away from River. When I snuck a look back at him, he had most definitely been paying attention and he had most definitely enjoyed it.

"Her curfew's at two," Taylor said, dropping his voice in a hilarious mimicry of our dad's deep tone. "No drinking. No drugs. And no hanky panky."

"No, of course," Grant stammered, and I tried not to smile at Taylor.

"Don't feed her after midnight and don't get her wet," Taylor continued.

"I'm not a fucking gremlin," I muttered as I rolled my eyes. "Right, we're going."

"You'll pull by later?" Taylor asked and I nodded.

"Yeah, sometime." I shrugged.

I took Grant's hand and led him out of the house.

"Oh, and no sex after midnight!" River called after us. "Her vag grows teeth and will never let you go!"

I heard Grant splutter in surprise, and I turned back to throw some death stare at River. He gave me a cheeky little wave, then Forbsy distracted him with something else as Taylor closed the door behind us.

As far as dates went, it could have been worse.

On the other hand, it also could have been better.

Grant had always seemed so animated in class. Passionate. Enthusiastic. I was looking forward to the same level of fervour on our date. I'd – in hindsight, very naively – thought we'd debate the finer points of Richard's latest lectures, get super horny from our mutual geek out, and have a perfectly satisfying quickie before I had to show my face at Taylor's party.

In reality, all I could think about was how close River had been to between my legs, the way he'd looked into my eyes as he ran his hand up the back of my naked leg, and Tansy's assurance that he was the best kiss of my life.

I knew it was all bullshit and frivolous and there was a perfectly good, decent and sexy guy in front of me who deserved my undivided attention…but he wasn't really doing anything to make me want to give it to him. So, when Tansy messaged to say she was heading to the McMansion, I used it as an excuse to say a prompt goodnight to Grant and went to meet her.

I walked in to hear, "Chug! Chug! Chug!" being shouted over the thumping music and, no surprises, found River in the middle of a drinking competition with Forbsy.

They both had bottles of something rather stronger than beer and, also unsurprisingly, River's bottle was only a quarter full to Forbsy's maybe half. I would bet that both bottles had been full when the competition started.

River drained the last of his bottle and pumped it in the air. He caught my eye across the room and there was that hint of something darker in him as he dragged his arm, of the hand holding the bottle, across his mouth.

He hid it as well as a guy, who partied as hard as a serious university soccer career would let him, could but there had always been something dark in River. It only showed occasionally, and only in the depths of his eyes or when a creeper was harassing me or Tansy. It hovered behind the propriety of looking out for his best mate's little sister, and I'd often wondered if he pretended to care about me as an excuse to let it out.

I gave River a nod. Whatever he thought it meant, he nodded back. Then someone was congratulating him on Forbsy's sudden inability to stand by himself and River was back to his usual piss-taking self.

Leaving him to whatever nonsense he would next get up to, I started my hunt for Tansy.

The Chasers' Mansion was big enough when the only people in it were me and the soccer team. Somehow, it felt even bigger when it was full of mostly-drunk people all shouting greetings to 'Mini Dev!'. Tansy could be anywhere and with anyone. I'd seen quite a few of the lacrosse players already, but couldn't for the life of me remember which ones she'd slept with or not. She'd told me about each one in technicolour detail, of course, but that didn't mean I could recognise them by sight.

Oh, except for the big guy with the rose tattoo. He was *very* memorable. He gave me an odd look at the unbidden smile that blossomed on my face at the memory of Tansy's debrief, and I hurried on my way before he came to see if I was interested.

After what felt like forever, but was probably only about half an hour, I finally saw Tansy on the other side of the games room, at the wet bar, drinks in hand. She saw me and made her way to me through the throng.

"They're fighting in the other room," she said as she passed me a beer.

I nodded. "River?"

"How did you know?"

"You ask this like I haven't known him for years."

Tansy nodded. "Yeah, I guess. Some guy took a swing at him. I assume he felt obliged to swing back."

Of course, he had. "River probably slept with his girlfriend," I said.

"Are you not in the least bit worried?"

"Why should I be?"

"Because he's your brother's best friend."

"He's also an arse and deserves every punch he gets."

"Yeah," I heard Taylor's amused voice as he appeared beside me. "Except the other guy hasn't landed a single hit."

Either the challenger was *very* drunk, or River was surpassing even his usual abilities. Feigning disinterest, I followed Tansy and Taylor back to the other room and saw a circle had formed around the two fighters. Although, 'fighters' was perhaps a generous descriptor.

River was goading on the guy, who was clearly livid about something that River no doubt fully brought upon himself. River looked as in his element as he did on a soccer pitch, with his fists up in front of his provocative smirk.

"Come on, Riv!" Taylor laughed.

River's eyes flitted to my brother in amusement, but then they alighted on me standing next to him. I couldn't read on River's face what might have been going through his head, but he seemed to pause, and it was just the opportunity his challenger needed to land a solid hit to River's cheek. River took it like he hadn't even felt it and it was more annoyance than anything else.

There went that darkness again in his eyes. His jaw set. His face more sneer than smirk. And his eyes. So cold and distant and angry.

Like it had been all my fault, River frowned at me and clearly decided it was time to stop playing with his challenger. River threw his fist at the other guy, who stumbled back and fell onto his arse. He shook his head like he was trying to clear it of cartooned birdies, and it was pretty obvious he was done with trying to get one over River.

"River!" some girl squealed, pushing me out of her way to run at him.

"Hit and run, officer," Tansy muttered to me, and I huffed a laugh.

The random girl launched herself quite literally at River and he caught her easily. She clamped her legs around his waist, and his hands were tight on her arse. She wrapped her arms around his neck as she kissed him.

A chorus of, "River, River, River!" proceeded an answering cry of "Oi, oi, oi!" in the traditional Aussie chant, accompanied by cheering and laughter. Meanwhile, Hank and Taylor were dealing with the guy on the floor.

River's lips didn't leave hers, but he threw both his fists into the air in victory. The girl in question was holding onto him so tightly, she was in no danger of sliding off him.

"Really gives meaning to the term 'clinger'," Tansy commented dryly.

I snickered and shrugged as I pulled my eyes off River. "A week of dishes says he's in the bathroom with a different girl in five minutes."

"Five minutes?" Tansy scoffed.

I nodded. "Five minutes."

"Fine. I'll call that bet. I obviously have more faith in him than you."

I huffed as I put my beer bottle to my lips. "Clearly."

Three minutes later, Tansy was conceding defeat as River dragged a different girl past us and into the downstairs bathroom. Yes, his room was upstairs, but none of his countless girls had ever set foot over the threshold.

"I should really stop betting against you," Tansy admitted mournfully.

"I know River better than he knows himself," I told her ruefully.

♥2♥
River

The Chasers had a code. It had been that way since long before the current formation and had better stay that damned way until long after I'm dead or I was going fuck someone up.

The code was the only reason I hadn't given in to the raging insane heat that lingered and teased between me and Skye-fucking-Devereux.

In the last year.

There was the slight issue that she was three years younger than me. Which had honestly felt pretty irrelevant since she'd started at Chester the year earlier, and was only going to be an excuse for another week anyway when she turned eighteen and there was no grey area in which to err on the side of caution.

There was the fact she hated me, and I didn't exactly love her. Not that I'd found that to be a hindrance to amazing sex before. As far as the Chasers knew, Skye was relatively innocent – relative to us, that is – but I had no doubts that she'd rock my damned world.

She was witty. She was so smart. She was sexy. She didn't put up with my crap. She called me out when I was being a dick – which was most of the time. She went after everything she wanted in life. She was unashamedly only herself, and what a phenomenal self it was. And she had no problems intimidating me. Or trying. She was a walking wet dream and got me hard just thinking about her, to say nothing of the effect she had on me whenever I saw her.

Which meant all I had to hold onto, to keep me from doing something unbelievably stupid, was the Chasers fucking code.

I loved Taylor Devereux like he was my own brother. But then, if he had been my actual brother, maybe I wouldn't have lusted after his sister quite as much as I did. Regardless of that, I still wanted Skye.

Even knowing I was the worst kind of shit, terrible for her in every way and incapable of being a guy she deserved, I still wanted her. Badly.

But the code was clear; you didn't touch a teammate's ex. Casual hook-up exchanges were fine but, if a Chaser had properly dated them, then they were no-go. No ifs, buts, or maybes. And Skye had dated Jax for a good four months the year before.

The penalties for breaking that code were even clearer; you go the next month of practices in nothing but a G-string and cleats, as well as forfeit game time for the rest of the season. And if that wasn't bad enough, you were stuck cleaning the whole McMansion for three months.

So, there were some pretty hefty consequences for giving into the way she made me feel. The rock-hard predicament was made even harder because I knew she wanted me as much as I wanted her. I'd go so far as to say she wanted me almost as much as she hated me. And I was very proud to say that she didn't hate anyone the way she hated me. Tension sizzled to a crisp between us in every discussion, insult, or argument.

Did that mean I didn't go out of my way to annoy her at every possible moment? Of course not. I lived to annoy Skye nearly as much as I lived to make sure Taylor kept his spot at Chester University; something I risked if I forfeited my game time for the rest of the season.

Which is why I could be found lying on the couch in her apartment, playing on my phone as I waited for her to get back from classes.

The Chester Uni Senior College kids had dorms closest to the main buildings proper and what classified as the uni proper. The buildings were just for CUSC students, and they rented their places for a two-year lease. The individual apartments came in one- to six-bedroom places, with a kitchenette and enough room for a small table and a living space.

Compared to the Chasers' Mansion, it was fucking tiny. Their whole apartment was barely bigger than my bedroom, but Skye and Tansy had made the place damned cosy. And there was something nice about not having like twenty-odd guys under the same roof. Not that I would ever risk even thinking either of those things outside the relative safety of my head.

The doors used codes rather than keys for locks and Tansy had very kindly given me the code to their door. I liked to use it as often as possible to aid in annoying Skye. I had to think there was a part of her that didn't actually mind because she hadn't changed the code on me yet.

"He can have me however he wants me as long as he fucks me hard," I heard, and I was sure my brain had spasmed or something.

"What?" I sat up and looked at her over the back of the couch.

As usual, she was temptation walking, even with her satchel and two shopping bags. Skinny jeans and ugg boots, a baggy jumper under a chunky, mid-calf-length puffer jacket, and the big, warm scarf Tansy had made when she spent that semester thinking she'd take up crochet. I could barely see the outline of

Skye's body, but I didn't need it. Her body was gorgeous and I'd committed it to memory, but it was the quirkiness of her mind and that flash of sass in her eyes that made her dangerously close to irresistible.

She saw me and those dazzling blue eyes widened.

Was it worry? Shock? Horror I'd not only heard her swear, but heard evidence that the good little future librarian was maybe not as good as we thought she was?

Please say it was true.

"Shit," Skye muttered. "Tanz, I'll talk to you later." She dropped her phone from her ear and forced a glared for me. "What are you doing on my couch, Pond Scum?"

"Finding out Little Miss Perfect has a dirty streak apparently." I bounced my eyebrows at her cheekily.

She rolled her eyes as she dropped her satchel by the kitchenette. "You don't need to be on my couch to discover that. And I'm not Little Miss Perfect."

"You are. What *do* I need to do, then?"

She shrugged as she took her shopping to the bench. "You've already uncovered the mystery, so you don't have to do anything else."

"Okay, but say I wanted to find out more of your secrets…" I pressed.

"*Had* I any secrets that you'd be even vaguely interested in, you'd have to be far less full of your own self-importance."

"I'd have agreed with you, but then I heard you say you like to get it hard." She was getting me hard just thinking about it. She got me hard just by existing, but hearing she liked it hard had me straining in my jeans. I took the opportunity to rearrange.

She was trying not to smile at me, but I saw it in her eyes before she turned away and busied herself in the fridge. "What's the matter, River? You have trouble with getting it hard?”

I had to pay that. “Touché,” I said as I jumped over the back of the couch to see what deliciousness she was putting in the freezer. “But,” I said as I reached over her and took the new box of ice creams back out, “erectile dysfunction is the least of my issues.” I took one out and offered her the box.

Goddamn, but I loved it when she was exasperated with me. It was only one reason that I annoyed her as often as possible.

After nabbing the box back from me, she stuck it in the freezer and closed the door. “No, any excuse to pop a pill, huh?”

I less loved the fact she could read me like one of those books she so loved burying her nose in. Well, maybe not quite. Of all my demons, she hadn’t even considered the most damning. The truth I’d nearly managed to bury in my past wasn’t something she’d ever even think of. I guess I had to be lucky for small mercies. But she saw my addictions for what they were. I had to give her kudos for having the balls to call me out on them.

“I prefer to self-medicate with liquids,” I admitted as I opened my pilfered ice cream and pointed it at her, “but I’m sure a pill would work just as well.”

She wasn’t impressed and I didn’t need her to be. “Still doesn’t explain what you’re doing on my couch.”

“It’s Thursday.”

“So?”

“Thursday’s when you get the good ice creams,” I said through an obnoxious mouthful of said ice cream.

“Pretending that we do have the same taste in ice cream, you’re not here for ice cream.”

“Taylor’s busy. I’m bored.”

She snorted as she went to the couch. “And all your booty calls are busy?”

"I'm offended, Gaol-bait," I said as I sat beside her. "To even imply you'd be the last person on my Boredom Busting list."

Her laugh was like fucking rainbows, and I loved it. "You have a Boredom Busting list?"

"It beats calling it a little black book. Feels so…nineties."

"Be honest for once and just admit I'm the last person you want to be hanging out with."

It'd be a lie, but… "Fine. Yes. I am scraping the dregs of the barrel to lower myself to hanging out with my best mate's nerdy little sister."

"There. Was that so hard?"

I rearranged my crotch. "Soft as."

She smacked me as she failed to hide a laugh. "So gross."

I grinned as I finished the ice cream. For some reason, her favourite was good-old savings brand vanilla ice cream on a stick covered in a chocolate shell. It was good, don't get me wrong, but there were so many better ice creams available.

"So?" she started.

"So?" I asked.

"Did you have any expectations beyond stealing ice creams and being in the way?"

I laced my fingers behind my head and put my feet up on the coffee table. "Nah. I honestly didn't think I'd achieve both my goals quite so quickly. Genuinely don't know what to do with myself now."

She spluttered a laugh, and I joined her with a warm smile. When we weren't arguing or insulting each other, which was ninety percent of the time, things were unbelievably easy with her. We'd spent three years with me at their house as often as her parents would allow without me actually moving in, and then another three of having to double annoy each other during holidays when she and Taylor spent every second they could together. The last year and a half we'd had the freedom and ability to just walk into each other's homes with a very different vibe than there had been before Taylor and I left for Chester.

Chester had changed everything. It didn't just mean I was working my way out of the shitty life I'd left behind the day my father went to gaol. But it also forced us to grow up faster than we would have had we just gone to one of the unis in Adelaide like most of the people we knew. Which meant that, by the time Skye had walked through the portal into Chester's basically gated community, neither she nor I were quite so naive and innocent as we'd been the last time we'd seen each other on a daily basis.

Skye had taken to life at Chester better than anyone I knew. She'd grown and blossomed into an even more competent young woman with a tonne of confidence, an excess of sass, and she'd just excelled at managing her studies without any real parental supervision.

I made no secret of the fact that I thought she was a nerd. The girl spent more time in the library than the whole soccer team put together. Which wasn't hard. Every member of a sport team at Chester was there for sport reasons and our GPA requirements were lower than the academics. Just. But, if us sports' students could pass the entrance exam, then we could keep our grades up with little effort.

"What time's your game this week?" Skye asked as we both sat and stared out the window overlooking one of the lawns leading to the main uni buildings.

I looked at my watch like that held any answers. "About two. Why? You got plans?"

She scoffed. "Of course." She shook her head. "No. Taylor just didn't tell me."

"You can find it out on the website," I reminded her.

She nodded. "Yeah. Or one of you idiots could let me know. It costs nothing but a couple of seconds of your time. Surely you have a couple of seconds in your week to make sure the unofficial mascot is at your games?"

I snorted, but she wasn't wrong.

Since she'd found out that she was the Chaser's unofficial mascot – more meaning that we would all go to war for her even when it wasn't strictly necessary – she'd taken her duties very seriously. Every game, she was dressed up head to toe in Chaser's merchandise, complete with banners and pennants and flags. Her and Tansy travelled in the bus with us to away games and took Taylor's designated room when there was a sleepover while he bunked with me. And they stood in every stand screaming their lungs out.

Skye wasn't just infamous at Chester Uni, but every soccer team in the competition knew who she was. I wasn't afraid to admit that I'd hit more than a couple of guys who'd said some less than respectful things about her. If any other soccer player was going to touch her, it was going to be me. And it couldn't be me, so it wouldn't be any of them.

"Okay," I said, pulling my head out of the many dangerous paths that train of thought could take me. "I promise I'll text you every week."

She frowned at me. "I can just nipple cripple Taylor until he no longer forgets."

"Is this about me being in your DMs?" I asked cheekily.

"This is about you being in my DMs," she agreed. "You don't need to be in there."

I leant towards her and whispered in her ear. "Where would you rather me…in?"

Fuck, but that was a bad idea. She smelled fantastic. She always did. Any time I vaguely caught a trace of it, my heart did this weird thing in my chest, my stomach bottomed out, and I imagined for a moment a future where everything was perfect.

She smelled like books and that perfume she'd used since she was fifteen. It was something like orange, rose and vanilla. I'd stolen a bottle once – not my finest moment. I'd read the label then hidden it at the back of my closet, and been so freaked out that someone would find it that I'd left it there.

She turned to look at me and I saw in her eyes the exact same way I was feeling. Heated desire. Craven need. Little bit of annoyance. Mostly just amused teasing.

Skye leant towards me, with her hand on my chest and I wondered where in the hell she managed to get her restraint because I needed some almost as much as I needed her. "I don't need you anywhere, Pond Scum."

I shouldn't have done it, but I trailed my fingers softly up her thigh as I reached over her to her other ear. Her leg lifted to almost hug me and I gripped her hip tightly. I felt her hand on my chest close around my tee. But was she holding me in place or trying not to pull me closer?

"Need and want are two very different things, Gaol-bait," I reminded her, not even that bothered by the breathiness in my voice.

She leant into my body, our heads over each other's shoulder. If anyone were to walk in, they definitely would have got the total wrong idea about us. I wondered what her dorky date from the week before would think about that, but she distracted me from asking by replying.

"I want you, River…" she practically moaned, her lips brushing my ear, "…to stop stealing my ice creams," she finished before pushing away from me and fixing me with a teasing half-smile.

Jesus fucking Christ.

Skye was going to be the death of me. Of all the condemnable things I'd done in my life, it was going to be her. She was going to kill me. I had no doubts that not having her was almost as good as actually having her would be.

"That's not a promise I can make you," I said easily.

"Can't or won't?"

I shrugged. "Either. Both."

She sighed as she got up. "Fine, but you owe me."

"What's your price?"

"Nothing you want to pay," she sassed.

I grinned. "You don't know that. Maybe I've got a dirty streak, too." And I winked.

She tried and failed to hide a chuckle. "I am one hundred percent certain you do."

"So how do you know I won't want to pay?"

"Because it won't be sexual."

"Well, that's no fun."

She nodded. "That's the point."

"Sorry," we both heard Tansy say absently as she opened the door. "That guy with the hands..." She paused like she was thinking. "Whatever-his-name-is bumped into me in the library and– Fuck! River, what are you doing here?"

"Learning more about the sex life of apartment 3D than I ever dreamed of."

Tansy looked to Skye in question, and Skye just rolled her eyes in answer.

"He's just being River," was Skye's verbal answer.

Tansy smiled. "Oh, well, that's all right, then."

I huffed an amused laugh at her relief. "Why? Did you think I was a ravaging her raw on your couch?"

"In all our dreams," Tansy said, looking at Skye pointedly.

I watched their interaction with interest.

Skye frowned at Tansy, but not in her usual 'oh my god, get over me and River' kind of way. There was something else there. Something new. Something I was very interested in knowing more about. They seemed to be having a conversation in nothing but facial twitches. Tansy kicked her head to me. Skye's eyebrows rose. Tansy's eyebrows jumped a couple of times as she grinned widely. Skye's mouth rippled. Tansy pouted. And Skye rolled her eyes.

"Not happening," Skye muttered, then she picked up her satchel and walked out.

"Care to clue me in?" I asked Tansy.

Her smirk was arrogantly knowing as she shook her head. "Nope."

I nodded. "Figures," I sighed as I stood up. "I guess that's the end of that round."

Tansy nodded. "I guess so."

"Catch you later, Tanz."

"Later, Riv."

As I pulled open the door, Tansy gifted me with a, "Just keep being you and I'm sure you'll find out."

I turned my head back to look at her and had to catch my lip in my teeth to stop myself looking so fucking desperate. It's not like Tansy didn't know how desperate I was for her roommate – I knew they talked about me, even if Skye denied it on a regular basis – but knowing it and seeing me like it were two very different things.

I gave her a nod of thanks and made my way out.

Later that night, I saw Skye walking past my door.

"Oi, Gaol-bait!" I called.

She paused and retraced her steps to poke her head in the door. Her eyes travelled to my naked torso, lingering satisfactorily. I flexed my pecs, and she rolled her eyes before they rose to my face again.

"What do you want?" she asked.

I kicked my head to indicate she come in. She did, helping herself to sitting on my bed expectantly, with her legs crossed. Despite the only thing I'd ever used that bed for was sleeping, it was huge, and she looked right at home on it.

I held up two of my shirts. "Which one makes me more fuckable?"

"Neither," she told me simply.

I flexed my pecs again and she noticed. "Should I just go *au natural*?" I teased.

She leant forward. "I think you should go with less manwhore," she suggested.

"You only say that because you haven't benefitted from my experience and expertise."

She scoffed. "I say that as a self-respecting member of my sex."

I snorted. "You said sex."

She was trying not to laugh. "You're so juvenile."

"Says the minor."

She rolled her eyes. "I can vote in a week," she protested.

"Figures that would be what excites you," I laughed. "Not being legal for the armed services or drinking…" I leant towards her, "or fucking." I winked.

She smirked. "Age of consent is seventeen here, Pond Scum."

Fuck. *Do not remind me.*

She was in my room. On my bed. Looking utterly kissable, lickable, fuckable, and like she belonged there. The last thing I needed to remember was that she wasn't as off-limits as she used to be.

Too many scenarios played out in my head of the many ways we could hook up from here. The ways I could get her on her back with me over her. Getting her on top of me. The options were limitless, and none of them were allowed.

"And yet, you're more concerned with voting," I answered. "Now help me out. Which shirt?"

"What does it matter? How long are you planning to be in it?" She leant back on her hands, and I shouldn't have liked the view as much as I did. But she knew I would.

I smirked at her with all the cockiness I possessed. "I don't waste time getting anything off that doesn't have to come off."

"I'll bet," she sighed as she uncurled herself from my bed and stood up. "Wear the black one. It clings more and is much sexier."

"Naw, you think I'm sexy in it?"

She headed for the door. "You know you're sexy in it, River."

"Yeah. But *you* think I'm sexy in it."

She looked at me and I saw her trying not to smile. "We both know you're sexy in anything. You're probably sexier in nothing. It doesn't matter what I think."

"On the contrary. It is very important to me what you think of me."

"You know what I think of you."

"Pretend I'm stupid," I begged.

"I'm not convinced you're not."

She turned to go, and I caught her hand. She looked back at it, then at me and I watched her eyebrow rise in question.

"Tell me more," I pled.

There was a smile in her eyes as she walked towards me, her hand still in mine.

"You're an idiot," she purred sexily. "You're obnoxious." She walked her fingers up my naked chest. "You have no morals and are one of the most annoying people I know."

I groaned appreciatively as my hands went to her hips. "I love it when you talk dirty to me, Gaol-bait."

The corner of her lip tipped in a wry smirk as she stepped closer to me. "You're the bane of my existence, River," she whispered as her fingers reached my chin and she reached up like she was going to kiss me.

Her lips were so damned close to mine. I just had to drop my head a single centimetre and I'd be kissing her. But the code was the code and, for all our flirtatious insults, I couldn't be sure she wanted me enough to overcome just how much she hated me. Teasing fighting was one thing, kissing her was another.

Had she bridged the gap, I wouldn't have hesitated. If she gave me any excuse and certainty it was what she wanted, the code and everything that meant could get fucked. But until that time…I would maintain some self-control.

"And you're the bane of mine," I told her with a cheeky smirk. God, if only she knew just how true that was, though.

She huffed a laugh and pushed against my chest. Part of me knew it was an excuse to touch me again because she could just as easily move away as me. She'd been the one who'd invaded my space after all. But I stepped back anyway.

"So, the black one's gonna get me laid quicker?" I clarified.

She shrugged. "Since when do you listen to me?"

"Dude," I heard Forbsy's chuckle. "There's a girl in your room!"

I grinned at him, then pretended I was shocked. "Wait! Skye's a girl?" I put my hands on my cheeks and dropped my mouth in a big 'O'.

Forbsy laughed and Skye just looked at me like I was an idiot.

"Sorry," she said sarcastically. "I forgot there were no girls allowed in Chez Torres. I'll leave my girl-card at the door next time."

"No one wants that, Gaol-bait," I told her honestly.

"Naw," she teased. "You gonna break all your rules for me, Pond Scum?"

Forbsy snorted like that was the most ridiculous concept in the world and of course I wouldn't, and I shot him a glare.

Skye nodded like that was all the answer she needed. "Yeah. Didn't think so," she huffed and walked out.

"Skye!" I glared harder at Forbsy like it was his fault she'd walked out of my room.

"What?" he asked with a shrug.

"Just…" I sighed. "Never mind."

I scrubbed a hand over my chin and considered running after her, but what in the hell would I say? What could I do? She didn't want to hear anything I had to say to her, and I couldn't tell her anything I actually wanted to. Nothing could happen between us without messing with a mountain of shit.

"You watch yourself," Forbsy joked. "Or you'll give a whole new meaning to being a Chaser."

I frowned at him. "And how's it going with Tansy?" I shot back at him.

"Low blow, dude," he said with a shake of his head before he walked out.

I knew it was a low blow. But I was nothing if not good at lashing out at those who didn't deserve it. I grabbed the bottle off my desk and took a large swing of whiskey before putting it down again. As though it was some penance or something, I pulled on the blue shirt and pushed up my sleeves.

"You nearly ready, Ken?" Taylor laughed as he appeared in my door.

"All sorted, Barbie," I replied. "Where's your sister?"

Taylor shrugged. "Dunno. Why? You piss her off again?"

"Mate," I laughed. "I piss her off just breathing."

Taylor grinned. "Better than anyone she's met. Let's go. I heard a few of the basketball cheerleaders were going to be there tonight."

I smiled. "Oh, noice."

No cheerleader would ever be Skye Devereux, but she'd be enough to distract me for one more night.

♡ **3** ♡
Skye

Stupid. God. Damned. Tansy.

All I could think about was her idiotic hypothetical. I'd got far too close to River the week before and actually contemplated something as ridiculous as kissing him.

Kissing him was one of those things that I'd put on my bucket list out of morbid curiosity. Was he as good as everyone said? What would it be like? Was my gut instinct right that our chemistry would be electric? Purely scientific, of course. I had no physical requirement to find out. It was all a mental exercise.

Yeah, right.

I could lie to anyone out loud, but lying to myself was dumb.

I wanted River, pure and simple. For nothing more than one night of no-holds-barred gratuitous pleasure, naturally. But I still wanted to give him a go.

Except there wasn't a chance in hell I'd ever be in a situation where I could give him a go without him making a big deal of it meaning something. Without it changing everything, not just for us but the people around us.

Was I thinking about that when I got dressed to meet the guys at the Mad Kitty, the uni bar at Chester, for my first ever legal drinks on my eighteenth birthday? Maybe. Either way, I walked out of there in a simple little black dress, with a cropped, chunky grey knit sweater over the top. I paired it with my black boots and a cross body bag under my sweater for my phone and incidentals.

The closer we got to the Mad Kitty, the more excited I was. Which was ridiculous because it wasn't like it was the first time I'd ever been to a bar and had one – or more – drinks. But, somehow, actually being legal now made it ten times more exciting.

"ID?" the bouncer said, and I showed him my driver's licence very proudly, complete with dicky excited grin. He just gave me a nod, showing I could go on in. "Happy birthday," he said, his voice sounding as dead as his bored eyes looked.

Tansy and I laughed and made our way in to find Taylor and River.

The Mad Kitty was packed, as one would expect on a Friday night.

"Drinks?" Tansy asked in my ear, and I nodded.

We made our way to the bar, nodding hellos to people as we passed. If anyone thought it was weird that I smiled back and even waved to a couple of them, then they didn't seem to dwell on it.

"Two beers, please!" I said, grinning widely.

"ID?" the guy behind the bar said, and I showed him my licence in the exact same dicky way I'd shown the bouncer. Except he grinned. "Happy birthday…" His eyes darted to my ID again. "Skye. First round's on me." Then he winked and moved away to serve the next person.

"Um, your birthday is awesome!" Tansy cried.

I leant over the bar and had a proper perve on the barman. As he went about his work, he threw me a side look and his lips rose in a cheeky smirk. I mean, yeah, I liked what I saw, and he clearly felt the same. In that, yes, he was interested in me, but I got the feeling he was more interested in himself. Or, at least, me being interested in him.

As if it was possible, the guy screamed even more narcissistic than River.

I shook my head as I picked up our drinks. "Nah, pass."

Tansy shrugged. "Guess we get Riv alone then."

I spluttered into my beer and frowned at her. She gave me an innocent bat of her eyelids and I couldn't help smiling at her. "Shut up," I told her as she laughed.

As we enjoyed my first legal drink in a bar, we sat on the stools and people watched. Most people we knew by sight, if not by acquaintance. There were kids from our classes, from Taylor's and River's classes, sport players, musicians, artists, scientists, all majors were accounted for.

River and Taylor were already dancing with a couple of girls in barely-there outfits. My eyes didn't linger on Taylor. I had no interest in watching my brother get groped on the dancefloor. Which is the excuse I told myself for staring at River.

As River danced with the girl, his eyes found me, and his lips curved in a wicked smirk. He whispered something to her, and I expected to watch him pull her to the bathroom. Instead, he left her there and came over to me.

"What are you doing?" I asked him, leaning up to his ear so he could hear me over the music. "I think you broke her heart."

His hand went to my waist as he stepped closer. "Better hers than yours. You can't dance by yourself on your birthday."

"Who said I was planning to dance?"

"You always dance."

"Are you asking me to dance?" I sassed him.

"Insisting," was his vehement reply.

With his eyes on mine, his hand trailed over my skin until he found my hand, like he knew exactly where to find it, like he knew my body better than me. As our fingers entwined, his cheeky smirk grew, and he tugged me gently. My eyebrow rose in question, and he inclined his head encouragingly.

"For the love of God!" Tansy yelled over the music and shoved against me.

I slipped off the stool and River stepped forward to catch my body against his.

Everything in me was fluttering and there was a decided heat zinging between us that I would never be able to ignore, no matter what I tried to tell myself. River ducked his face to press a lingering kiss to my cheek, then stepped back and turned to drag me onto the dance floor. Wanting to see where this was going, I let him lead. I'd heard it was typical practice when dancing and, since I was sure he'd had far more experience than me, I figured I'd let him utilise that experience.

River found a spot he seemed to like and pulled me to him. He touched his forehead to mine as his hands went to my waist and mine went around his shoulders as our bodies swayed together. His smile was warm in his eyes, and he looked at me with actual affection. I had to say that the feeling was mutual, really. Much like a brother, I had to admit I did love River. I just didn't really *like* him all that often.

"How do you make a sweater sexy?" he purred in my ear, and I laughed.

"It's cropped," was my argument.

His arm slid around my back to pull me closer, and we were practically rubbing together right there in the middle of everyone. "It's still a knitted sweater, my future librarian."

"Any complaints about the dress?" I asked and I felt his smile against the side of my head.

"Oh, that wasn't a complaint," he said, and I heard the humour in his voice. "I'm legitimately confused how you make anything sexy."

"Maybe it's not the clothes, River," I suggested. "Maybe it's the person in them."

He held me tightly. "I have no doubt."

I didn't know what to say to that and the music seemed to rise in volume which made talking difficult, so we just danced. Although, dance was a generous description of our movements. Dry humping might have been closer to the truth. I lost track of the number of songs but, eventually, a slower one came on and we simultaneously parted and decided it was time for drinks.

Although, River's idea of drinks was shots. Taylor and Tansy were totally on board.

After a couple of rounds, I watched as River grabbed the microphone, climbed up on the bar, and raised his shot glass. "To it finally being legal to fantasise about your best friend's sister," he cried, throwing me a wink.

"Oi!" Taylor laughed and shoved his leg companionably.

"To Skye!" everyone shouted before throwing back their drinks.

Taylor and River, who'd jumped unnecessarily effortlessly off the bar and given the mic back, squeezed their way over to me and Tansy. Taylor was carrying far too many shots than any four people should ever get through.

"I know this is legal now," I told them over the music, "but I don't think that makes it sensible."

Taylor shrugged. "More for Riv, then."

I put my hand over River's as he reached for one, and our eyes caught. Tansy's little seven minutes in heaven scenario was playing in my head at the look in his eyes. I very nearly believed that we could manage seven minutes in heaven. I could get my taste and it didn't have to change anything. But I also knew that was the previous round of shots talking. So, clearly, another round would put me to rights.

River's eyes were full of mischief and mayhem as he looked at me over the current shots. To match his eyes, he wore a cheeky smirk. It was a dare. I could see where this was heading, but I still didn't stop it.

Sure enough, soon the drinks had devolved into Truth or Shots. Basically, it was Never Have I Ever but you get asked a question instead. If you refused, you took a shot. If you got caught out in a lie, you did a dare. A mature and sensible, adult kind of game.

"Okay!" Taylor said. "This one's for Riv. How many times have you tragically spanked it to my sister?"

"Dude, I can't count that high and you know it," River laughed.

"Ballpark," Tansy pressed with a smirk.

River shrugged. "Once a week for…three years?" he guessed. "Round up to the nearest hundred for a few extras. What's that?"

"Two hundred," Tansy said immediately. That's a STEM major for you.

I spluttered my drink. "What?"

River shrugged again like it was nothing. "What, what? Skye same question."

"How many times have I spanked it to myself?" I sassed.

River leant forward with a sexy grin. "To me. Obviously."

I played coy. "I don't know. Maybe three."

"That is a bold-face lie, madam!" Tansy outed me.

"Excuse me?" I cried. "Traitor!"

"I don't make the rules," she reminded me.

I huffed and took a drink for good measure.

"Right, I dare you…" Taylor said slowly, looking around.

Before he could decide, River jumped in. "My question, my dare," he reminded us. "I dare you to go into the bathroom, remove your panties, and bring them back here."

Now I leant towards him. "And who says I'm wearing any?"

He smirked. "Take the dare, Gaol-bait."

So I did. Five minutes later, I put my black lace briefs on the table and River gave me a nod of surprised approval. He actually didn't think I'd do it.

The drunker we got, the more ridiculous the questions and the more lies we told. Tansy dared Taylor to pretend he was dancing on a stripper pole. Taylor dared River to crank call their assistant coach or their captain, Ajax (River chose the coach as the less scary option). River dared Taylor to kiss Tansy, as long as Tansy agreed – the alternative was for Taylor to kiss River. And I dared Tansy to sing 'Supercalifragilisticexpialidocious' on the karaoke machine, knowing full well that she'd just end up stringing together swear words. We'd been kicked out of the uni bar at closing time and had retired with a couple of bottles to Tansy and my apartment.

"River," I said after my next turn. "Tell us the real reason you won't be tied down by a girl."

For a moment, there was a flash of something hard in his eyes, then it was replaced by his usual easy cockiness. "There's just so much I can give to the world. It would be unfair to keep it all just for one person."

Even Taylor snorted. "Dare this bitch."

Was this my chance? It was like the fates had aligned to give it to me. I had the power to dare River to do anything. Conveniently, *I* was anything and there was a hypothetical that was just begging to be made real.

I pinned River's eyes with mine. I felt totally calm despite knowing what I was about to do was utter lunacy. "Seven Minutes in Heaven. With me."

I'd been prepared for a lot of reactions, but an unblinking, "Done," as he stood up and held his hand out for mine wasn't one of them. "Where?"

"In her room," Tansy told him, not missing a beat.

Sounded fine to me. I took River's hand and started pulling him to my room.

"Standard rules, I assume?" River asked.

"Of course," I replied casually, internally panicking that there might have actually been standard rules, and dear God what rules had I played by?

"Be nice!" Taylor called, clearly drunk enough to see this for the harmless nonsense it was.

"I'll be a perfect gentleman," River assured him.

"I was talking to Skye," Taylor chuckled, and I smiled.

I took a step into my room, then River wasted absolutely no time. He used my body to close my door and his hands were hot against the skin of my hips.

"I haven't started timing yet!" Tansy yelled in objection.

River's eyebrows jumped suggestively. "More time for me, then."

He pressed his body into mine as one hand went to cup my jaw. I didn't have time to be nervous that I was finally going to live, in real life, the fantasy that had been playing out in my head on repeat since Tansy had given me the damned hypothetical, and for years before that to be honest, because River's lips were on mine.

He tasted like smooth, rich whiskey – his drink of choice – and something sweet. He felt like perfection. Hard and soft in all the right places as he utterly claimed me. He kissed me like there was nowhere in the whole world he'd rather be, and no one else in the whole world he wanted to be locked in an embrace with. He kissed me with fire and passion and a mutual want that it felt like no one else could sate for either of us.

It was probably a good thing he was holding me up against the door. His touch heated my whole body, but his kiss knocked the wind out of me. My heart fluttered wildly and, as Tansy had predicted, my clit throbbed. My stomach bottomed out and I felt a desperate need to wrap my legs around him. My arms wound around his neck instead, as his hand blazed a white-hot trail up my side.

I had never been so turned on, so quickly, from just a kiss. But then, how many guys had I kissed with something like three years of bantering foreplay?

Our kiss deepened and I felt him groan against me. He dropped his hands to my arse and picked me up effortlessly. My skirt rode up and his fingers slid further up my skin, reminding us both I was still naked under there.

I felt him smile. "I forgot about that dare," he murmured, spinning us so he could place me on my conveniently heighted chest of drawers, knocking the books I'd had there onto the floor.

My hand ran over the huge bulge in his jeans as my knees clamped around his waist. As he pinched a nipple through my shirt and bra, I took his lip in my teeth and moaned his name, pulling him closer with my leg.

His erection rubbed against me in far too tantalising a way, and I felt my knee grip him harder. He slid his hand from my knee down my thigh and held onto my hip firmly. My hands slid up his body, memorising every ridge and contour, over his shoulders and into his hair. It was softer than I'd expected as I ran my fingers through it.

River's hands roamed my body with a delicious pressure that made my nipples tighten and my skin break out in goosebumps. His lips didn't leave mine as he coaxed my leg higher around his waist and pressed against me closer. His zip rubbed me, and a moaned sigh escaped me as our breaths mingled.

That seemed to unlock something in him as a new fervour gripped us. Our bodies moved together as our kiss was hard and fast and deep. Our arms wrapped around each other tightly like we knew that our time was limited.

And I did know our time was limited. I'd dared him to do this, and he'd thrown everything into it, but I knew this was it. This was our chance.

Even ignoring his friendship with my brother, and the fact that we had never been in a room together and not argued about even the smallest nonsense, the Chasers' code wouldn't let him touch me again. That he was touching me now spoke volumes about this until-now unresolved tension between us.

But Jesus. How was I supposed to go about my life now I knew – not just guessed or assumed or believed the rumours – how good he felt? How good we felt together.

"And that's seven minutes!" Tansy called as there was a thump on the door.

River grunted in annoyance and leant his forehead to mine. "Jesus, Gaol-bait. Where has that kiss been all my life?"

"I'm eighteen, River. I'm not gaol-bait anymore."

He smirked. "No…" he mused. "I'll have to find a new name for you now."

"You could always use my *actual* name," I suggested with a smile.

He finally pushed away from me, and I was glad I wasn't the only one who seemed reluctant for him to do so. "Nah, I couldn't do that. Far too familiar."

"You done, or you going for round two?" Taylor shouted teasingly.

River pulled the door open with a shit-eating grin. "Mate, you trying to say something about my stamina?" he asked as he walked out.

"Or lack thereof," my brother answered.

I took a breath and slid off my drawers. My legs were embarrassingly shaky for a second.

"You good?" Tansy asked with a laugh, and I looked up to see her in the doorway.

I nodded. "I don't know what kind of school he went to before Chester, but *that* is not how we played Seven Minutes in Heaven at my old school."

"Good, then?" she teased.

I nodded. "Um. So good."

Just thinking about it had my heart beating way too quickly, like a flight of butterflies had taken home in there. My lips were hot and there was a rawness to my face from his stubble that felt nothing short of amazing and totally worth it.

My brain was suddenly imagining how that stubble would feel against my inner thigh while he…

"Okay!" I said loudly as I pulled my head from that dangerous fantasy. "And I'm good."

"You sure?" she asked.

I nodded, feigning a coolness she would have seen right through. "Yeah. Totally."

We went back out to find Taylor and River back on the couch and looking for a soccer game, no doubt, on the TV. They were laughing and chatting like absolutely nothing happened. But, when River looked at me, I saw the heat in his eyes and the stark reality of the situation hit me.

What was supposed to have been a joke, an excuse to harmlessly get a taste of him to tick off my bucket list, was obviously not quite as innocuous after all. All I could think about was what might have happened if he hadn't opened the door. What if Tansy and Taylor had been distracted and forgotten about us? What if we found ourselves locked in another room together?

All I could think about was how soon could we do it again?

And, by the look in his eyes, he was wondering the exact same thing.

♥**4**♥
River

I woke up the next morning and my body hated me.

Why had I slept in a chair?

I actually groaned in resistance as I tried to sit up properly, and I heard a soft laugh. Recognising it instantly, my eyes flew to look for her. She was sitting at their kitchen table, sipping a cup of tea as she read a book, looking totally hangover-free.

"Clearly, I did a terrible job last night," I said, careful not to wake Taylor as I got up and went over to her.

Like we shared one brain, we both seemed to freeze and look each other over. Something was niggling at me, and it didn't take me long to remember why my morning wood had hardened even more at the sight of her.

The kiss.

We'd kissed.

Skye Devereux, the girl of my dreams, and I had finally locked lips. Not just lips. My hands had committed her to memory in a way that made them tingle and itch to feel her again. Our bodies had fit together like they were made for each other. And the way she'd bitten my lip? She'd taken me to literal Heaven, and it had blown my goddamned mind.

Then, like she hadn't been remembering the same thing as me, she smiled and got up to get me a coffee. "Or I'm not as Cadbury as you thought I was."

Still not sure if she remembered or not, I decided not to make a thing out of it. "I get the distinct feeling you're not a lot of things as I thought."

She threw me a grin over her shoulder as she got the milk out of the fridge. "And did that make sense in your hungover mind?"

I nodded. "Definitely."

"How long have you got to sober up?"

I checked the time on my watch. "Uh, make that two hours until we have to be in the changeroom?" I guessed.

She laughed and my cock strained in my jeans. "Thank God, you're playing home this week."

I nodded as she passed me my mug. Our fingers brushed and we both froze again. Those gorgeous blue eyes seemed to search mine for something. I just didn't know what. There had always been heat between us. It had always flared to life stronger when we touched. But there was something else here. Not just unresolved tension that was slowly burning away at the edges of our frenemies connection. I was almost certain she was acting like it hadn't happened. I just couldn't work out whether she didn't remember it or if she didn't want to.

Fuck, had she ruined me for all other girls, and she just seriously regretted it?

Well, I wasn't about to bring it up and risk having all my hopes and dreams utterly crushed. No. Much better that I fantasise about a world in which we could be together, while keeping my hands off her and our interactions no less platonic than usual.

"I'm sure the team would give you a pass if you wanted to pike out today," I told her as I sat back and focussed on keeping my hands to myself and my eyes on her face.

She shook her head as she sat down opposite me and picked her cup up. "I can't do that."

I was *not* thinking about the way her hands wrapped around the cup in just the same way she'd had her hand on my dick the night before. So not thinking about it. Because she deserved my undivided attention on the words coming out of her mouth.

That mouth that had moaned my name in a way I'd never heard it moaned before. In a way I'd never heard her moan before. Oh, she'd moaned in my ear, but I knew she'd been teasing. Last night, it hadn't been teasing, it had been full of need, begging me to ease the ache in her.

Goddamn it, arsehole! I snapped at myself.

I nodded. "You can. It's the day after your birthday. I'm sure most of the guys fully expect you to be worshipping the porcelain goddess for the majority of the day."

Another laugh, and her eyes sparkled.

I wanted to say that the hangover was addling my brain, turning it to mush and making me more of a chauvinistic dick than usual. But it wasn't the hangover. I'd had far worse and not for a long time. These days, if I pulled up with more than a slight headache and serious dehydration, I'd overdone it, even for me.

"I'll be fine. Thanks."

I nodded, feeling very not fine myself. "I guess I'd better get this arsehole home to the shower." I kicked my head at her brother where he was sprawled on the couch.

It was too small, even for him. My body would have been even more furious at me if I'd tried to sleep on it.

Skye looked over to Taylor, a fond smile at her lips. The way those two loved each other had always got to me. They bickered and fought like nobody's business. I'd seen screaming matches. I'd seen them throw things at each other, including punches.

There had been blood drawn more than once. But no matter how serious the argument, it was nothing more than a small blip on their relationship. Like, the worse the fight, the quicker they were over it and everything was back to normal.

I'd never had that growing up. There had been fighting and just so much blood, but no love that would hold everything together even through the fucking apocalypse. No love at all. Not until the Devereuxs had come into my life and not hesitated to make me one of their own. Even the ten-year-old spitfire Skye had been then.

Not much had changed except our ages…

And the single best kiss of my life.

Before I spent more time up my own arse than necessary, I drained my coffee and got up to kick Taylor awake.

"Huh, what?" he yelped as he rolled off the couch in surprise.

"Courtesy dictates we shower, mate," I said, throwing a smile to Skye.

She grinned over the rim of her cup. I could see it in her eyes. God, her eyes and the way she'd…

Fuck's sake!

Taylor wiped the drool off his face and nodded. "Yeah. Good point." He looked over to his sister and smiled. "Good morning, old woman."

She inclined her head. "Old man."

He snorted as he dragged himself off the floor. "See you after the game?"

She nodded. "Of course. I will be ready to commiserate with you."

He huffed as he waved a hand at her. "Pfft. Lotta faith you have in the Chasers."

She shrugged. "What can I say? I know them far too well."

Ugh. She just had to stir shit this morning, didn't she? Worse, why did I have to love it so much? I'd loved it before our kiss. Now? Forget the porcelain goddess, I'd worship at Skye's feet all day and every day if she let me.

Fucking. Stop.

Before I delved into total jerk territory, I grabbed Taylor and hauled his arse out of there. I opted to shower last out of the whole team, which was mainly an excuse to try to ease the raging boner in my pants that wouldn't let up any other way.

I didn't need any help. The image and feeling of Skye was still visceral. I could feel the press of her body against mine. Her boobs pushed up against my chest between us. The feel of her heat – enough that I'd nearly blown my load in as little as seven minutes with nothing but a tantalising pressure – as it ran over my dick.

I freed my dick from my boxers, and it was only the start of the relief.

Lubed up, I ran my hand over it and, shamelessly, imagined it was Skye's hand. I replayed her hand on it over and over again, and it took me an embarrassingly short time to finish. Even as I started to go limp, I'd only satisfied half the problem; no more boner, but I still craved something that was just out of reach.

And it didn't get better over time.

My head was a mess for the rest of the week.

We barely won our game because I was too busy constantly forcing my eyes off Skye in the stands. If anyone noticed I wasn't at my usual level, they didn't make a mention of it, which meant they didn't suspect who was actually to blame. I had managed to score the winning goal to a great uproarious cheer of my on-field nickname.

But that was the closest to satisfaction I got because every girl I thought about picking up just wasn't doing it for me. I was horny as hell. I had girls lining up and willing. But there was no spark of excitement or anticipation when they touched me. I felt antsy to move on and find something else. I wanted to say I didn't know what the something else was, but I totally did.

And Skye was just going along, acting like nothing happened.

So, I was also just going along, acting like nothing happened.

Tansy was hilariously frustrated. Which made the act all the more appealing.

Every time something like the kiss had been brought up, Tansy was all, "Like when River and Skye kissed?", the rest of us just asked "What, when?" Because Taylor was either in on the joke or also didn't remember it. The other option was that, as okay as he'd been with it at the time, maybe the only way he was okay with it was pretending it had never happened.

So, I couldn't let on that I'd been thinking of nothing but his sister all week.

Because I had.

The next Saturday, I was still at it. Sitting on my bed in our hotel room after an away match, drunk off my arse, I was still thinking about such a simple little thing.

One kiss.

One single kiss.

That was all it took to turn my whole world upside down.

I couldn't stop thinking about it. No, I couldn't stop thinking about *her*. My best friend's little sister. My teammate's ex. A girl who hated me. She got me hard in a way no one ever had. She had for years. Our sexual chemistry had been visible from space for the last like three or four years. Not quite long enough for it to be creepy, but before it was probably okay.

But this was different. This wasn't hypothetical anymore. I'd heard her moan my name while my body rubbed between her legs.

I'd felt her hands in my hair as she bit my lip. I'd felt that spark in my chest ignite when my lips touched hers.

Resisting her had been hell. And it wasn't like any of the reasons I shouldn't touch her had gone away, but I couldn't do it anymore. I couldn't make myself believe they were still more important than having her in my arms.

She might not have been gaol-bait anymore, but that didn't mean wanting her like this was okay. It didn't mean it was something she wanted. And that was the only thing that was keeping my hold on the raging fire she'd fanned to life in me. Because, without that, I was willing to throw away every other connection and meaning in my life for her.

I might now be a part of the love could keep the Devereuxs glued together through the apocalypse, but Skye was the catalyst to my own personal apocalypse. And I was one drink away from texting her and begging her to come over and ease this torrid desire in me. I was fully ready to set my world to implode, to risk everything that came with that, for just one more taste. But, if I put the bottle down now, then I'd still have the restraint to do the right thing.

I lay down on my bed, sighing heavily. Then I smirked at my dramatics.

My own personal apocalypse?

Huh.

I needed a new nickname for her now.

I snorted. "Calypso," I said to myself. "She's my Calypso."

"What, mate?" Taylor mumbled, half asleep.

I shook my head as I put my arm behind it. "Nothing, mate. Go back to sleep."

"Okay."

I looked over at him and wanted to feel guilty for wanting his sister. For the team's sake, it was easy. After years of doling out punishments for breaking code, I knew them far too well. But for Taylor's sake? It was getting harder. For Skye's sake, it was about as hard as it could be.

This deep in a bottle, I knew the number one reason I'd kept my distance from her all these years. It was the same reason I was this deep in a bottle, and so often was. And I didn't want to hurt her. It would kill me to hurt her.

So, I couldn't let one kiss change anything. It had been fantastic and, in a perfect world, I'd be a one-woman man. But we lived in the real world and that meant nothing had changed.

Not being with Skye was going to take every ounce of willpower I had, and my track record with giving up my addictions wasn't great, but she wasn't just an addiction. She was so much more.

♡5♡
Skye

It had been over a week – ten days, but who was counting? – since I'd dared River to Seven Minutes in Heaven, and I wasn't sure he even remembered it.

Literally nothing between us had changed. Nothing except I was sure I was going to combust or throw myself at him every time he was near me. It was stupid. I was horrified with myself. One kiss and I was reduced to absolute cavewoman insanity. But, at the same time, I loved it. I had never been like that. Sure, I enjoyed sex, but I'd never been so crazy about it before. And I was crazy about it with the one guy it was so complicated to want. Which made me annoyed with myself all over again.

It was made all the worse because I couldn't tell if River didn't remember it even happened or if he was just *pretending* he couldn't remember. The morning after my birthday, there was a moment I almost thought we were going to talk about it, but neither of us had said anything, we'd both just been acting like nothing happened, so I hadn't had the guts to say anything first.

If he was pretending, why? Did he regret it? Because it was awful? Because there was no spark for him? Or because he thought Taylor – no doubt with his fist – and the rest of the Chasers – with G-strings and cleaning products – would have something to say about that? Or was it something else? I just couldn't think what that something else might be other than he regretted it.

Oh, God.

Did he regret the single best kiss of my entire life to date?

It would, honestly, be just my luck.

So, I went along with the act. I pretended it hadn't happened either.

I went from not being sure how we were going to handle it, to acting like it hadn't happened and, the more time that passed, the less I felt like I could bring it up. What was I going to do? Suddenly, a week later, be all like 'so, that kiss, huh?'

I pretended that every little touch, every look – that before we kissed would have been utterly natural – didn't make me freeze up just so I wouldn't act on the sudden wave of lust that enveloped me. I acted normal. As normal as I could while overthinking exactly what actions *were* normal and how would I normally interact with him?

I pretended even with Tansy, and she was about done with my shit those ten days later.

"I get why Taylor and Riv aren't talking about it," she said to me as we walked in the same general direction as each other to class that morning. "But I don't understand why *we're* not talking about it. I mean, it was *my* idea!"

I shrugged as I sipped the tea in my travel cup. "I don't know what you're talking about."

"Seven. Minutes. In. Heaven," she said slowly, and I felt like she was going to kill me.

I shook my head. "Doesn't ring a bell."

"You and River," she said. "K-I-S-S-I-N-G."

"Oh, you mean your hypothetical from the other week? Yeah,

okay, it was a good one. I can admit it. Happy now?"

"No!" she cried. "No, not happy now. Very not happy, Jan!" she snapped, then peeled off earlier than necessary to get to the science building.

I sighed and prayed she'd forgive me. I knew she would, I just wasn't sure how much it was going to take to make up to her. But if I couldn't talk about it with River, and it had somehow – maybe – become a bit of a joke that we acted like it hadn't happened, then I didn't know how I could talk about it with Tansy.

Usually, Tansy and I talked about everything. And I didn't mind her knowing that I remembered the kiss perfectly well or that it had turned my whole world upside down for a guy I couldn't have. No. I was more concerned that talking to her about it would just make me pine for him more. She'd be full of best friend support like 'Just go and climb that manwhore mountain' and 'screw the Chaser Code *and* River' *wink, wink*. And it wouldn't take her long to convince me to do it. But without knowing that River felt the same, it – he – meant too much to me and the people around us to risk him turning me down and all the awkwardness that would cause.

Tansy ignored me for the rest of the day. Fairly simple considering we both had pretty full Mondays – she had a few practicals – and we barely crossed paths. But she didn't even read my DMs, and I wasn't quite so sadistic that I was going to call her and be hung up on.

So, I went about my day and was glad I didn't run into anyone at risk of talking to me. Until I did.

From the corner of my eye, I spotted River coming from the other direction. My mind and body went haywire. I desperately wanted to talk to him like I always did, but I also really didn't want to talk to him, and I wasn't really sure why. There was no hiding now, though.

"You in a hurry, Calypso?" he asked, and I almost missed he was talking to me.

Then I registered that he'd said 'Calypso' in the exact same sultry yet insulting tone of voice that he usually reserved for 'Gaol-bait'. I came to a stop, and we met in the middle of the path.

"Calypso?" I clarified, wondering if this was my new nickname, and he nodded. "Have you been doing a Pirates marathon and got lazy?"

He shrugged, for all intents and purposes totally nonchalant and devastatingly gorgeous as usual. "I thought it suited you."

"I'm far too uncoordinated to be associated with any form of music or dance," I reminded him as my heart beat too fast.

He was effortlessly sexy. Like he always was. Jeans and a hoody, with one strap of his bag over one shoulder, his hair obviously just left to dry after his last shower. Which made me instantly picture him naked and dripping wet, with those bedroom eyes and the cocky, expectant half-smile lighting up his face while he beckoned....

Making me dripping wet as well.

Good lord, woman, I huffed in the privacy of my own head.

"I was thinking more the goddess of the seas cursing men," he quipped, and I knew it was a dig – even a fond one – at the more acerbic parts of my personality.

But it did the job of distracting me from mental images of him in the shower. Just. They were at least shoved to the background.

"If that were the case, I'd have had your heart long ago," I told him.

"Who says you didn't?" he answered, easily and without missing a beat.

I tried not to smile an absolutely unbidden, goofy smile at that idea. Because this was just River being River after all. This was normal pre-mind-blowing-kiss behaviour. It meant nothing more than our interactions usually did. And I'd tell myself as often as it took to believe it.

"Then I'd have far more control over you than I actually do," I retorted hotly and pointedly.

He stepped up to me, the toes of our shoes touching, and looked down at me with a sinful intensity. "What would be your first command?" he asked, his tone low and pleading.

Goddamn him. Goddamn everything he was, then send me right after him.

Everything in me responded. Holy hells, but I didn't care we were in the middle of the quad. I wanted him to prop me up on the closest surface and kiss me like he had on my birthday. And I didn't want him to stop there.

As I looked into his eyes, I saw the shining proof in them that he did remember. He remembered, he didn't – I hoped it wasn't just wish-fulfilment speaking – regret it, but he wasn't doing anything about it.

Ugh!

Why the hell not?

Was he waiting for me to do something about it? Waiting for me to make the next move? Well, why in the hell had he – finally – let me know in the middle of a public space when he knew far too intimately exactly who I was as a person?

Maybe that was the point? Maybe the point was to give me time to think about it. To not make rash decisions. An 'I'm here and willing if you want it'. A no pressure kind of thing. Because I felt like we both knew, had he tried that on in private, neither of us would have any clothes on right now and give zero cares for the consequences. Probably sensible to let the larger brains make such a big decision.

And I hated him for being the rational one.

Uncharacteristically nervous around him suddenly, I tucked an invisible piece of hair behind my ear as I looked down. He put his finger to my chin and tilted my face back to look at him. His eyes were searching mine, and I think his were the most clear I'd ever seen them. Whatever he was feeling, he was one hundred percent certain about it.

My heart pounded.

"Speechless, Calypso?" he teased.

"Not wasting a command on the first thing to pop into my head," I corrected him.

He gave a nod. "Very godlike. Sensible. Out of interest, what was the first thing to pop into your head?" God, how did he say that in such a seductive way? How did he manage to heavily insinuate ALL the good things would happen to me if I told him?

But my cheeks didn't heat. We'd done a similar dance to this enough times that I wasn't embarrassed by how or what I felt for him. The only difference to the way I felt around him was that I actually wanted to act on it with him now.

"I was just wondering if you kiss…other lips so well. Purely scientifically, of course."

Heat pooled in his eyes as he caught my meaning. "Of course. Well, in the interests of science, I'd be very happy to test your hypothesis."

I bit my lip against a full smile. "That doesn't surprise me at all."

He took a step back. "Any time you want to do…science, I'm at your beck and call."

We both knew he hadn't mean 'science'. I gave him a nod as my mouth went dry. "I'll remember that."

"I'd be very happy to remind you. As often as you want."

"That seems like it could get very annoying for you," I pointed out.

He shrugged, that cocky gleam in his eye like a siren call. "Not really. You might not want reminding at all."

I think it said a lot about what I wanted him to do to me that I hadn't actually considered that a likely option. "And if I want reminding…" I tried to think of the most annoying thing I could. "On the hour, every hour?"

The corner of his lips tipped up and it made his eyes crinkle pleasantly. "You lifting the ban on me being in your DMs?"

Now, I shrugged. "It wasn't really a ban, was it?"

"Wasn't it?"

I shook my head. "I knew I could never keep you out."

The humour left his face. "If you really wanted me out, I'd stay out."

I searched his eyes and knew he was totally sincere. We might tease and goad and shamelessly flirt with each other in the guise of insults and mutual dislike, but all of that was welcome. It's what we wanted from each other. At least, we both got off on it. I hadn't really thought about it, but I guess I'd sort of just assumed that, even if things changed for me, River would always be River like that.

Now, I was certain that, if I honestly told him to stop or get out, then he would do it. Unhesitatingly. Any sign that I was uncomfortable or it wasn't fun anymore, and that would be the end of it.

Quite frankly, it made me want him more. And I don't think that was the reason he felt that way. It didn't feel like there was an ulterior motive. I wondered, for probably the first time since I'd met him, how much the chauvinistic arsehole was a play, a mask. And, if it was a mask, what was it hiding?

Jesus, but I couldn't even begin to wonder if River had depths that didn't just include how far, how quickly he could get into a bottle. I was having enough trouble taking my eyes off those full lips as he did nothing but talk to me the same way he'd always talked to me as I imagined them all over my body.

I could almost feel them on me now and I had to force myself to take a steadying breath. As I looked into his eyes, I saw the heat there and I felt my teeth catch my lower lip. Something in his eyes sparked – it was knowing, it was humoured, and it was desire.

I took another deep breath and nodded to him. "If you stay out, how will you do your job? That's two things you're supposed to remind me about now."

He inclined his head as his tongue trailed painfully slowly over his top teeth. "That's right. I've got to tell you what time our games are and *now* I've got to remind you about my availability for scientific experiments. I'll be reduced in your phone to 'Reminder Man'."

I huffed a laugh. "Sounds like a terrible superhero."

"He's annoyingly persistent and his phone bills are massive, but at least he doesn't destroy the city on his quest for universal punctuality."

A wide smile blossomed across my face, unbidden, and his followed suit. My heart beat hard, but it was so nice. It was times like this I was reminded that things with River were crazy easy. We knew each other so well, it was effortless to make the other smile. No matter how nasty we got with each other, we could always end on a smile if we wanted. He knew my ticks – for good and bad – and I knew his. And, when we used our powers for good, it felt amazingly simple and good.

After we'd just stood there for I didn't even know how much

time, he finally nodded again. "Richard waiting on you?" he asked cheekily.

Out of sheer panicked habit, I looked at the clock on the Lincoln building. He laughed and I frowned at him.

"Don't use Richard to diffuse the sexual tension!" popped out of my mouth.

Humour danced in his eyes. "I wouldn't dare, but I'm pretty sure even Richard couldn't dampen what we have."

Everything in me fluttered. My heart. My stomach. Every nerve dancing down my arms and legs. One went down my spine. Another burst between my legs.

"It must be pretty strong then," I said, embarrassingly breathless and he cocked his head to the side. "This thing…we have."

As he understood my meaning, his eyebrows bounced up. "Oh. The strongest."

Another forced, deep, steadying breath as his words slid over my skin and wrapped around me seductively. "Well, wouldn't want to get in the way of that."

Was this what I was reduced to now? What our witty banter and scathing foreplay was reduced to? This weird semi-sincere, 'am I on the cusp of asking him to make this official?' nonsense. On one hand, I hated it. I'd thought I was stronger than lust. On the other, it was weirdly empowering and flooded me with these anticipatory tingles that I couldn't get enough of.

"No," he said slowly. "No. We couldn't have that."

I bit my lip. "But I do have to get back to Tansy. I promised her I'd go out with her tonight."

The humour in his eyes went dark and my heart skipped a beat. "Anywhere exciting?"

I shrugged. "Probably the Mad Kitty? I dunno. My idea of a

wild night is a quickie in the library stacks and getting my next assignment finished." I was pretty sure he was about to offer. "Tansy's in charge of date night."

He went stiff. "Date night?"

Did I imagine a slight strangled quality to his voice? Or was it actually there?

"It's like girls' night, only we've made it an obligation so our relationship doesn't suffer and stagnate." Tansy firmly believed that *all* relationships should have designated hangouts.

"Oh, you and Tanz?" I was definitely not imagining how much he had to force the casual quality to his voice.

I nodded. "Yes. Me and Tanz. There will no doubt be dicks involved later in the night. But we always start out pretending that it's girls only."

There went the cheeky half-smile. "I'll remember that."

"Well, if you're there, dicks will definitely be involved."

"Oh, baby," he chuckled, and I felt it in *places*. "There will *definitely* be dicks involved."

I smiled at him, trying to keep it from being the goofy smile of the enamoured. "I guess I'll see you tonight then, Pond Scum."

"I guess you will, Calypso."

A shiver of a whole different kind skittered over my body. My nipples tingled and I had to wonder how one word had such power over my body's reactions. The way he said 'Calypso' was a hundred times more evocative and dirty and exciting than 'Gaol-bait'.

All I could do was nod once to him, then hurry off to my dorm room. I felt his eyes on me long after I would have disappeared from sight.

"Okay," I said as I burst into our dorm and was gratified when Tansy wasn't only in the room, but looked at me expectantly.

"Okay, what?" she asked, like she hadn't stormed off and been ignoring me since.

"We're officially talking about it."

She grinned, no longer mad at me. "We are?"

I nodded. "Yes."

"What happened?"

Of course, she knew that we were only talking about it now because something had happened.

"He's got a new nickname for me."

She scooted closer to me over the back of the couch. "Pray tell?"

"Calypso."

She frowned as she tried to work it out. "What?"

I shrugged. "Something to do with goddess of the sea cursing men."

She nodded. "Oh. Drunk Pirates marathon."

"No doubt."

"No doubt."

"But…" I started and she perked up again. "It's the *way* he says it."

"Oh, yes?"

I nodded. "Oh, yes."

"So, he remembers?"

"He has to."

"Why hasn't he said anything?"

"I don't know. I get the feeling – maybe – like he's letting me make the next move. Like he wants to be sure it's something I want."

"Of course, you want it!" she yelled, then grinned sheepishly. "I mean," she said more softly. "Of course, you want it. And he knows this?"

"I *think* so?"

"Oh, my God! What are you two waiting for?"

"I don't know. But Tanz, it's a big thing."

"I mean, I guessed. You hear stories about how well he satisfies–"

I snorted and she stopped. "I didn't mean his cock. Although, that did feel pretty good. But him and me, it's so freaking complicated."

"Well, uncomplicate it."

"How? Just hop in my pilfered TARDIS and turn Jax down then throw myself on River and this whole thing could have been done with a year ago?"

Tansy nodded. "Ideally, yes."

I rolled my eyes. "I'll get right on that."

"Do."

As I went to my room to get changed, I casually remarked, "He suggested he – and presumably the boys – will meet us out tonight. He seemed to think dicks needed to be involved."

"WHAT?" she cried excitedly. "Where did you tell them we're going?"

"I told him I didn't know what you had planned."

"Where did you tell him we were going?" she practically shrieked, and I smirked even as I winced.

"I told him I thought you were planning on the Mad Kitty. Why? Where were you planning?"

"Who fucking cares! We're going to the Mad Kitty!" Then she came running after me. "What are you wearing?"

"Something comfortable," I said as I looked back as though I was daring her to disagree.

For the space of a single heartbeat, she thought about it. Then she looked resigned. "Well, that's less fun."

"Why?" I laughed.

"Because River's boner rages for you no matter what you wear."

I shrugged coyly. "That doesn't mean I won't let you choose my outfit tonight."

Her eyes bugged. "Really? Seriously? Actually? For real life?"

I laughed. "For real life." I gave her another shrug. "Maybe he does want me in anything, but there's no harm making him want me more."

"I don't even care what the aliens did with you," she said frankly. "Or the fae. Changeling likely to eat my face off in my sleep? Sure, why not? I'll take it."

"You suck," I said with a smile as we opened my wardrobe.

"That's why I get third dates."

I snorted, completely undignified. "I like my third dates to be based on more than my fellatio skills."

"Spoken like someone who has none," she said with a wink.

I shoved her companionably, knowing her ribbing was mostly all talk. Tansy liked hooking up almost as much as I did, and she was more vocal about it than I was. She was also more talk than she was walk. She liked being shocking and amusing. She felt like it was her duty as a feminist to normalise women talking about sex the same way men did; namely making it sound like we got far more and far dirtier than we actually did (in our experience at least).

It was a good atmosphere to start a night out, especially if River and the guys were going to meet us.

♥6♥
River

Okay, so coming up with a new nickname for her and then making some kind of in-joke bordering on some of the hottest oral sexting had perhaps not been the best idea.

Or, it had been my best idea yet.

Because the heat had cranked up between us.

It's not like we hadn't been flirty before The Kiss. We had, obviously. I was a naturally flirty guy and she had always reciprocated, and then some. But now we'd made the unspoken acknowledgement that we both remembered The Kiss and we'd been thinking about it. A lot.

I'd thought the idea she regretted it was the worst possible outcome?

Colour me very wrong, indeed.

Turns out, the worst thing was knowing that it had affected her as much as it had affected me. That she thought about it as often as me. That she wanted to do it again – and more – as much as me. And then she was doing absolutely nothing about it.

I'd dragged Taylor and the boys to the Mad Kitty every night for the last week.

Tansy had dragged a very willing-but-pretending-otherwise Skye to the Mad Kitty every night for the last week.

And Jesus Christ, I thought I'd known what blue balls were before that week. It's not like I hadn't gone through dry spells. Despite the stories about me, there was actually a time when my hand had been my only company, and it was now once again. By that next weekend, my balls actually ached. They fucking ached. And it wasn't just with how much I wanted her and only her. I'd spent three years aching with how much I wanted her. This was different. This was physical torsion or some shit I knew nothing about because, despite what I was willing to do for Skye, I didn't do science.

But I wouldn't change a fucking thing. I literally couldn't. Taylor kept trying to wingman chicks into my pants, but I didn't goddamn care. I didn't want them. I could have pretended I did, for his sake and theirs, but I just didn't. I appreciated their aesthetic, I could appreciate they were gorgeous and sexy and probably great people, but they did nothing for me. And they deserved to be told that straight out so they didn't waste their time or mine.

I had never had to lie about my ability to pull before. I'd never been one of those guys who lied about how many people I hooked up with. By the time I felt like it mattered how many hook ups I had, I was getting more than everyone else around me. And I just didn't care what others thought anyway – each to their own and all that.

That week, I lied.

Well, not lied, but I stretched the truth within an inch of its life.

Taylor asked me how the girl was the night before. I told him, 'fine'. I never flat out told him we'd both gone our separate ways while he had his tongue down some girl's throat. Let him think he was getting me laid.

In reality, I was spending every minute I could with Skye and, by extension, Tansy.

And not just at the Mad Kitty while Taylor was hooking up. I didn't so much make excuses to have lunch with them, but I sat down at their table, leaving Taylor and the guys to either sit with them as well or not. I took the long route to fucking everywhere just so I had more chances of running into Skye between classes. I did as I'd told her, and I sent her the time for that week's game – an away – as well as the occasional – not quite every hour on the hour – reminder that I quite liked scientific experiments. Because, for her, I'd fucking do it.

She rewarded me with nothing but perfect Skye smiles all week. Even when she was trying to reprimand me, she was smiling. I could see it in her eyes. There was something different about the way we interacted now. Some unspoken thing between us that was just simmering away and waiting to fully combust. I'd given her the message that the ball was in her court, and she gave me all the signs that she felt the same. But still nothing.

On Friday, a bunch of the Chasers were going out to dinner before going to the Mad Kitty. It was pizza and burgers, but still counted. Me, Taylor, Lachy, Jax, Frankie D, Robbie and Forbsy. The existence of Frankie D implied there were other Frankies, or had been other Frankies. There weren't and there hadn't. As far as anyone knew.

Our captain, Ajax, watched us as we traipsed out. I saluted him and he shook his head with a knowing smirk.

"Remember, bus leaves at nine. I'm not taking vom bags and we're not fucking stopping," he said.

We all grinned at him, assuring him that we'd behave, not drink too much, and be home by midnight.

"Sure," he said. "I've fucking heard that before."

I shrugged as the others went on ahead. "You can come with? Keep your ever watchful Captain eye on us?" I teased.

I knew full-well he wouldn't; we were old enough to make our own mistakes and it was Ajax's last year. He was out of there and off to a team in Europe after graduation so what did he care if we fucked up the rest of this season? It only hurt us and was, hands down, the best way of teaching us to do better.

"I'll fucking see you on the bus at nine," was his answer as he headed up to his room.

I gave him one more salute, and hurried out after the guys.

"Skye coming out tonight?" Jax asked and I felt a pang of guilt at how non-nonchalant he sounded.

Taylor shrugged. "Dunno."

"You asked?" I said, far more nonchalant.

"I didn't. You've been texting her all week. Didn't you?"

"You've been texting Skye all week?" Frankie D said with obvious confusion.

My shrug was too defensive. "Not *all* week."

The guys laughed.

"Not *all* week," Lachy teased, and I shoved him.

"Did you ask her, though?" Taylor asked, either seeing no more in my texting Skye than there needed to be, or being okay if there was more.

Which was a mind fuck, and I was going to walk away from that train of thought.

"I didn't. Want me to?"

"I don't care. We've just seen them a bit this week. I kinda assumed you'd organised something with her."

I huffed a laugh. "Why would I organise anything with her?"

Taylor looked at me weirdly. "Why would you not?"

Right. Because it was actually normal for me to organise shit with her. Because we always had. Because us talking and being close was actually not abnormal and there shouldn't be anything wrong with it.

I nodded as I went to pull my phone out of my pocket. "No. Sure. I'll see if they're free."

Riv.Torn
We're heading out for za
and burgers. You and Tansy
down?

She wasn't long in replying.

Sky'mDevestated
Ha! Great minds. We're already there.

Riv.Torn
Save us a booth?

Sky'mDevestated
That will highly depend on how many 'us' is.

Riv.Torn
Why? If it was just the two
of us, it'd be fine?

Sky'mDevestated
...
It would be easier.

Jesus. How had she meant that? And what did it say about me that I was wondering? Did I want to date her? Romance her? Be an exclusive, forever kind of thing? But then, I'd gone and started it, so I really only had me on which to blame my rapidly beating heart.

Riv.Torn
We might need two.

Sky'mDevestated
smirk GIF
What's the matter, Pond
Scum? You risk being real for
a second there?

Riv.Torn
Bold of you to call me out
over message.

Sky'mDevestated
Weak of you to pike out over
message.

Riv.Torn
What do you want me to
say, Calypso? You want me
to tell you how fantastic it
would be, just the two of us
insulting each other over
good food while we both
pretended we didn't want it
to be so much more? You
want me to say that, after,
I'd take you back to your
room? You want me to tell
you all the dirty things I
want to do to you once I
get you there? Or do you
want me to warn you that
we'll probably need two
booths?

Sky'mDevestated
por que no los dos GIF
A very undignified snort left my person and I had to put my

phone in my pocket while I tried to school the goofy smile on my face.

"What?" Taylor asked. "Some chick send you a nude?"

I shook my head. "Nah. Just... Nah. The girls are already there. Said they'd try and get a couple of booths."

Taylor nodded. "Sweet."

When we walked in, my eyes found her instantly and she was grinning at me. Humour lit those brilliant sapphire eyes and she nibbled on her lip like she was trying not to smile even wider.

A few of us headed straight to order, Lachy, Jax and I went over to the girls.

"What?" Skye laughed at me. "Too chicken shit?"

"Maybe..." I started as I slid in next to her, "...your GIF game is just too good for me."

I went to steal a fry and she tried to bat my hand away. But I managed to snag one and held it up between us with a shit-stirring grin. I bounced my eyebrows at her suggestively and her frown was fighting a losing battle against her amusement.

"Give that back, Pond Scum," she said.

I leant towards her. "Make me, Calypso," I purred at her.

Heat flooded her eyes and God, but I wished it was just the two of us.

"Give it back." Her tone was more warning now.

I licked it and held it out to her. "Sure."

Her tongue darted out to lick her lip before her nose wrinkled. "You owe me a whole new order."

I ducked my head to her ear. "You don't want my spit, Calypso?"

I felt her body lean closer to mine and her hand went to my chest. "Not on my *food*, Pond Scum."

Fuck, but the way she purred in my ear. I felt like she may as well have just kissed the fucking daylights out of me. Ugh. What was the GIF with the swooning? I mean, there were a million of them, but they all had nothing on me. Nothing. I was about ready to float to the ground like a feather over this girl.

Tansy cleared her throat loudly and I realised the others had stopped talking.

Skye and I extricated ourselves from each other and looked at them all. The rest were back as well, and everyone was looking between me and Skye like we'd been full-on just macking out and fondling right there in the middle of the place.

"You ordering?" Taylor asked me as he sat beside Tansy.

I shrugged. "You girls want anything more?"

Skye glared at me. "Fries. Many fries."

"Onion rings?"

She shook her head.

"What?" I scoffed. "You love onion rings. Or do you not want to risk onion breath tonight?"

She gave me a small, reluctant smile. "I've come to the realisation that they cool too quickly and then they're gross. I'm an adult now, so I feel like maybe I'm too old to be wasting my own time like that."

Was that a subtle reminder she was legal now? God, I hoped so.

I nodded. "Okay. Boring, but okay. Fries. Tanz?"

"Sundae. Large. Chocolate. With nuts."

Skye nodded eagerly. "Yes. Sundae, too. No! Thickshake."

She and Tansy shared a look and a smile.

"Yes," they both said together.

I shook my head. "Whatever you want, you delightful weirdos." I elbowed Skye. "You wanna help me out?"

Skye grumbled, but was out of her seat instantly. "But you're paying."

I rolled my eyes. "Duh."

By the time we'd jostled each other to the line to order, Jax and Lachy were done and heading back to the table. I had Skye's arms behind her back and smiled at them.

"You need help with that?" Lachy asked with a smirk.

"Nah. I know how to make her behave."

"You going to cuff me, officer?" she asked with a teasing lilt to her voice.

I pulled her back to my front and said, "I'll spank you if you beg for it," before I thought about what came out of my mouth.

"Promises, promises," Skye laughed.

My eyes flickered to Jax and Lachy. Lachy was looking between me and Skye with interest and Jax's face was unreadable. I relaxed my grip on Skye and casually threw an arm over her shoulder that even more casually turned into a headlock.

"Oi!" she chuckled and Lachy grinned.

Even Jax gave me a smile, although I could guess what was running through his head. By the lack of expression or emotion he was giving me, I could guess what was running through his head. Knowing him, he thought he was being paranoid and didn't want to look like the jealous ex. On this one occasion, I would have given him a pass. But admitting that to him would mean inadvertently admitting to a whole lot more I couldn't.

Jax and Lachy went to the tables, and I felt far more self-conscious about how I was acting with Skye. We'd never really watched how we were with each other before. There had been an almost unspoken agreement that we didn't purposefully feel each other up in front of other people, especially her brother, but that had felt like second nature and a good excuse not to let things get too far. Now, it felt more like second nature to let things go too far no matter who was looking.

"Okay," Skye said, her voice still humoured like she hadn't noticed if anything was weird. She leant into me. "We need thickshakes and fries."

I smirked down at her. "I know what you're planning to do with those, and I am not condoning it."

She grinned. "Oh, come on, River. How else am I going to practice my fellatio skills?"

I felt something lodge in my throat and realised it was my own spit. "Excuse me?"

God, her humour was all cheeky and evil, and I knew it was expressly designed to turn me on. And she knew it was working.

The problem was, we knew each other too damned well. She knew what and where every single one of my buttons was. What turned me on. What made me angry. What made me smile. And she wasn't afraid to press them all when it suited her; she always went right up to too far but never any further. I think that was one of the things I liked about her the most. The fact she wasn't afraid to play me like a finely tuned instrument for both our amusement, but she also wasn't cruel about it.

With the exception of one incident from my past, she knew everything about me. There was good, but plenty more bad. She had the power to emotionally ruin me, even without knowing the full story, and she'd never used it. She'd done it to Taylor when they were younger – and he'd returned the favour – but she'd never done it to me.

I felt her finger under my chin and brought my focus back to her.

"Speechless, River?" she teased.

"Just not willing to risk my chances on the first thing that popped into my head," I told her, which wasn't that far from the truth; if she knew what lay in my past, there was no way in hell she'd be looking at me the way she was now.

She smirked. "And what was that, then?"

I shook my head as I frogmarched her closer to the register to order. "Oh, no. I won't give it up that easily."

"No," she said as she pulled away from me. Her tone was all piss-taking wistfulness. "You need a dare for that."

I stepped up behind her, my hands on her waist as I leant down to her ear. "Just say the words."

I felt her shiver slightly and my cock stirred in my jeans. "So, if I dared you to kiss me right here, you'd do it in front of everyone? Taylor?" She paused and looked back at me. "Jax?"

Were I a better man, no. But I wasn't a better man. Most days, I wasn't even sure I was a good man. Looking into her eyes now, I could convince myself I was a good man. For her, how could I not be? But rationally, I knew that was shit. Even knowing that was shit, if she dared me, I'd fucking do it and already be mentally putting on the G-string of punishment.

"Just…say…the…words…" I told her slowly, a dare of my own.

She searched my eyes, and I wasn't sure if she had the balls to go through with it or not.

"Next!" the person at the register said and we were both saved the answer of whether this would happen or not.

Skye pulled away from me, looking suddenly self-conscious and it still didn't tell me what her answer might have been. I longed to know. Ached to know. To grab her arm, tell the server to wait, and demand she make a decision. But, if she'd wanted to make a decision, she would have made it. That, or that *was* her decision. And as much as I needed to know what the hell was starting to happen between us – if she felt as mad about me as I did about her – I wasn't going to rush her or ask her to give me something she didn't want to or wasn't ready to.

Consent was fundamental.

Expecting things that you weren't owed was the lowest form of shittery.

My whole body might have buzzed for her next touch, but that was a me problem.

Being ninety-eight percent certain that she felt the same gave me no right to make her feel like I was demanding answers or action.

It was fucking hard – in more ways than one – to not just pull her to me and kiss her in a way that told her exactly how she made me feel by just existing, but I wasn't going to be that guy. Skye was amazing and it wasn't settling to accept she might not want to act on it, even if she felt it.

We ordered and headed back to the tables.

"Bathroom," Tansy said to Skye, and they disappeared instantly.

I dropped into the seat next to where Skye had been sitting and picked absently at her remaining fries.

Lachy checked to make sure the girls were gone, then leant towards me conspiratorially. "What in the hell is going on between you two?" he laughed. "You act all weird around each other for like two weeks and now there's a sizzle?"

I scoffed. "There's no sizzle." Fuck, there was so much fucking sizzle.

"It's all damned sizzle," Frankie D said.

I shrugged. "I don't know what you guys are on, but I'll take some."

"It's Skye and River," Taylor said, like, 'duh, what else did you expect?'. "Besides, if Torres was stupid enough to break the fucking code, then it'd be for nothing less than true love."

"That'd be right," Forbsy chuckled. "If he's gonna fall, he's gonna make it as hard for himself as possible."

Taylor looked like he couldn't care less. "I'mma leave him to sort his own shit."

Jax was all bravado and said, like it was all a good joke, "Aren't you worried he'll break her heart?"

I knew it was bravado because I was pretty sure he was still nursing that exact wound after he and Skye had broken up. He hid it well, but he was a dater, and he hadn't really been with anyone since, as though no one compared. I had to agree with him, I just wasn't allowed to. Because of him.

Taylor scoffed, "Oh, he's a piece of shit who'll never be good enough for my sister, but I'm under no delusion that Skye wouldn't wipe the fucking floor with him. She doesn't need me throwing down for her, she can do that for herself." He nudged me. "He knows what I'd do to him if he actually touched my sister."

I had a pretty good idea, yeah. Taylor knew me better than anyone else. He knew the darkness. He knew my past as well as I did. Skye and me as frenemies with him as a buffer was one thing. Skye and me in an actual relationship? Code, be damned. There were more pressing concerns. I didn't blame Taylor for being worried about what that would do to his sister long-term.

"I heard a rumour they kissed on her birthday," Jax pressed.

How? I barely believed it anymore and I'd been there. How in the hell had Jax heard about it?

Taylor nodded and it was the first confirmation in nearly two weeks I'd had that he remembered it. "Yeah, but Seven Minutes in Heaven on a dare doesn't count."

Didn't it?

How far did that extend?

One Hour in Heaven?

What about Seven Hours in Heaven?

Was that my free pass to be with her?

Fuck! What was wrong with me?

I'd never been that guy. Hung up on one girl when it went against the Code. Well, no. I'd always been that guy. But I'd never let it get to me before. Never let it get the better of me.

I was the guy beating all the other guys to make them stick to the Code. But then, I'd had to. Because if they broke the Code, then I should be allowed to break it, too. And if I was being a very good boy and not breaking the Code – when it went against everything in me telling me it was right to – then I would die before anyone else broke the Code.

I would be the world's biggest hypocrite if I broke Code now. It would be worse if I broke it because I'd spent so long upholding it. And because it was Skye Devereux. A teammate's sibling. She was an honorary member of the Chasers. If the Code was going to apply to anyone, it double applied to her. The Chasers worked because we were a tight knit bunch, and we couldn't be creating issues between us because we all ended up falling for the same person just by the law of proximity.

Familiarity bred fondness after all, and I'd seen teams ripped apart because some sibling did a Tansy and ended up dating half of them just because they hung out with them all the time. There was no intention to hurt people or date half the team but, being around them all the time, feels got caught.

"Who dared who?" Jax asked.

I looked up at Taylor and it felt like we had an unspoken agreement to not tell Jax the truth. I didn't know if Taylor was on my side or if he just knew that Jax would take it the wrong way.

And it didn't matter. All that mattered was Taylor's answer.

"Probably Tanz. What does it matter anyway?"

"What are you blaming me for now?" Tansy asked as they appeared again and took their seats.

Taylor shrugged and gave her a shit-eating grin. "World hunger. War. The Dean's ban on Water Wednesdays in November."

Tansy frowned at him. "That wasn't my fault. I was only…"

My eyes darted to Skye as she leapt to her best friend's defence. I knew it was as much about giving Taylor shit as it was solidarity. I didn't care about her reasons, I just loved the way she lit up, the animated way she stuck to her guns and wouldn't back down for anyone.

It didn't matter that I'd just been given a very visceral warning about the Code, even under the guise of friendly shit-stirring. I didn't give a single fuck that Jax and Lachy were watching me closely. That they were watching me watching Skye. I couldn't take my goddamned eyes off her.

She was just wearing trackies and a long-sleeved tee under a chunky cardigan with ugg boots – one of her favourite outfits – but she was the most beautiful thing in the world to me. I didn't have to see her to think she was the most beautiful thing in the world. She could have been in a cardboard box, and I'd still be unable to keep my eyes off her.

"So, Mad Kitty?" Taylor asked Skye and Tansy when everyone was finally done eating.

Tansy nodded straight away but Skye shook her head ruefully.

"What?" Taylor asked her. "Why not?"

"What about my outfit suggests I was planning on heading to Mad Kitty after this?" she asked him.

He shrugged. "I don't know. I don't see outfits, I just see my sister."

Skye rolled her eyes. "Progressive, bro. But no. We're gonna be wiped after all day away tomorrow, and you lot have already made me so far behind on my assignment this week."

"Oh," I said dramatically. "One of those wild nights, then?"

The corner of her lips tipped up at the in-joke. "One of those wild nights, then," she agreed. "Because I know you won't let me study tomorrow night."

"There is more in the world than just study," Forbsy said, and Skye nodded.

"Yeah, for all of you who find this shit easy. Unlike the rest of you, I have to work to keep my place here. There's no way in hell I'm risking you leaving me behind because my grades start slipping and they kick me out."

Tansy's eyes were tight, like this was an argument they'd recently had and there was much more to it than that. "But I'm coming out," she told us cheerfully.

Taylor obviously realised not to push either and just smiled. "Okay. Great. You want someone to walk you back?" he asked Skye, and she shook her head.

"We're close enough. I'll be fine."

"You sure?" I asked her as the others all started getting up.

She smiled at me, more in her eyes than at her lips. "I am. Thanks."

I paused. It wasn't lost on me that accepting my offer might have made me think it was an invitation. So, refusing my offer could have been a very pointed message that she was giving me the very opposite of an invitation. I didn't know if I was reading too much or too little into anything, so I could only nod.

"Cool. Have a good night."

She gave me a nod as well. "Will do. You, too. Don't go

jumping into any dares."

Dangerously, I let my eyes show her exactly what I was thinking. Hers answered in the positive and I couldn't stop myself murmuring, "Just say the words, Calypso."

I saw in those deep sapphire blues the acknowledgement that she would do just that. Just, obviously not right now.

Outside, we said our goodnights and promised to keep an eye on Tansy. As the others headed off, I snuck one last look back to Skye, and saw she was looking back too. I gave her a small wave. She turned to walk backwards and gave me a bigger wave in return before wrapping herself in her cardigan, turning back around, and hurrying to her dorm.

It felt the worst to be walking away from her when I wanted to do the opposite, even if we just sat on her couch watching movies all night while she complained about how much of her food I was eating. As I jogged after the others, I couldn't help smiling at the mere idea.

I was so far gone for this girl that just being friends with her made my fucking day on a daily basis. And, if I was lucky enough that she felt the same, I couldn't do a damned thing about it.

So, I did what I always did, and lost myself in booze.

I'd been fortunate that I had not just my soccer scholarship, but also an equal opportunity scholarship. When I'd applied to the Senior College, I hadn't thought about how I'd pay for anything if I got in. I acted naïve and applied all the same. So, when I got a place and had to seriously consider passing it up, the Dean decided my skills could not be allowed to play anywhere but Chester. So, for a kid from a dubious background, they started the Chester Discretionary Scholarship in my name.

They'd always had academic scholarships that were intended to help disadvantaged kids, but I wasn't academically gifted –

compared to a lot of the students at Chester – and even my soccer scholarship was hardly going to help me when I'd just been emancipated from my parents. So, the CDS gave those of us, without family money to bankroll our lives, enough of an income to pay to live, as well as save a bit for living once we left Chester. Because, weirdly, Chester realised it wasn't actually enough to leave us in the lurch once we graduated.

Living in the McMansion with the other Chasers, my costs were low. So, I could afford to buy rounds of drinks for my teammates and friends. Which is what I did that night as I felt awful for pining after a girl who I was pretty sure didn't want to act on any feelings she may or may not have for me.

I was a few drinks in when I noticed Forbsy doing his own pining, his eyes firmly on Tansy. I felt bad for giving him shit about his crush on her the other night, and I resolved to make it up to him.

I went over and put my arm around Forbsy's shoulder. "I think it's about time we got you the woman of your dreams, mate."

He shook his head. "Everyone knows she does teams. And I don't want to risk losing her to you or Dev."

I sniggered. "Yeah, not going to be a problem, mate. Our Code's stronger than any of those other wankers."

Forbsy didn't look convinced. I gave his shoulders a squeeze.

"Dude, the Code is all. You know this. Dev's never shown interest in Tansy and I'm too hung up on–" *Fuck.* "The single life." *Good save, me.* "The Chasers don't do another guy's person."

Forbsy smiled. "I think she could be my person."

I nodded. "Good. Then let's get you your person!"

I dragged him over to Tansy, not caring how obvious I was being to anyone who might be watching. I tapped her on the arm, and she turned to us. A brilliant smile blossomed across her face as she saw it was us.

I leant down to her. "Have you met Forbsy?" I asked cheekily.

As Tansy searched my eyes, she knew exactly what I was doing; namely, making a move on her for a guy who was too gentlemanly and shy to do it himself. She slid a sensual smile to Forbsy before reaching up to my ear.

"Calypso says, 'I dare you'," she said to me, almost like it was repayment for the favour I'd just paid her.

I pulled back to look at her, in clear shock. Her grin was so knowing as she nodded at me slowly and I dipped to her again.

"Seriously?"

I felt her nod again. "Seriously, River. The offer might not be there anymore if you fuck about too much longer."

Oh, I wasn't going to fuck about too much longer.

I looked at her again and she nodded encouragingly. I gave her a single nod.

"Don't go home any time soon?" I suggested, not sure if it was my place or I was pre-empting anything.

She nodded. "Okay, I won't."

One more nod, like a total prat, then I was out of there and running to their dorm room as fast as I could.

If River had actually been giving me some kind of hint about making the next move, he certainly wasn't making it easy for me.

As though fate herself was lining up against me, it felt like there were no accidental run-ins with River. He didn't come to my dorm on the flimsy excuse of staking out the new ice creams. The only times I saw him, we were surrounded by people. No one but Tansy made any indication that they noticed anything different between us, but I felt like I was constantly thinking about what I was inadvertently giving away.

Except that night.

While we'd waited to order, I hadn't thought anything of it. It had felt normal and natural, and I hadn't second guessed myself. Then I'd got home and sat at my desk, and I suddenly realised things. Things like Lachy's and Jax's eyes on us. The way River and I touched each other more. How close we were. Me licking thickshake off his finger a little too suggestively, even for us. Constantly nudging each other as we ate and talked. Somehow touching the whole time, even when it wasn't even conscious.

Had I not known it was me and River, I'd have said we were acting like a couple. And not just a couple, but a couple who'd been together for a while. A couple comfortable with each other, whose very second nature was to be together.

Much like the last few weeks, on one hand, I loved it. On the other, I had to wonder why I had to make life so difficult for myself. Not just myself, but for River. He was a stickler for the Code, the first to enforce punishment on anyone who broke it. Even though he was pretty much fucking me with his eyes every time he looked at me, he wasn't making any moves to act on this thing, despite that we'd both admitted it was the strongest.

Which told me he wasn't going to. It told me the Code was more important. That his relationship with Taylor was more important. And I couldn't blame him. We'd spent seven years with our main motivation being to antagonise and annoy each other, to suddenly turn around and risk blowing up both our worlds for a case of serious lust was folly.

But knowing it and accepting it were two very different things.

So, I spent a good couple of hours staring at my textbooks and laptop, having to force myself to stop getting distracted. I'd been texting Tansy, telling her all about the whole 'say the words' thing that I desperately wanted to act on but didn't have the guts. She'd threatened to out me and I'd put my phone down in fear she might actually do that. Thus, naturally, it was when I was finally, actually getting on with my work that I was interrupted.

There was a knock on the door, and I looked at the time. It was nearly midnight, and I smiled.

"If you're so drunk you've forgotten the door code again…" I started as I went to open the door. My words died on my lips when I saw it wasn't Tansy after all. "River?"

He nodded and stepped forward. My heart pounded in my chest and my stomach fluttered wildly. There was only one reason he was in my dorm room, at this time of night, by himself, with no warning. Wasn't there?

Please say there was only one reason he was there.

His breathing seemed purposefully deep, like he had to force it to stay relatively even. His eyes were hard, but heat raged in them as he took me in like I was the only one who could soothe that fire that burned in him. He was holding himself rigid like he didn't trust himself otherwise.

I didn't care. I didn't want him to hold back. I didn't want to hold back any longer. Two weeks of this new sizzle between us had me at the very edge of sanity and I was sure, if I didn't act now, then I was going to lose the last shred that remained. My nerves had been on high alert for far too long, just waiting for that moment he touched me – really touched me – again.

So, I didn't say anything to him. I just stepped forward, grabbed the front of his tee, and pulled our faces together. River reacted instantly. His arm wound around my back as the other hand went to my neck. Every nerve ending flared to bright and beautiful life, sending a flutter of tingles racing through my body like I'd only been half-alive until now.

We both took a couple of bumbled steps into my dorm and got the door closed behind us, our lips never parting. My hands were in his hair. His were on my back, one up my shirt, warm and firm on my skin.

Relief flooded me. All the uncertainty I'd been feeling was just gone.

It was me and River, and everything, finally, made sense again.

Gratifying tingles shot through me that I wasn't just right that we both felt this thing, but that we did both want to act on it as well. Whatever the reason we hadn't until now didn't matter anymore because our kiss was definitely making up for lost time. It was frenzied and rushed and so uncoordinated. But it didn't matter because, what we lacked in finesse, we more than made up for in passion.

We stumbled again and my legs hit something. We pulled apart and I looked down to see I'd run into a dining chair. We shared a laugh, and I took the opportunity to pull off my shirt, leaving me in my daggiest t-shirt bra and oversized trackies.

Not that River seemed to care. His eyes took me in and that heat only intensified further. There was nothing sexier than a guy wanting you when you were at your most comfortable, than a guy not caring about the clothes you wore or when you last shaved or if you were in the middle of a breakout. And River was a guy who wanted me, perfectly imperfect and just as I was. He wanted me. The heart, the mind, the soul, as well as the body. And I wanted him.

Our hands reached for each other again and we pressed our foreheads together. The rest of our bodies followed suit like we were lining up perfectly. Like we'd been made specifically for each other. River groaned, low, guttural, and so damn primal. It was so sexy.

"Just say the words," he begged.

I was so ready. "I dare you," I told him.

I had never seen him look so relieved by anything. By the look in his eyes, he'd just been waiting for me to give him permission. Had he spent the last two weeks thinking I didn't want this, the same way I had about him?

God, I hoped we weren't that stupid.

"I'm breaking all the rules for you, Calypso," he said against my lips, and I wondered if it was a reference to the other week in his room when he'd asked me about his shirt.

"How?" I asked, feeling myself smile.

"The team was giving me grief about breaking the Code just

for flirting with you."

"You always flirt with me."

"Yeah, but it's different now, isn't it?"

It was. I felt it. I pulled back only enough to look at him. "Then, is kissing me a good idea?"

As he pulled off his shirt, he shook his head and said, "Hell no, but I'm not going to stop now, baby."

And he wrapped me in his arms and kissed me even harder, like he was making a point. I was very happy for him to make it. I knew all about the Code, of course I did. You didn't get to being the unofficial team mascot and not know about the Code. It was one reason I'd never thought seriously about hooking up with River earlier. But the Code was between the team. If River was willing to risk it, then it wasn't up to me to tell him otherwise.

His fingers trailed their way into my trackies, and I felt him smile when he realised I had nothing on underneath.

"I didn't even have to dare you this time," he chuckled.

"Not every underwear decision I make is based around you," I told him.

He dragged a finger over my clit, and I arched my body into his. "Are you sure? Because you are so damn wet, Calypso."

"Of course, I am. Three years of foreplay led to a mind-blowing kiss, and then nothing for two goddamned weeks, Pond Scum."

He picked me up and I loved how effortless it was. "You been thinking about me?"

I ran my nose over his face. "You know I have."

The smile was warm and bright in his eyes. "How much?"

I wrapped my arms tight around his shoulders, my fingers playing with his hair. "Maybe even as much as you've been thinking about me," I sassed, and he grinned.

"That's an awful fucking lot," he said.

I pressed closer to him and nipped his earlobe before saying, "How many times have you spanked it to me in the last two weeks, River?"

"You know I can't count that high," he said, his voice somewhat breathless. "How many times have you spanked it to me?"

"What's three times a day for two weeks rounded up to the nearest ten?"

He groaned again and sat me on the back of the couch. "Why are you so fucking sexy?"

I ran my hands over his chest. "Why are you?"

"You're like my own personal brand of heroine."

I snorted. "Was that a *Twilight* quote?"

His eyes went wide. "Fuck, I hope not."

I nodded. "It was," I whispered.

He dropped his head to my shoulder. "You have ruined me, woman!" he moaned, and I laughed.

Then he flipped us over the back of the couch, so he was lying on his back on it, and I was lying over him.

"Practise that one, do you?" I asked, still laughing.

I had never seen his eyes that crinkled with happiness, and it made my heart melt. "Actually, I panicked half-way through and was pretty sure we were both going through the coffee table."

"Your big boy brain not in charge?" I teased.

His hand skimmed up my side. "My big boy brain is never in charge when you're around, baby."

"God damn it, River," I mumbled as we nuzzled.

"What?" he asked softly.

"Just fucking kiss me."

He sat us up, making sure my legs were on either side of his, so I straddled his lap. I expected hot and heavy, but he just put his bent finger under my chin and touched his lips to mine so softly and so reverently. After all the build-up we'd had, it was enough to make me nearly shatter for him. My heart felt like it was crumbling only to be rebuilt all over again, somehow stronger.

Our kiss was slower now. More like proper making out. Our bodies rocked together as our hands roamed purposelessly. We just enjoyed it. There was no rush for more, it was just enjoying what we had in the moment. It was like being fifteen again, before that hormonal switch had flipped and it was like everyone's instinct was suddenly to fumble around in the other person's pants as soon as lips made contact.

My fingers found the huge scar running across his back. I'd seen it enough over the years that it wasn't a surprise to me. It wasn't a thing to shy away from, it was just part of him. A rock-climbing accident from when he was younger. I didn't pay any special attention to it, but I didn't avoid it either.

Just as River's fingers were heading for my bra clasp, there was a noise at the door.

I sat up quickly and launched myself off River's lap so quickly that Tansy would have known exactly what we'd been doing, even without the fact we were both topless.

She paused in the doorway, looking between us, and her face clearly wasn't sure how it felt. She looked like she was about to cheer in excitement and like we were leading ourselves to the gallows.

"Taylor's on his way up…" she said slowly, which explained the latter look.

"Fuck," muttered River.

I blinked and hunted around for my top. "What? Why?"

"Pitstop. Said he had to pee, so I let him in, and he figured he'd come say hi when he was done."

I found my top and pulled it on hurriedly, noting that River was much slower about the whole thing. I glared at him, and I was sure he was getting off on it. A whole new wave of lust hit me, and I really wished my drunken brother wasn't on his way up.

Then I turned to look at Tansy. "You don't seem surprised to see him here."

River made a noise, and Tansy and I both looked at him.

"You," he said to her, giving her a small salute.

"Me," she agreed with a nod.

"You, what?" I asked, having no idea what was going on.

"Me was sick of this dance you've both been doing," Tansy said pointedly.

I looked at her and realised what she'd done. "You didn't!" I accused.

She nodded. "I did. And you can thank me after your brother's left."

I looked between them, and honestly couldn't bring myself to be angry with her. If River and I had just been too stupid to be the first one to make a move when we both wanted it, then maybe we did need a meddling best friend to sort our shit out for us.

"Ugh, his timing!" I muttered.

River chuckled and pressed a quick kiss to my lips. "Talk to me this time?" he asked.

"You could talk to me," I reminded him.

He smirked. "And I will. If I can't be all up in you tonight, I'll be all up in your DMs."

"How is that sexy and gross at the same time?" I asked, scrunching my nose.

"Because you want him all up in you," Tansy pointed out. "And because he manages to make everything sound sexy."

I nodded in agreement. "Yeah, true."

"Riv!" Taylor said as he swung in the door. "Is this where I left you?"

"Clearly he's going to be ready for the bus at nine," I said sardonically.

River smirked. "Yeah, we've had worse." He turned to my brother. "Mate, I thought you'd fallen in. Let's head back to the mansion, yeah?"

Taylor nodded, his eyes closing. "Good idea. Ajax is going to kill me."

"Why?" we all asked him.

"I think I was a little bit sick in the bathroom."

I tried not to laugh at him in his drunken misfortune. "I'm sure it'll be fine."

Tansy waved her hand dismissively. "Nick'll probably think it was Craig."

Nick was our Dorm Dad, for lack of a better term. He was a student at the uni, so more of a big brother figure, but it didn't have the same alliteration, or annoyed him quite as much.

"Poor Craig." Taylor shook his head.

"All right, I'd better get him back," River said, and we exchanged a meaningful look.

I gave him a small nod and that seemed all the answer he needed.

"We'll see you at the bus?" Taylor asked.

I gave him a playful punch on the arm. "I'll see your hungover arse at the bus."

"It's not a sleepover," River reminded us.

I nodded. "Got it. No sleeping over."

He looked at me and his eyes burned hot. "It's not a rule. You just won't need to bring bags…on the bus."

I nodded so he knew I'd heard his message. "Okay, then."

"Okay, then. We'll see you lovely ladies in the morning."

"Night, boys," Tansy said loudly.

Taylor's eyes had lost focus. "Goodnight, ladies."

As soon as we had the door closed on them, Tansy turned to me, and I knew she was about to settle in for the gossip.

"You saw the extent of it," I said, pre-emptively.

She deflated a little. "Seriously?"

I nodded. "Seriously."

"I thought you'd have combusted the dorm in a fit of sexual passion and he'd left ages ago."

I shrugged and looked at the time. "Yeah, apparently we just kissed for like two hours."

She blinked. "Seriously?"

I smiled. "Yes. Seriously."

"He must kiss really well," she said, obviously not sure if she believed me, but then not seeing why I'd lie.

"I mean, he does."

"No more goss?"

"Even if I did, you're going to have to wait."

"What? Why? What if I have goss?"

I nodded. "Okay, give me yours real quick, but then I need to have a conversation with a man about some kisses."

Understanding dawned in her eyes. "No. Okay. Fair. I'm not going to stand in the way of healthy, grown-up communication."

I snorted. "Your goss?"

"Oh, Forbsy and I hooked up."

I blinked. "Really?"

"Don't act like it's weird."

I shook my head. "I'm not. I don't think it's weird, you've just never hooked up with any of the soccer team before."

"If you're worried I'm going to try to collect them all, you need not. I know the Code is thicker than blood. I'm not stupid."

I was going to ignore the way she said that like me going out with Jax in the first place, when River and I clearly had chemistry, *was* stupid.

"And you picked Forbsy?" I teased.

"What is wrong with Forbsy?" she asked,

My phone went off and I smiled at her as I pulled it out of my pocket. "Nothing. I just wanted to see your reaction. And the blush tells me everything."

"Don't you start. Work out what's happening with your own hook-ups before you start sticking your nose in mine."

I inclined my head. "Fair. I'm going to go do that now."

"Night," she said with a laugh.

"Night," I answered as I went to my room, closed the door and unlocked my phone.

Riv.Torn
So, I feel like we should talk?

Sky'mDevestated
What gives you that
impression?

Riv.Torn
That I'm not going another
two weeks hoping you want
to kiss me again but not
wanting   to   make
assumptions   while   our
chemistry is clearly off the
charts.

I smiled to myself as I lay down on my bed.

Sky'mDevestated

I want to kiss you again,
River.

Riv.Torn

I want to kiss *you* again.

Sky'mDevestated

Even though it's a bad idea?
Or *because* it's a bad
idea?

Riv.Torn

I've spent the whole last two
weeks asking myself that
question, Calypso.

Sky'mDevestated

And what was your
conclusion?

Riv.Torn

The only way I can resist you
is obligation. Wanting you is
so fucking messy. Having
you is messier. It breaks the
Chasers Code. Taylor would
kick my arse. I have all the
reasons to not want you.

Sky'mDevestated

Please say there's a 'but'
coming...

Riv.Torn

BUT I still want you anyway.

Sky'mDevestated

So, what do we do about it?

Riv.Torn

I don't know.
I don't want to rush anything
and fuck it up.

> **Sky'mDevestated**
>
> I get that.

Riv.Torn

What do you want to do
about it?

> **Sky'mDevestated**
>
> I don't know either.
> I want you to rip my
> goddamn clothes off and
> have me hard.

Riv.Torn

Jesus, Calypso.

> **Sky'mDevestated**
>
> What's the matter, River?
> Too much for you?

Riv.Torn

Not enough.
Never enough.

> **Sky'mDevestated**
>
> Do you want me to wrap my
> hand around it, River?

Riv.Torn

You want me to jizz in my
pants without me having to
even touch it?

> **Sky'mDevestated**
>
> Anyone else managed that?

Riv.Torn

Of course, not.

> **Sky'mDevestated**
>
> So, I'm special?

Riv.Torn

Never think otherwise, baby.

> **Sky'mDevestated**
>
> Are you thinking about me?

Riv.Torn

Oh, I'm thinking about you.

Are you thinking about me?

Was I thinking about him? Only the fact that made twice that he'd managed to stoke a burning fire inside me that I wasn't getting any relief from. That I could feel his body against mine, his lips on my neck and his hands hot on my skin, and I couldn't give myself a satisfying enough orgasm to get over it for five seconds.

> **Sky'mDevestated**
>
> I can still feel your lips on
>
> my skin.
>
> How hard you were
>
> between my legs.

Riv.Torn

I think I've been that hard for

two weeks.

I liked that more than I should have. It implied he hadn't been with anyone else and that any relief he was giving himself was just as useless as my efforts.

> **Sky'mDevestated**
>
> You say that like I haven't
>
> been this wet for two weeks.

Riv.Torn

Really?

> **Sky'mDevestated**
>
> I mean, not literally. That's
> not how vaginas work. But
> like, figuratively.

Riv.Torn

How's your hand holding
up?

> **Sky'mDevestated**
>
> Cramping. Yours?

Riv.Torn

Boring. I'm not sure I can
even be bothered anymore.
On the flip side, I don't
imagine how else I'm going
to get to sleep tonight.

> **Sky'mDevestated**
>
> And we've gotta be on the
> bus in like seven hours or
> Ajax will leave without us.

Riv.Torn

I should be sleeping,
shouldn't I?

> **Sky'mDevestated**
>
> You should.

Riv.Torn

This would be easier if you
were here.

> **Sky'mDevestated**
>
> In your bed? I thought girls
> weren't allowed in your bed,

River.

Riv.Torn

You're not girls, Skye.

You know that.

Sky'mDevestated

If I was there, what would

you be doing to me?

I shouldn't have asked, but I couldn't help myself and River didn't hesitate to answer.

After turning each other on more than we already had, River eventually couldn't put sleep off any longer. We agreed that we'd play this thing between us cool and take it slow. We wanted each other, but the practicalities of being together would ruin any enjoyment we got from finally admitting we both felt the same. So, it was going to be business as usual, just without all the denial and doubt. Maybe we'd never work out if it could work, but at least we were being honest with each other.

Knowing that, if he was anything like me, he was going to need some self-love before he went to sleep, I took a chance and sent him a picture of me in my bra. He didn't reply for a few minutes but, when he did, it was with a picture of his abs. It made for only slightly more relief than usual.

♥8♥
River

I walked into my room, closing the door as I started pulling my tee off. The lack of sleep before the game, all the travel there and back, and Ajax's lengthy post-match recap had wiped me out and I just wanted to crawl into bed, spank it a couple times, and get a decent sleep for once. Ha! As if my demons would let it be that easy.

Halfway across my room, though, I paused mid-step.

Because my bed wasn't empty.

There had never once been a single time where I wasn't in my bed, and it wasn't empty.

But there it was, with a young woman in nothing but short shorts and a singlet, that left nothing to the imagination, lying in it. Her hand was behind her head and her naked knee was bent up. At least she'd taken her shoes off before she made herself at home in my freaking bed.

Under any normal circumstances, I'd have lost my shit and roared the house down to get them out. But these weren't normal circumstances, and this was no average woman.

"The fuck are you doing in my bed, Gaol-bait?" I huffed an easy laugh, then reminded myself she wasn't gaol-bait anymore and my restraint was hanging by a very fine thread indeed.

Even after our chat the night before, I wasn't sure where we stood. She'd let me in. She'd kissed me. She'd seemed reluctant for me to leave. We'd had an adult conversation and admitted we wanted each other but were going to take it slow. Whatever that meant. But that didn't mean she was here for more now.

She glared at me and was clearly not going anywhere soon. "The fuck is Forbsy doing in my roommate?" was her counter-argument.

I snickered, all my worry leaving me. She was here to do exactly what I'd hoped getting Forbsy and Tansy together would make her want to do; annoy me. "Yeah. I thought you'd like that."

She pushed herself up indignantly and leant on her elbows. My eyes darted to her chest which now pushed out, amplifying what was perfectly ample. My already hard cock throbbed against the band of my boxer-briefs. She rolled her eyes, knowing exactly or at least very nearly what was going through my head, and sat up properly.

"So that *is* your fault?" she accused, focussed on the matter at hand and not the still-unresolved tension between us.

I liked – no, loved – that we'd admitted we both wanted each other and basically sexted the night before, and now were acting like it wasn't the only thing that mattered. Because it wasn't. Teasing each other and insulting each other and still being ourselves together was far more important than any sexual gratification I might get from or because of her.

"Call me Cupid," I told her lazily.

"I'll call you giving up your bed every time he's over. Do you *know* how thin our walls are, Pond Scum?"

I whipped off my trackies, and dropped onto my bed and lay beside her. She huffed and scooched over to give me room. Not that she really needed to because it was a damn big bed.

"What?" I laughed at her indignant huff. "You didn't think I was sleeping on the floor, did you?"

"No, of course not. I do know you," she muttered as she lay down again, acting for all the world like this – a girl, and her no less, in my bed – was the most normal thing in the world.

"What I don't know is how thin your walls are," I said, leaving the question hanging.

"They are so thin, I need a muffler." Her voice was bordering on seductive and, if she was shifting the mood, then I wasn't going to shift it back.

I very much liked that image and seriously regretted not being able to discover that the night before. "One pillow or two?" I teased, turning my head on *my* pillows to look at her.

She turned hers to look at me and deadpanned, "No one is good enough to require *two* pillows."

I leant towards her, too late realising how big a mistake that was if we were keeping this PG. "I'd make you need three."

Molten heat made her eyes liquid sapphire, then she scoffed and lay back down, closing her eyes like she was settling in for the night. "Yeah. Sure, you would."

I trailed my fingers over the space between her shorts and singlet. "You want to put that to the test?"

"Despite this decided sizzle between us, I am not here to sleep with you, River," she sighed, but she didn't bat my hand away. "I'm here to annoy you at least half as much as you annoy me just by breathing."

"*Por que no los dos*?" I asked.

Her eyes opened and she sat up unbearably slowly, turning over onto her side and towards me until her nose was brushing my cheek. "If it's annoying, then you're not doing it right."

I dropped my fingers to brush up along the inner thigh of her right leg, the one lying flush with the mattress. "You want to test that theory?" I asked again, stirring shit.

"If you want to sleep with me, River," she purred, her lips brushing over mine, then pinning my eyes with hers, "then you just have to beg for it."

Shit. Was that all it would take? Gladly.

My fingers trailed closer to her centre, and I felt her legs part for me. I dropped my lips to her neck and grazed them over her skin ever so lightly.

"You're all I think about, Skye," I told her. My hand went to the knee of her left leg and started running up the outside of it to her arse. I coaxed that leg around my hip. "I want to feel you." I ran my nose over her cheek. "I have so many reasons to not touch you, to not want you, but I can't resist you anymore, Calypso." It was pretty much what we'd said to each other the night before, but saying something in person never hurt.

I felt her head drop back and she sighed, her hand sliding onto my body and up my back. Her fingers didn't pause or hesitate as they passed over my scar, they danced over it like it was just a part of me that deserved as much attention as the rest of me.

"Is this a bad idea, River?" she asked.

I dropped a kiss to her chest. "Probably. You want me to stop?"

Her hand ran up my body to cup my cheek, her eyes following the movement until she was looking into my eyes. I saw the smile in them, and my heart hitched. As she bit her lip, she shook her head.

"No," she told me. "I don't want you to stop, River."

I was happier than I had a right to be, but just then I wasn't going to let my shit tarnish this or tarnish us. She wanted me? She could have me.

Our lips found each other, and her hand slid from my cheek into my hair. Fuck, I loved the feeling of her fingers in my hair. Deep in a kiss, she had a tendency to clench her fist around it, making it tug in a sexily domineering kind of way, and I didn't think she even knew she was doing it.

I trailed my fingers between her legs and rubbed over her shorts, gratified when her hips bucked to meet them. Her other hand joined the other in my hair and our kiss deepened. I didn't give a shit how many people she'd kissed before me, but she was damn good at it. I'd never been a big kisser. I hadn't initiated a kiss in years. Not until her. My lips couldn't get enough of her. And every time they met hers, my heart felt like it was restarting.

Of all my addictions, her kiss felt like the best – and safest – one.

She rolled her hips against my hand again, and I could take a hint. I felt myself smile against her lips as I slid my hand into her shorts.

"This what you want?" I asked her and she nodded as I found her clit.

She was so wet. It was easy to lubricate her, my fingers gliding between her folds, finding the places she reacted to the most. Whenever I ran circles over her clit, she seemed to relax, she breathed out heavily and her back arched slightly. It was the most natural and satisfying response. So, I kept doing it, varying my pressure and speed to gauge what she liked.

I was marvelling at how needy her whimper was in my ear, how I felt it in places I didn't know I still had, when her breathing got short and shallow and she started rocking her pelvis, grinding against my hand. Her hands fisted in my hair and her kisses became less smooth.

"Yes, River. Like that. Please."

Her whole body moved against mine until she crushed her lips to mine to stifle her moan and tensed. She'd clamped her legs around my hand, so I stroked her gently and she spasmed as she chuckled, pressing a kiss to my lips.

"Shit," she breathed, and I heard the joy in her voice.

She looked up at me, her cheeks absolutely flushed with pleasure as her chest rose and fell heavily. She shook her head before touching her forehead to mine.

"I'm supposed to be here to annoy you, not sleep with you, River," she reminded me, although I was pretty sure she was reminding herself more.

"And you think stopping now would annoy me?" I asked, guessing where she was going with this.

She nodded as her hand dropped to the raging hard-on in my briefs. "I think it would be *very* annoying," she said, a shit-stirring humour in her voice that I fucking loved.

I grinned. "If it's not what you want, it's not annoying. The boner is annoying, but not you stopping."

A frown crossed her features. "What? Why not?"

I chuckled. "Gee. Sorry to disappoint."

She shook her head. "No. I mean. Fine. Yes. But why isn't that annoying? *I* would be annoyed."

I shrugged as I got up. "Call me old-fashioned, but I like it when she's into it and she wants it. You don't want it? Cool."

She rolled onto her side and leant her head on her hand. "I think you'll find that's the *literal* opposite of old-fashioned. And where are you going?"

"To rediscover the joys of peeing upside down with a boner."

She smirked. "Are you going for a wank?"

I failed to hide my smile. "If the mood takes me while I'm there, maybe." *Yes.*

"You don't have to leave to…"

I didn't know if she wasn't sure how to finish that sentence or she wished she hadn't started it. There was a slightly darker flush to her cheeks as she bit her lip almost nervously. I watched as she went from hesitant to decided. She knelt up on her knees on the bed, crawled over to the edge, and crooked a finger at me, beckoning me over. I wasn't going to say no.

"I thought you weren't here to sleep with me?" I teased as I stopped in front of her.

She smirked up at me. "I don't have to sleep with you to deal with this. Do I, River?"

I shook my head far too quickly and excitedly, and her smirk grew.

Skye reached into my briefs and gently took my dick out. She looked it over as she ran her hands along the shaft, and I felt myself twitch.

"Before I blow my load," I said carefully. "Did you have a plan here?"

Her hands were so damn soft and hot and sexy. She seemed to be thinking, but I was pretty sure it was a ploy. "If you could cum anywhere on…someone's body," her eyes darted up to my face and I was very eager to know where this was going, "where would you choose?"

"Stomach," popped out of my mouth in an embarrassing strangle. I cleared my throat. "What are you proposing, Calypso?" I asked her.

She crawled back to the middle of my bed, and she was full of heightened sexual confidence. I'd never seen this side to her before. She was fucking seducing me to insanity in my own damned bed, and I wasn't just not complaining, I was a willing accomplice.

"Last night, you had a picture," she said slowly. "Tonight, you can have the real thing, if you want."

Had all my dreams come true?

Okay. No.

Not all of them.

Very decidedly *not* all of them.

But was she actually suggesting that I could wank to her body? Over her body? In person. Jesus, what had I done to get so lucky?

She lay back against the pillows, and slowly spread her legs as she dragged her singlet up under her boobs, leaving the smooth skin of her stomach on display. Her eyes burned with a 'come hither' look that I was powerless to resist.

"What are you waiting for, baby?" she asked.

The speed with which I clambered onto the bed and between her legs showed a desperation I hadn't felt about sex for a long time. She made me feel like everything was new and exciting again.

As I knelt between her legs, she smiled up at me. One hand slid up the muscles of my leg and I tingled at her touch. My hand was, naturally, wrapped around my shaft and slowly running over it.

"Are you sure about this?" I asked, more because I just couldn't believe it.

She nodded and resettled so her centre was closer to me. "If you want to."

"You know I want to."

She bit her lip as humour flashed in her eyes. "I do know you want to. That's why I offered. I figured we both had to go solo last night." She shrugged. "But we don't have to tonight."

I leant over to the bedside table and grabbed the lube, and her smile widened.

"You're fucking gorgeous, you know," I told her.

She looked up at me. "If you were anyone else, I'd take exception."

I paused. "Why? You don't want people to think you're beautiful?"

She shook her head. "No. Because I don't want to just be my physical features."

I felt like she'd kicked me in the gut, and not in a good way. I put my hands on the bed on either side of her and leant down. "Skye, I don't–"

She leant up to meet me, our noses bumping. "I know, River," she said, her voice soft and sweet. "You don't just see my face or my body. I know, when you tell me I'm beautiful or sexy or gorgeous, that you mean all of me, but that you mostly mean what's in here." She put her hand over my heart and it fucking skipped.

I lay my hand over hers. "How do you know me so well?" I asked her, a reverence about me I didn't feel around anyone else but her.

She searched my eyes. "How do you know *me* so well?"

I had to kiss her, or I would have said something stupid like, 'Because I love you,' but that ran the risk of her either walking out in disgust or, worse, returning the sentiment. Even if a large part of me meant that platonically, I couldn't really bring myself to finding out that she'd never feel the same while I had my cock out over her half-naked body.

That thought alone had me at risk of deflating but, like she realised the turn my mood had taken, she stroked her hand over me as she kissed me hard. I groaned against her, and her hand slid up to my neck.

"I love it when you do that," she murmured.

"Do what?" I asked her.

"That groan."

"Why?"

"Something about it is so sexy. Like you just can't help yourself. Like I make you crazy."

"Because you fucking do," I chuckled.

She took my lip in her teeth and pulled gently. When she let it go, she said, "Show me how you think about me, River." She leant back on her elbows, her stomach still bare.

I wasted no time lubing up, and she watched my ministrations avidly. I didn't feel self-conscious under her gaze. I felt more like I wanted to put on a fucking good show for her. So, I did my best.

Long, strong strokes as I imagined it was her wrapped around me. Her slick warmth covering me.

She put her hands on my legs, on my stomach, she drew me down for a kiss before pushing me back up so she could watch it all again. She was in charge, and I was at her mercy.

As my strokes got faster, she slid her hand into her shorts and her eyes pinned mine.

There we were, both masturbating, to each other, and it was so hot.

"Are you going to cum for me, River?" she asked, desire hazy in her eyes.

"You going to cum for *me*, baby?" I countered and she nodded.

Her hips bucked and her head pressed back into my pillows. "I'm so close, River."

My hand worked faster as she writhed under me. She was the single sexiest thing I had ever seen. She was so unapologetic and self-confidant. There wasn't a part of her that was self-conscious about masturbating in front of me while I was doing the same.

Instead of awkwardness, we were both getting off on it.

She put her arm over her mouth but that did next to nothing to stifle her cry as she came, and her pleasure was enough to send me over the edge. I fell forwards, catching myself with a hand beside her on the bed as I came on her stomach.

The hand in her shorts was still moving slowly as her other one reached up to my face and she kissed me softly. I kissed her back hungrily, feeling more satisfied than I had in two weeks, but still so on edge over her. But it was an awesome feeling now, not the blue balls aching of that whole week.

I grabbed some tissues and helped her clean up.

"It's so sticky," she chuckled as she found some on her arm. "And it's gone everywhere."

"Yeah, sorry."

She shook her head as her eyes found mine, a happy smile deep in them. "No. It's fine."

There was no talk of her going back to her place. She ducked out to the bathroom, and I'd expected she'd pull on the trackies and hoody lying on my floor that I assumed had been her protection from the elements on her way over. But she didn't. She just climbed into my bed and snuggled in under the blankets. So, I just went to the bathroom as well, closed the door and turned out the light on my way back, and did the exact same thing.

She was facing away from me, and I slid my arm under her neck. She rearranged to get comfortable and took my hand in hers. It would so be worth the risk of dead arm in the night.

"Was that better than a picture?" she asked me, and I laughed as I pulled her closer.

"Yeah, it was better than a picture," I said as I kissed her temple.

She snuggled into me, and I was threatening to get hard again.

"River," she said suddenly.

"Mm?" I answered absently, just enjoying having here there.

"There's a girl in your room."

I hugged her tight. "You're a girl?" I asked sarcastically.

She nodded. "In your bed and everything."

My heart did this weird fizzling thing in my chest, but I liked it. "I'd keep you here forever if I could," I told her, the dark making me bold.

"River?"

"Mm?"

"Did we just make things more complicated?"

I kissed her shoulder. "Probably."

"Do you mind?"

"I'm old and mature, and you're wise and smart. I think we'll figure it out."

"River?" There was humour in her voice, but also something else.

I gave her a gentle squeeze around the stomach. "Skye?"

"What are we doing?"

I coaxed her to roll over and look at me, even though it was almost impossible in the dark. "We're not rushing into anything."

"This isn't rushing?" she asked.

I shrugged. "I don't think so. If you do, we can slow it down more.”

“I don’t think I can handle any *slower*,” she said, and her voice was rueful.

My fingers trailed across her stomach. “Thank God, me either.”

“I have another proposition,” she said as her knee rubbed over my hip.

“Is it as enjoyable as mutual masturbation?”

I felt her humour. “I hope so…”

There was a slight hesitancy to her voice, and I knew I just needed to wait for her to think about what she wanted to say.

“I want to suggest we could do a friends with benefits sort of situation…” she started.

“But…?” I couldn’t help asking when she petered off. At least I managed to sound less desperate than I was feeling to just say ‘yes’.

“But the Code means no one can know about it, and…”

“You are killing me with these pauses, baby,” I laughed.

“And,” she said, and I heard the smile in her voice, “as much as I want to fool around with you, I feel like actual sex will…”

I felt her hesitation here. “Will be a line we can’t uncross?” I suggested.

“Something like that.”

I didn’t understand it, but I felt it, too. “I think we just proved we can get plenty of satisfaction without actual sex.”

I could feel hesitation in her still.

"What?" I asked, nuzzling my nose under her jaw. "Talk to me."

"If we did this–"

"I was liking the proposition until now."

"If we did this, I wouldn't want… I'm not the kind of girl to… Casual is one thing–"

"Exclusive," I said simply.

"Uh, yeah." She sounded so unsure, and I would not stand for that.

"Skye," I started, wanting her to know how sincere I was.

"Yeah?"

"I will be with you however you will have me. You want it to be just platonic while you bitch and moan through the latest Action movie and I eat all your ice creams? I'm down. You don't want me to even touch myself unless I'm on my knees in front of you in a gimp mask and you give me permission? I'm there. You want to never talk to me again? No questions asked. You want me totally celibate and only bring you to the heights of pleasure? Where do I sign?" I sighed as I leant my head to hers. "You want a secret friends with benefits situation without actually having sex? Baby, that sounds perfect."

"Really?"

I nodded. "I understand why that surprises you, but yes, Skye. God, yes."

She laughed and wrapped her arms around my neck. "I'm not saying never."

"You can if you want."

"I just…don't want to complicate things more than we already have, but I can't…"

"Ignore this anymore?" I offered and felt her nod.

"Not anymore."

"Then our decision of last night stands. With one change," I told her.

"What's that?" Panic gripped her voice.

"Exclusive," I said with a laugh. "Or did you forget already."

"Maybe I need Reminder Man all up in me."

I nuzzled into her neck. "Exclusive," I purred. "Exclusive." I grazed my teeth over her skin. "Exclusive." I pressed a kiss under her jaw. "Exclusive." Another one on her cheek. "Exclusive." I got to her lips.

"Exclusive?" she sassed.

I smiled against her. "Exclusive," I agreed.

♡9♡
Skye

I woke up at some point and had a mild panic about the arm draped over my waist. Then he shifted with a sleepy mutter and his smell enveloped me, and I didn't have to open my eyes to remember where I was or who I was with.

Had we complicated things? Hell, yes. But we also had a plan. Of sorts. An understanding. Sure, it would either be a funny story to tell our grandkids, or risk imploding both our worlds, but the way River made me feel was worth it.

I'd spent years thinking I hated him. Or, at least, loving but decidedly not liking aspects of him. In truth, nothing had changed, but I saw now that was just what it was like to love someone. Whether platonically, romantically or in a familial way. You could not like someone for a bit, but that didn't mean you stopped loving them and would never like them again.

As I slid out from under River's arm to find my phone and see what the time was, he suddenly yelled and thrashed in his sleep. Nothing discernible, just noise but, whatever he was dreaming, he wasn't having a good time of it.

My instincts had me shift over to his side and lay next to him while half sitting, kind of hugging his head awkwardly.

"Shh," I whispered. "You're okay. It's okay, River."

Like he heard my voice, he rolled over and burrowed into me. I saw his face scrunched in utter pain and my heart lurched. His head found refuge on my lap, his arm around my legs, and he finally settled again. His breathing eventually getting deep again.

I saw a clock on his bedside table, and saw it was only half four. There was a part of me who knew I'd need to sneak out before risking any of the other Chasers seeing me; I'd arrived while they were all at post-match recap for a reason. But I couldn't bring myself to leave him just yet.

Despite the awkward position, I dozed against his headboard until I felt him stir. The clock read almost six now. Explaining the slight light peeking around his curtains.

"What are you doing up there?" he mumbled, and I smiled.

"You had a bad dream," I told him as I ran my hand over his hair.

He was still wrapped around me, so I felt his body stiffen, then he pulled away quickly. "Sorry. I guess you were sneaking out?" I couldn't tell if he was awkward about the dream or pissed at the idea I was leaving.

"Just checking the time," I said slowly, wondering how I could make him less wary around me again.

He sat up and huffed. "It's getting late. Early. You should probably head out."

"Kicking a girl out. Sounds far more like you," I said, aiming for teasing. Sort of.

"Yeah?" was his acidic response as he stood up. "Good, dependable River, then."

I shuffled over to his side of the bed. "Riv…" I started.

"It's fine, Skye. Can't possibly risk anyone seeing you." His voice was still hard, and darkly sarcastic.

He turned on the lamp and I blinked against the light.

Then he was grabbing the clothes he'd dropped on the floor the night before and was getting dressed.

"River," I begged him. "What's–"

"Nothing, Calypso," he said quickly. "Stupid of us to pretend I did sleepovers."

Excuse you? "Oh, no," I huffed a humourless laugh. "Oh, you are not doing this, Pond Scum."

He whirled on me, and I saw his eyes. Something ugly gripped my heart, but I wouldn't let it put me off. His eyes were as dark as they ever were. The kind of dark when he was about to do something unbelievably stupid. Like letting the other guy beat him unconscious or opening a new bottle of whiskey when he could already barely stand.

"Not doing what, Gaol-bait?" he snarled.

I stood up, not that it helped much because it only seemed to highlight exactly how unintimidating I was next to this River. But I made up for it in attitude, assertion, and sheer force of will.

"You're not going to push me away now for… I don't even know what. Some misguided assumption I was rejecting you? Or I saw you in a moment of vulnerability? No. That's bullshit, River. I'm not doing this."

He shrugged wildly. "Fine. No one's asking you to. Leave, then."

I plopped back down on his bed, and I saw some of his bravado fade in confusion.

"What are you doing?"

"Not doing this," I said simply. "You're not kicking me out because you think I'm about to leave."

"If anyone sees–"

I nodded. "Yeah, I know. Shit hits the fan, and we are nowhere near ready to deal with that yet. But I'm not leaving 'til *this* shit is sorted. What the fuck has got your panties in a knot?"

He completely deflated and ran a defeated hand through his hair as he looked at me. A war waged in his eyes and I didn't know what it was about. All I could do was wait semi-patiently and hope that he explained himself when he had his thoughts together.

"I… I don't want to hurt you, Skye."

"So, you think making up a bullshit fight and kicking me out is going to solve that?"

He waggled his head noncommittally then came and dropped to a crouch between my legs. "No. Yes!" He lay his head on my leg. "I don't know."

"Talk to me, River," I pled.

He sighed heavily and pressed his face into my thigh like it was both a comfort and a hiding place. "You know there's a darkness in me, Skye."

I nodded as I ran my hand over his hair in what I hoped was a comforting pat. "I know."

"My dream–"

"I don't need specifics if you don't want to give them, Riv."

I knew there was some epic shit in his history. Everyone did. Taylor had never given me the details, said it wasn't his place but, whenever it came up, Taylor's eyes got this look in them that told me just hearing about them was disturbing. Whatever River and I were, we didn't need to go into it ever if he didn't want to. It was enough to know he'd dealt with his unfair share of something, and it had left a mark on his soul. One that, just at that moment, I would do anything to heal. But healing it wasn't up to me no matter how much I wished it was.

He shook his head and looked up at me again, still leaning on my leg. "I don't want it to hurt you. I don't want it to…infect you."

I leant down to him and took his face in my hands to nudge his nose with mine. "And what if it doesn't?"

"What if it does?" he said, and I heard in his voice just how much the idea alone pained him.

I gave him a smile. "Making up bullshit fights and pushing me away is only self-fulfilling prophecy, not proof of anything, baby."

I finally saw the hint of smile tugging at his lips. "I couldn't bear it if I hurt you."

"Then don't push me away over nothing. When you get bored or you're done or you fall for someone else, then we have a discussion, and we end it amicably."

"You think I'm going to get bored or be done or find someone else?" he asked, sounding more like his usual, cocky, teasing self.

I shrugged. "I'm not making assumptions about what this is, River. What if it doesn't work out?"

"What if it does?"

I smirked. "Well, it's not going to if you're all dramatic and tragic."

He snorted and knelt up so he could reach my face. "I'm sorry I was all dramatic and tragic."

I nodded. "You should be." And pressed a kiss to his lips.

"It doesn't change the fact you probably should leave me."

I laughed. "I thought you weren't going to be dramatic and tragic?"

"I didn't say I wouldn't be. I just apologised for it."

"Don't be pedantic."

"Besides, you're the one who didn't use a pillow last night. The rest of the house probably knows I've had someone in here."

I bit my lip. "Yeah. Sorry."

He shrugged. "I don't fucking care. It was sexy."

"You don't care that I might have given away that the guy, who doesn't have people in his room, had someone in his room?"

He shrugged again. "You keep reacting like that, and they can think what they want."

"Still wasn't three pillows' worth," I sassed, and his eyes flashed.

"You probably don't have to leave for a few more minutes," he said slowly, and I felt a million flutters.

"You really want to advertise how quick you're going to be?" I teased him and his smirk grew.

Slowly and purposefully, he put his hands on my hips and tugged me to the edge of his bed.

"River…?" I said slowly.

"Skye…?" he said equally slowly, molten heat firing in his eyes as he lowered himself between my legs.

"River…?" I said again as his head disappeared.

Then he'd pushed my shorts to the side as he very deliberately mumbled, "Skye?" so his lips brushed over me.

"What are you planning here?" I asked him as his tongue ran up over my clit.

"I'm aiming for one pillow minimum," I heard him say, then he gripped my hip harder before using one hand to coax me down into lying on the bed.

I was distracted from any reply I'd lined up as I felt him gently run his tongue over my clit again before sucking on it hard. My back arched slightly off the bed, and I felt the smile in his cheeks against my thighs.

God, but that was the most intimate thing I think I'd ever felt in my whole damned life. It was at once the most amazing feeling, but it also made my heart flutter wildly and a flicker of doubt hit for the briefest of seconds.

Was this going too far?

Was this one of those lines we couldn't uncross?

But then, if this thing with River was ever going to be a real thing, we had to take steps forward or risk stagnating and fucking it up anyway. And, God, but he was really good at it. Like *really* good at it. Who was I to say no to a man willing to inflict those levels of pleasure on me? It would just be rude to stop now.

The hand that, moments earlier, I'd been sure was going to grab his hair and pull him away instead held him closer as I ground against his mouth.

My heart pounded in my chest. I couldn't escape the knowledge that my brother's best friend and my life-long annoyance had his face buried between my legs. But it felt right. I didn't feel like I was doing anything wrong or taboo or that we were heading for the kind of hard and fast that only ever ends in a fatal crash.

No. It was just all gratifying. Heart, soul and…carnal. The kind of gratifying that an arm would in no way even pretend to suffice.

"River. River," I panted. "Jesus…"

My left arm searched the bed desperately, and I finally found one of his pillows. I grabbed it and shoved it over my face as I came hard and legit cried out his name. My back full-on arched off the bed involuntarily, and my legs shook as they tried to clamp around his head. I felt his huff of laughter and the smile on his face, and forced myself to relax again.

"Still…" I said as I breathed heavily and removed the pillow. "…only counts as one."

He stood up and looked down at me. There was a hunger in his eyes as he dragged his hand over his chin. It was deep and there was something about it that made my nipples pinch and tingles shoot down my spine. It made me nervous, in a really good way. I bit my lip as I let him pull me to sitting.

"I'm building up, baby. Can't give you everything all at once, can I?"

I smirked. "No. We couldn't have that."

He dipped down and pressed a deep, lingering, needy kiss to my lips. I very nearly grabbed him, turned us around and threw him on his bed to climb on board, sailor. But I refrained, by the thinnest thread that was about one touch away from snapping.

River finally moved away, scooped up my trackies and deftly threw them to me. I less deftly caught them with my shoulder as my hand closed over empty space. He gave me a shit-stirring smile.

"What are your plans today?" he asked as he reached to the floor for my hoody.

"I told Taylor I'd call in later," I said as I pulled on my trackies and my ugg boots, still very aware of the blissful tingles bursting between my legs at the slightest brush or movement.

He nodded as he absently ran my hoody through his hands. "Okay."

"Why?"

He shrugged as he chucked me the hoody. "Nah. Just wondering, is all."

"You've had one sleepover and suddenly you want to do breakfast?" I teased.

He grinned. "No. I like hanging out with you." He shrugged again. "I've always liked hanging out with you."

"You've always like giving me shit," I corrected him, but it was good-natured.

"It's our love language," he answered, and I paused in my tracks. "What?" he laughed.

I shook my head. "Nothing. I guess that just should have been more obvious to me."

He frowned quizzically and I was the one shrugging.

"I mean, it makes a scary amount of sense."

He shook his head. "No. Because you hate me," he seemed to be reminding me.

"I hate some of your behaviour, River. I don't hate *you*." Then, I added as shit-stirring, "Most of the time."

There was a fleck of humour in his eyes, but his jaw was tight. "I *am* my behaviour, Skye."

I stood up, pocketing my phone. "No. You *want* people to think you're your behaviour."

"Are you really starting a fight over who I think I am?"

I smirked. "No. I'm not starting a fight."

"You sure sound like you are."

I leant up to his lips. "It's not a fight when I'm right, baby," I sassed, then kissed him.

Before I pulled away, I felt the smile on his lips. "Oh, is that how we're playing it?"

I nodded as I headed for his door. "That's how we're playing it, Pond Scum."

Humour flashed bright in his eyes, and he licked his bottom lip. "All right. Game on, baby."

"Game on, baby," I agreed. "I'll see you later."

"Not if I see you first."

I gave him a wink and then slunk out his door, pulling it closed behind me.

The mansion was dead quiet, except for the whir of a machine in their small home gym that I knew was probably Ajax up and at it already. I saw no Chasers, and barely anyone else, as I snuck out the front door and back to my apartment.

I got maybe a couple of hours of sleep in my own bed before Tansy woke me up demanding answers. She insisted she'd spontaneously combust if she had to wait any longer.

Whatever was happening between River and I, it wasn't so much changing our dynamic as building on it. Yeah, there was a whole new sexual aspect to us now, but that wasn't all it was. We were still us.

I'd done as I'd said and met Taylor at the McMansion later that day, and we were hanging in one of the lounge rooms, playing some Sports on the console, when River strolled in.

"No one told me Mini Dev was in the house," he said as he dropped into one of the chairs to watch us.

"That's because I'm *dev*astating Taylor," I said pointedly, and River chuckled.

"Need to sub me in, mate?" he asked my brother.

"She's wiping the fucking floor with me," Taylor grumbled.

River snorted. "It's the three-pointer shoot off, it's like the easiest."

"Shut up," Taylor muttered.

"I mean, that's the only reason Skye's any good at it," River continued. "Now, table tennis? Skye is horrendous at table tennis."

"You want to talk about the golf?" I suggested, throwing him a look as I took my shot.

His eyes darted to where my clothes parted and showed bare stomach. While his eyes heated a little, it was far more important to give me shit about my Wii Sports skills – or lack thereof – than to think about how much we wanted each other just then.

"Windsurfing, Calypso?" he countered.

He had me there, I was legitimately terrible at the windsurfing.

"What happened to the girl?" Taylor asked like he knew River and I could go at it for the rest of the afternoon if left unchecked. If he was aiming for nonchalant, he was doing a piss poor job of it.

"What girl?" River replied, sounding as casual as you please. My heart, meanwhile, was trying to crawl out of my chest. Thankfully, it had no negative impacts on my shooting.

"The one heard *actually* screaming your name all night?" My brother laughed as he shook his head. "Damn, dude. But you know how to make a guy jealous."

"Aw," River teased him. "You want me to make you scream my name, mate?"

Taylor shot him a look. "I'd be lying if I said it hadn't crossed my mind. Short of that, teach me your secrets."

River snorted. "My secrets, I will teach you, young padawan, when ready you are."

Taylor laughed. "Fine. Who needs your secrets?"

"Based on Claire's feedback last week, you," River said and only just caught the cushion Taylor threw at his face.

He lowered the cushion to show us the biggest teasing grin River Torres owned.

"Shut up. As soon as I'm done getting my arse kicked by my little sister, we're bowling."

"Okay, you're on. But I need snacks first," River said.

Taylor was finishing his last couple of dismal shots so River stood up and headed for the kitchen. As Taylor was then navigating to the bowling, I watched River's retreating arse. When he was far enough away that I could say he was out of earshot, I turned to my brother.

"Drinks?" I asked him.

He nodded. "Sure. Sounds good."

I rolled my eyes. "Anything in particular?" I said, sounding an awful lot like our mother when she wanted us to be more helpful.

"Nah. Whatever you want is good."

I nodded. "Cool."

I hurried as inconspicuously as possible to the kitchen and thankfully found River alone in there. He had a bag of chips and was getting a bowl out of the cupboard. Suddenly an awkward fog descended over me, even as he gave me an easy, welcoming grin over his shoulder.

"You ready for the game next week?" I asked him as I lounged against the bench.

Next week's round was no different to any other round in terms of gameplay or fanfare, but the Hornets were the Chasers' main rivals, and it meant a lot to beat them.

"Blake's out with an injury, but I heard Perez is out for the rest of the season," River answered as he poured the chips into a bowl.

"Yes, because Blake and Perez are on the same level," I joked.

River threw me another grin and came to put the bowl on the bench beside me. "I don't think anyone's on the same level as Perez."

"Don't tell Ajax that," I said with a grin.

He leant towards me and pressed a quick kiss to my lips. "And here I thought you were going to compliment me," he teased.

"Compliment *you*?" I scoffed humouredly. "You think me sleeping in your bed one night means I'm going to start complimenting you?"

He leant his nose to mine. "How many nights will it take?" he asked suggestively, peppering each word with its own kiss.

I laughed. "Why don't we see when – if! – it happens a second time?"

"When?" he asked cheekily.

"If," I clarified, both of us knowing I was only teasing.

"What *if* tonight?" he asked, his eyebrows bouncing.

I shook my head. "I have class tomorrow. No sleepovers on a school night."

As he looked me over, I saw the warmth in his eyes. The teasing. The humour. The shared joke. The desire. The love.

There was so much history between us and things were changing. I wasn't scared of them changing or not working out, but I was scared of us running into this way too quickly and ruining whatever chance we had. An organic ending was entirely different to us fucking it up and forever wondering what might have been.

So, as much as I wanted to wrap my whole body around his and make him take me straight up to his room for much, much more than we'd had the night before, I just picked up the bowl of chips and kicked my head to him.

"Grab the drinks."

It wasn't a question and his eyes flashed hotter as though he liked me bossing him around.

"Game fucking on, baby," he chuckled.

I licked my lip and threw him a wink. "Game on."

10
River

I had never been happier, and I hadn't gone this long without actual sex since before I lost my virginity.

True to her word, Skye refused to do sleepovers on school nights. She wasn't, however, averse to late nights. Or, to put it more accurately, she seemed as incapable of kicking me out as I was of leaving her.

So, to be texting her of an afternoon to see what she was up to because I was jonesing for my next hit was not out of the ordinary. Given that it was an afternoon on which I didn't have soccer practice, I actually had some free time to relax.

Riv.Torn

What are you up to?

Sky'mDevestated

Studying.

Riv.Torn

Boring.

Sky'mDevestated

Necessary.

What are you doing?

Riv.Torn

Considering joining you.

Because I was now. So much for relaxing. If she was studying,

I was thinking about studying. The idea was, as long as she was involved, attractive to me. I both hated and loved what she brought out in me.

Sky'mDevestated

I REALLY need to get this homework finished, Pond Scum.

Riv.Torn

Like I don't have assignments to do as well.

Sky'mDevestated

This isn't code for hooking up, Torres.
I need to get some work done.
Sorry xx

Riv.Torn

I honestly wasn't suggesting it was. I am literally considering joining you while we both study.
Just so I can spend some time with you.
Meet you in the library in fifteen?

Sky'mDevestated

Lol. Why? You worried you won't be able to focus if we're in my room?

Riv.Torn

I'm worried I won't be able to focus if we're in the

library.

I'm still planning on it.

Did I make it a habit of studying with girls? Fuck, no.

When it came to any other girl than Skye, I was a chauvinistic arsehole. I knew what I was, and I never pretended to be otherwise. I didn't make friends with girls easily and, as arrogant as it was, most girls who tried to befriend me only wanted one thing. Which was convenient, because it was the same – and only – thing I wanted from them.

But not Skye.

Never Skye.

With absolutely zero hesitation, I packed up some books and my laptop and headed towards the library. I was on my way out the front door of the mansion when I got her reply.

Sky'mDevestated

Fine. But no funny business.
First sign of funny business
and I won't be able to
control myself reciprocating,
but you can explain to
Richard why my grades are
slipping.

I wasn't going anywhere near Richard I didn't have to, so I'd be a good boy and keep myself to myself. After Skye's little comment to Tansy the other week, I wasn't going to take her warning with as much flippancy as I might have previously. Maybe I was distracting her too much. Was if I was the cause of her losing her spot at Chester? Quite aside from the fact that *my* life would suck without her in it basically every day, I didn't want to be the reason her future came crashing down around her.

Of course, keeping myself to myself was a lot harder when we were sitting at a table together in one of the most out of the way corners in the library and she was right fucking there. But she'd explicitly stated no funny business and I was nothing if not good at following the rules it was beneficial for me to follow.

She let me run my finger over the back of her hand, and she nudged my knee with hers every now and then like she was reminding me that we might have been doing separate study, but we were doing it together.

And it was the easiest thing in the world. Sitting with her in silence – but for the tapping of laptop keys, the flicking of textbook pages, the occasional mutter of annoyance at something being stupid – was the most natural, normal, perfect thing in my life. Like we did it all the time. Like I did it ever. If this was what it was going to be like, I was pretty sure I could do it forever.

So of course my best mate had to come and ruin it.

"What in the hell are you doing here?" I heard Taylor's voice and looked up.

He was looking between me and Skye like the world had turned upside down. And I guess it kind of had.

"Bumped into each other," she said without looking up. "Seemed no reason to not sit together."

"I needed a steadying influence," I joked.

Taylor grinned, but I saw something in his eyes that told me he was trying to work out if there was anything else there. "The amount of study you've been doing lately, I wouldn't have thought you needed it. Or you already had it."

I shrugged. "Little extra never hurt anyone," I said as Skye sassed, "You've been *studying* lately, have you?"

I smirked. "A boy has to keep his grades up."

She scoffed. "That what the cool kids are calling it these days?"

"I am not at all surprised you don't know that," I retorted, implication heavy in my tone.

"Excuse you. I'm not uncool," she huffed.

"Doesn't make you cool."

Skye looked at her brother, who just shrugged.

"What?" he asked.

She looked indignant and I loved it. "What?" she repeated. "How about standing up for your poor, helpless little sister?"

Taylor snorted. "Helpless? You? Don't think so."

"You're still supposed to come to my defence."

Taylor shook his head. "Nu-uh. When it comes to you two, I'm impartial. I'm fucking Switzerland."

"What?" I cried sarcastically. "The whole country?"

He smirked. "Dry spell making you a little jealous, Torres?"

I scoffed. "Dry spell, Dev? Never."

He nodded his head, and I could tell he didn't believe me. "Sure. No, sure. I mean, there's that girl you have in your room. The rest of the team is totally not starting to think she's recorded and you're just reliving the glory days in a bout of depression."

The idea that the team was actually floating that idea made the whole thing so much more worth it. Of all the guys to be having a dry spell in the team, I was least likely. But then, weirdly, I actually kind of was. Not that it felt like it at all.

"Do you want it or not?" Skye asked, finally looking up at her brother.

He nodded. "Yes. Yes, I do want it."

I scoffed. "What is this? Some kind of back library drug deal?"

"Close," Taylor admitted.

"Mum sent shortbread," explained Skye.

"No way!" I hissed, aware that even tucked away in the library equalled being *in* the library, and there could be battle-ready librarians around any shelf ready to shush me within an inch of my life.

Skye nodded. "Way. But I've only got Tay's box. Yours is still at my place."

Fuck. I was overthinking things again. Because that sounded an awful lot like a code to get me back to hers after this. Or had Taylor somehow encroached and the box in her bag was meant to be mine? Or…

My eyes narrowed. "You sure you weren't just planning to eat mine and hope Taylor finished his before he got back to the mansion so I wouldn't know?" I asked her.

She shrugged, very coy. "What you didn't know couldn't hurt you."

I shook my head. "Not cool."

And, yeah, double standards and all that. It was the exact theory I was running on. But this was Mrs Devereux's shortbread we were talking about. Not something that was going to implode a relationship – sexual or platonic – before it even had a chance to get started. It wasn't something better left in the past so it didn't tarnish the present and future. We were talking about things that very definitely belonged in my stomach.

Skye gave me a look that told me in no uncertain terms that I was wrong. "We've been through this." She pointed to herself. "Very cool."

Taylor pointed at both of us. "Super uncool. Where are my biscuits?"

Skye huffed and rolled her eyes as she grabbed her bag and went hunting for biscuits.

"I don't know why you couldn't wait. This essay isn't going to finish itself," she muttered.

"Why do you only have my box?" Taylor asked, as though

suddenly suspicious.

Did I imagine the way Skye's eyes darted to me? Was I right that they were meant to be mine?

"Because I thought I'd see you first. And I knew River would kill me if I left his box with you or unprotected in the mansion."

Taylor shrugged as he took the box from her. "He'd sure be pissed if someone ate them first."

Skye nodded. "Okay. Great. So, now you can go away and let me study in peace." She waved her hand at him as she went back to her work.

"You coming or staying?" Taylor asked me.

I shrugged. "I've still got–"

Taylor scoffed. "Come on, man. Nina said she was finally getting Callie out of the house tonight. I don't care what excuses you've been using to avoid coming out lately, but you can't pass *that* up."

I mean, I could. I would. But studying with his sister was one thing, passing up the twins was going to raise a million red flags.

Skye shifted next to me, and I desperately wanted to know what she was thinking. We'd agreed to keep this thing on the downlow until we knew exactly what it was, and that it wasn't going to make a whole mess of everything only to end as quickly as it started and still leave us dealing with the shit it caused.

So, she had to know that I only had one choice if we didn't want to make Taylor suspicious. I was going to have to choose him.

I nodded. "No. Sure. Let me just finish this. I'll meet you back at the mansion in about half an hour?"

Taylor shrugged again and helped himself to a chair. "I can wait that long."

Skye sighed loudly and dramatically. "Just don't get in the

way, Tay, 'kay?"

Taylor crossed his heart. "Wouldn't dream of it, Nerd-guy Skye."

Her eyes darted up with a glare, but she said no more.

Taylor pulled his phone out and I felt stuck between a very literal rock and a hard place. I knew Taylor wasn't going anywhere until I was, totally innocuously because it was the kind of thing we always did. Then there was Skye, who I felt was owed an explanation as to why I'd agreed to hang out with the twins when we'd agreed to be exclusive.

How the hell had I got myself in this mess?

I'd have said no one was worth the absolute cluster-fuck I'd caused myself. But Skye was worth that and more. I understood why she didn't want to go public, but I also had a vested interest in keeping things to ourselves until we knew this was going to work long-time, if not forever.

"Oo," Taylor cooed. "You seen Callie's latest post?"

I smirked despite myself. "Dunno. When was it?"

"Ten minutes ago. And if that's a snap of what we can expect tonight, I call dibs."

I laughed. "Going for the coveted twin threesome, mate?"

Taylor looked at me with a knowing smirk. "You wanna race for it?"

Skye suddenly swept her shit together and stood up. "You two are disgusting. Those girls are people. They might not even be interested in you." The she rolled her eyes like she knew that was unlikely. "You can't call dibs on a girl."

Taylor sat back and crossed his arms. "You *can* call dibs on a girl."

Skye clearly wasn't impressed with that attitude. "No, you can't."

"Tell me you didn't call dibs on Freddie Sinclair, and I'll take it back."

Skye opened her mouth to argue, then snapped it closed. She shot me a look that in no uncertain terms told me to keep mine shut. I couldn't.

"Freddie Sinclair?" I spluttered, failing to not laugh. I remembered Freddie Sinclair and the idea Skye called dibs on him was hilarious.

Her glare deepened. "I was fourteen!" was her defence.

Taylor shrugged. "And I'm twenty. What's your point?"

"You're old enough to know better."

Taylor leant towards her. "Just because I call dibs, doesn't mean I expect anything."

"Oh, really?"

He nodded. "Really. It just means Magic Cock himself over here has to keep his hands to himself until I've had a chance. If she doesn't pick me? Fine, he gets his shot."

I watched Skye swallow hard at the mention of my dick. Fuck, I wished her brother wasn't here right now. But then, it was probably a good thing because I might have tried bending her over the table, rules or not.

"You're still a dick," Skye said, her tone suggesting even she thought it was a weak comeback.

Taylor grinned. "Never suggested otherwise."

She rolled her eyes in lieu of answering, because she was out of arguments. So, she just grunted in annoyance, spared us both a look that told us exactly what choice words she was thinking about us, and stormed out of the library.

"Du-ude!" I hissed, leaning over the table to him.

"What?" he asked.

I sighed and started packing up my shit. "I just needed a few more minutes—"

"To pine over my sister some more?" he teased. "Mate, you can do that whenever. Nina. And. Callie. This is a *once* in a semester thing."

I took a deep breath. "Taylor…" I started. *Rules be fucking damned.*

"Am I in trouble?" he laughed.

I scrubbed my hand over my chin in frustration. "Look, me and Skye—"

He held up a hand to stop me. "I know," he said softly.

I blinked. *Fuck.* "You know?"

He nodded. "Yeah, I know. You guys are who you are, and I love you both. Do I sometimes wish for a world where you two at least *pretended* to get along for my sake? Sure. But," he shrugged as he stood up, "that's family, man. Whole lotta love, but like isn't a requirement."

I didn't know what to say to that. I had actually totally been about to tell him that I'd been hooking up with his sister – and I thought it had the potential to be 'it' – but his certainty about what he thought I'd been going to say gave me pause. He who thought he knew better than anyone, could read my mind at the drop of a hat in any situation. And it wasn't anything like I'd been going to say.

What did it say about me that he didn't guess? Or, maybe, he was still in denial? Maybe he knew what was going on, but he didn't want to talk about it because that would mean he couldn't ignore it anymore?

Shit!

This whole thing was fucked up.

I was keeping secrets from my best friend AND I'd just accepted an offer to hang out with other girls from said best friend in front of the girl I was madly crushing on to keep those secrets.

But I plastered on the old Torres charming smirk as we headed to the mansion to get changed. "No doubt," I told him. "No doubt."

But there was doubt. Much doubt. None of which was assuaged when I texted Skye the moment I closed my bedroom door behind me.

Riv.Torn
You know nothing's going
to happen tonight.

My heart spent the whole minute it took her to reply trying to crawl out my throat. Her answer didn't make it feel any better.

Sky'mDevestated
Do I?

Riv.Torn
Come on, Calypso. Please
tell me you understood why
I did what I did.

Sky'mDevestated
I understand, but does that
mean I have to like it? Or
wonder what the
implications actually are?

Riv.Torn
We said exclusive. I meant
it.
Would you rather just tell
him about us?

Part of me hoped she'd say yes.

Sky'mDevestated
Sure.

Seriously?

    If you want to risk blowing
up both our lives and all our
important relationships.

Riv.Torn

What if it helps them?

Sky'mDevestated

If you need a reason to end
this before you leave the
mansion tonight, then man
the fuck up and just do it.

I scoffed, and part of it was humoured.

Riv.Torn

Now who's making up
bullshit fights?

Sky'mDevestated

…
You're right. I'm sorry. I just…
I feel bad lying to Taylor, but
we don't even know what
this is, River. I'm not ready to
unleash it on the world and
have to deal with all that shit
while we're still figuring it
out.
Because you know there's
going to be a mountain of
shit.

Riv.Torn

I do know that.

Sky'mDevestated

I'm scared that, if we have to

deal with all that as well,
then we won't get the
chance to figure it out. It will
all get in the way and ruin us
before we really even start.

I understood that. I really did. More than I was going to tell her.

Ignoring Taylor's thoughts on the matter, we had Jax and the Team standing between us. The shit I'd get for hooking up with her, even if they weren't actively trying to break us up, would take a toll. I wasn't a good guy, and I wasn't afraid to admit that I was scared I'd be too weak to stick through it. The only thing that made me feel better about that was that it sounded like she was saying a very similar thing. That and we had a workaround; keep keeping it to ourselves, and those external pressures weren't going to be a problem. Not yet, anyway.

Riv.Torn

I get it, babe. I really do.
Plus, I'm just selfish enough
to want to keep you to
myself.

Sky'mDevestated

Just promise me you won't
be stupid tonight.

Riv.Torn

I won't. Promise. I'll be
keeping an eye on Taylor.

Sky'mDevestated

Thanks.

Well, shit.

Clearly that hadn't been the right thing to say.

Riv.Torn

You're the only girl for me,

Calypso.

Sky'mDevestated

Fuuuuuck.

Was a yellow heart a good thing or a bad thing? Because it didn't feel like a good thing. It felt like the sort of reply that was meant to make me think everything was okay, but also testing me to see if I realised she wasn't happy. I mean, fucking mind games, but we all played them.

And if I hadn't realised she wasn't happy with me after that fucking yellow heart response, I'd have worked it out from the lack of seeing her or really talking to her the next two days.

That had been Wednesday. I didn't see her on Thursday or Friday. So much so, that I knew she was avoiding me. And I knew I kind of deserved it. She gave me the shortest replies to my texts, the bare minimum to show she wasn't totally ignoring me but also telling me I was in the shit house. Or she just needed space, so I was going to give it to her. She was the one who'd been against bullshit fights, and we were both new to this, so she'd reach out when she was ready.

We had a home game that Saturday and, true to form despite whatever bump in the road we might have been in the midst of, Skye and Tansy were in the stands behind the team's bench covered head to toe in Chaser's merchandise and waving signs with 'RIVER' and 'TAYLOR' on them.

Poor Forbsy.

As I ran past, I glanced at her again. She smiled at me, and I was pretty sure that was an apology on her face. She bit her lip and gave me a small shrug, and I nodded. Of course, I forgave her.

I'd done plenty of stupid shit in my life, and she was still here. If she was apologising, then we could talk about it and it was all going to be okay.

At half time, we were down two-nil and I had to admit, I hadn't been playing my best; we were at very real risk of losing to the fucking Hornets. Again. So, I was a very naughty boy and checked my phone and saw I was right. About Skye.

> **Sky'mDevestated**
> I'm sorry I've been a bit MIA.
> I overreacted. Maybe not
> quite a bullshit fight, but
> bullshit nonetheless. I was
> jealous and had no right to
> be. We agreed to keep this
> secret and we agreed to be
> exclusive. I don't doubt you,
> River, not really. But you've
> never done this before and I
> was scared you were getting
> bored. I'm going to try not to
> let my fears get in our way
> again. Forgive me?

As relieved as I was, I didn't have time to reply. I barely got the whole thing read before Ajax fair smacked my phone out of my hand.

"Get your fucking head out of your dick and onto the fucking game, Torres," he snarled.

"Aw, I love you, too, man," I teased, and he just growled at me.

As we jogged back onto the pitch, I looked to Skye and gave her a salute to show I'd got her text and understood. She broke out into a wide smile, but still chewed her lip like she was trying not to give too much away to anyone who might be watching us.

And, just like that, I was back to being my best again. In the fifty-first minute, I scored our first goal. Then, at sixty-eight minutes came the equaliser, and I celebrated accordingly.

"Killer! Killer! Killer!" the crowd cheered as I skidded towards the corner, my arms in the air.

Taylor jumped on my back, and we crumpled to the ground to louder cheering.

I ignored the way my on-field nickname always made my chest twinge and the shadows descend. I kicked the darkness off and took it for what it was supposed to be; a call of support for a good play made up as a joke about my penchant for getting laid and then moving on after.

"Killer, Killer, Killer!" it went again from one half of the fans.

"Oi, oi, oi!" came the answering call from the other half.

Forbsy joined the pileup and started shaking me in excitement.

"YES!" he laughed. "Come on, Killer. One more!"

We all heard the ref blow the whistle. "Come on. Don't make me card you now, Torres. You're just making this interesting again."

Taylor helped pull me off the grass and we all jogged back to the centre for kick off, my eyes on the Hornet's centre, Wilcox.

"RIVER! WOO!" I heard the unmistakable yell of Skye from the stands and smiled.

"Still not tapped that, Torres?" Wilcox drawled.

I frowned at him, but Skye yelled my name again, complete with absolutely over the top 'woo' and my smile fought through.

Wilcox smirked like he knew why I couldn't stop smiling. "Once she's done with the Chasers, she'll find the Hornets have the real men." Implication was heavy in his tone. Usually, I wouldn't stand for it and I'd be red-carded right off the pitch.

Instead, I laughed. "Yeah, nice try, mate. But not today."

The ref blew his whistle, and I was behind the ball the moment it left Wilcox's boot to pass it over to Ajax.

I had never been more focussed, less irritable, or had more energy despite how often Skye and I had been up late that week or how often I'd had to stop myself taking things too far with her. I felt like I bounced around the pitch like a fucking pinball machine. I showboated way worse than usual, pulling out my fanciest footwork and popping off some effortless shots that a whole three hours of training would never produce.

We cruised to a three-two win over the Hornets and I didn't even throw a punch at Wilcox for some less than savoury remarks at the end of the match. I didn't fucking care. He could say whatever he wanted about Skye to try to get a rise out of me, but I was far too high for it to touch me.

Ajax spared me a very reticent nod of approval for the part I played on the field and I, like the cocky bastard I was, nodded back with a shit-stirring grin. Ajax's eyebrows drew even closer and I knew I was pushing my luck.

"Killer in the house!" Frankie D cried as he jumped on my back.

"Mate, that last one. Stroke of fucking brilliance," Robbie said appreciatively.

I pointed at Robbie while giving Ajax, 'see? I'm a god' eyes. Ajax was not impressed. Unsurprisingly.

"You know what happens to cocky bastards," Ajax growled.

I nodded. "Extra practice?" I guessed.

"They get their entire fucking futures whipped out from under them like their arrogance deserves."

"Self-righteous much?" I teased him.

"It'd be you going pro next season instead of me if you weren't so fucking unfocussed."

I frowned as the rest of the team parted around us, paying no mind to the captain giving their star forward yet another talking to.

"I'm focussed, or did you not notice I hat-tricked our way to a win?"

Ajax shrugged. "Yeah, you're good, mate. But, you could be so much fucking better."

"What do you want me to do, Cap? Have no life? Live in fucking depressing solitary? Waking up at five to train, study, shit, sleep and do it all again?"

"If you want a shot at pro, then, yes."

I swallowed hard. I wasn't sure I did want a shot at pro. Not really. Not international levels anyway. Not now I had something to keep me at home. Or at least might have something to keep me at home. There was definitely someone I wanted to keep me at home.

Ajax nodded when I didn't say anything. "Yeah, I figured."

I bristled. "There's more to life than just a career going pro."

He nodded again. Once. "If that's what makes you happy, fine. But while you're on my team, you keep the kind of focus we saw in the second half."

"And what if the thing that makes me happy gives me that focus?" I asked, bold without the rest of the team in ear shot.

Ajax looked me over. "Then you fucking hold on to her and don't fuck it up."

It was me nodding now. "That was the plan."

"Good."

I snorted and his frown deepened.

"Sorry," I told him. "You just looked like spitting image of

Grumpy Cat just then."

There may have been a touch of humour in his eyes. "Go fucking shower."

"Yes, Cap."

By the time I was done with the ritual of a post-win shower in the locker rooms, there was a text on my phone from Skye.

> **Sky'mDevestated**
> I never gave you your shortbread. Want to come by when you're done and get it?

Did I? Yes.

> **Riv.Torn**
> Just getting dressed. I'll be there soon.

"Right. How many drinks are we being offered tonight, then?" Taylor asked and the rest of the guys laughed.

"I've got plans," Forbsy said. "But have a few for me."

"Oh, plans," Whistler teased and Forbsy grinned.

"Yeah, plans. Of the date variety. Thank you very much."

"Oh, Forbsy's got a date!" chorused around the room.

I smiled at Forbsy and gave him a nod. I might give him shit with the others – it was who we were – but that didn't mean I wasn't going to support him going after his person. After all, all we had in this world was giving it our very best and, even if it all went down in flames, at least we know we tried.

Better to have loved and lost and all that shit.

I knocked on Skye's door a little later and found her alone.

She was holding my box of shortbread from her mum and chewing her lip.

"I'm sorry," she said.

I shook my head. "Thanks, but I'm one hundred percent forgiving you. Already forgiven. And forgotten."

"I was a bit of an idiot."

"Not the first time. Won't be the last time."

"River..." she started and I stopped being flippant. "We said we'd talk to each other, and I didn't do that. It was stupid and meant I missed out on two days of seeing you."

I smirked. "You spend one night in my bed and now you're hooked?" I joked.

She was trying not to smile. "I like hanging out with you." She put her hand on my chest as she stepped closer, and I was in danger of messing up. "But I'm serious. I missed you. It gave me time to think. Too much time."

"Good or bad?" I asked, knowing a little something about that.

"Both," she admitted.

I nodded. "Anything I need to know?"

Her eyes dropped low. "Tanz said she and Forbsy were out tonight..." Skye started as she tucked a piece of hair behind her ear.

I poked my head into her apartment like I was double checking. "Oh, yeah?"

Skye nodded. "Yeah..."

I nodded as well. "Good for them. Anywhere nice?"

She smirked. "You could come in, if you want?"

I looked at her like I hadn't even thought about it. But, of course, I'd fucking thought about it. I'd thought about exactly where it could lead. Namely, Skye screaming my name in carnal pleasure again. And again. And again. But she'd said no sex. So, no sex it was going to be. To be honest, I just counted myself lucky I got to kiss her and touch her and have any kind of interaction with her that wasn't just us antagonising each other, as fun as that was.

"I've got a whole box of virgin ice creams begging to be stolen," she said as she took a step towards me.

Fuck me.

Except not, because that was the whole point.

I wasn't sure, at this point, if I was reading too much into the things she said or small actions she did because I'd gone without for a while and I wanted her badly. Or maybe she was testing me. That sounded like her. She might not have been intentionally cruel with her teasing, but she was going to step right up to the line and push me as far as she could.

Well, I could show her that I was stronger than that. I was better than that. Which was bullshit – I wasn't better than anything – but I'd do right by her and respect her wishes because it was the least she deserved. Just because I was a debased animal with a raging boner for her, that was my problem, not hers.

I nodded, keeping myself as calm as I could. "While I would love to deflower your box, baby, I don't have nearly enough time before Forbsy and Tanz get back to do them justice."

Oh, that had been quite possibly the worst thing to say. Her weres were liquid sapphire. Molten heat. She liked the idea of me deflowering her box – as it were – as much as me. But this wasn't like after our first kiss where we'd both wanted to act on it and thought the other one didn't. We'd talked, we'd communicated. She'd said no sex.

She's allowed to be horny and it not mean sex, idiot.

Fuck, this was one of those times where I was at risk of being a total douchebag again and I had to get it together. Not everything revolved around sex. And I was fighting to remember that.

"Oh," she said, leaving her mouth in a very suggestive little 'o'. She nodded. "Probably a good point." She took a step back.

"I guess you're going out with the guys tonight?"

Was that her asking me not to? No. Of course it wasn't. She'd have just said that, if that was the case. Fuck, why did I have to overthink this all the time? When I wasn't stuck in my head, it was so easy.

There was my answer; get out of my fucking head.

"We have a standing reservation at Dolce's after Hornet's matches," I said as though she didn't know. "Did…did Taylor not tell you we got you a seat?"

She smiled. "I meant after that."

I nodded like I was thinking. "I don't know. Don't have plans. Usually would, I guess. Are you not coming out with the guys after?"

She hugged the box of biscuits to her body. "I don't know. I was thinking about studying…unless I had a better offer."

"You want me to ask you out, Calypso?"

She shrugged. "Noo…" she said, totally believably.

I huffed a rough laugh. "You want to come out with me tonight?"

She nodded. "I want to go out with you tonight, River."

Fuuuck me.

I was in all sorts of trouble over this girl, and in no mood to change anything about that. So I nodded. "Great. I'll expect you to make an effort. The boys decided to suit up tonight in honour of our win."

Her eyes widened like she knew I was bullshitting that one. I was. But all it would take is me walking into the Chasers mansion yelling 'suit up' and it would be a done deal.

"Okay. Dressy it is. But I expect you to play the gentleman, then."

"Done. It's a date."

She bit her lip like she was trying to stop her smile from being so adorably goofy. She failed. "It's a date," she agreed.

"We'll see you at Dolce's," I told her.

"I'll see you there."

I pressed a quick kiss to her lips then made to head off.

"River!" she called.

I span back and the speed at which I returned to her would have been embarrassing if I'd not been so totally into her. "Yes?" I asked, my eyebrows bouncing like I was suggesting she wanted more than a kiss.

She held out the box of biscuits. "You forgot these."

I looked down at them, then back to her face. "I did, huh?"

"You did. There something you like more than my mum's shortbread?"

I grinned at her. "You know there is."

"You are so chees—"

I cut her off as I pressed her into the door and kissed her hard. I actually felt her melt against me, and my cock stirred. There was a burst of noise from the door to the stairwell and I reluctantly pulled away from her.

"Saved by the rabble," I teased.

"Saved or blocked?" she teased right back and fucking Jesus.

"I'm going to leave before something happens we might regret. See you at dinner?"

She nodded, but the way she chewed her lip didn't say she was trying to school a smile. It seemed more uncertain.

"Will do, and I'm going to knock your fucking socks off."

Fuck, yes. "Looking forward to it."

♡ **11** ♡
Skye

Something we might regret? Something we might regret!

Well, if that didn't have me all up in my head, I wasn't sure what would.

But then there was the whole 'it's a date' thing and that kiss! I was sure he was thinking about having sex with me as much as – if not more than – I was thinking about having sex with him, but then he avoided coming in and said things like 'something we might regret' and I suddenly panicked that he wasn't.

River was a flirty guy, it stood to reason that he could be thinking about how much he didn't want to have sex with me… But then why kiss me like that and kind of ask me out?

It was so fucking confusing and I had no one but myself to blame. Well, and River, but I'd been the one who'd drawn the line in the sand at no sex. Why had I done that to myself? Why? What was wrong with me? Like mutual masturbation and mind blowing – pun mildly intended – oral sex *wasn't* crossing a line?

For someone who had to have a certain level of intelligence to get into Chester, I was a Class A idiot. What was I trying to prove or do by saying no sex when it had been obvious that we'd wanted to fuck each other for years? Was I worried it would get too real too quick? Well, congrats, Past Me. It seemed to have done that anyway, and I'd left myself second-guessing his motivations instead of enjoying them.

So, mission the next was to get up the nerve to take back my 'no sex' rule.

I didn't know how I was going to do that because he'd literally just paved the way and I'd gone for ambiguous flirting rather than just open, honest communication. Seriously, why was it so terrifying to just come out and tell someone what you wanted, that you were finally ready for next steps even though you'd been the one to pump the brakes in the first place?

Wandering around my room, trying to find a good dressy outfit, I cussed myself out well and good. Now, in hindsight, it was perfectly obvious that River would be fine with me just literally saying 'hey, so I know I said, "no sex", but I'm up for it if you are. No pressure if you're not, just wanted to let you know'. Why then, in the moment, did I get frazzled and ridiculous?

I picked up my phone to message that exact thing to him, then paused.

Again, I didn't know why, but something was holding me back.

I was ninety-nine percent sure that he'd be fine with me saying it, even if he turned around and said he still wanted to wait. I'd be okay with that. But there was this one percent of me, niggling away, being all paranoid and self-conscious and thinking that what if he was playing, or just plain old confusing his feelings so having sex was the line he was drawing as well?

I threw my phone on my bed like it was all its fault and went back to my wardrobe.

"Slim pickings, Skye," I said to myself. "Slim god-damned pickings."

By the time I was dressed, clothes were strewn all over every surface of my room. I didn't even know I owned that many clothes. But I was dressed and I looked damned nice. At least as nice as the future librarian – and proud – liked to get.

Tights and heeled booties, and a tight-fitting knit dress with long sleeves and cut out shoulders. It was classy, it was chic, it was worthy of Dolce's, and it was weather appropriate. To be honest, it only hit all the marks because it was the middle of winter and my wardrobe was definitely winter friendly. Ask me to dress up in the height of summer, and I was calling in with an excuse fifteen minutes out.

I shot off a text to Tansy, hoping she was enjoying her actual date and letting her know I'd be with the team later if she and Forbsy weren't too busy to join, then shoved my phone in my pocket and saw I was already late.

"Of course, I am," I muttered to myself as I hurried out and made my way to Dolce's.

As I got there, a few of the guys were vaping out the front and nodded to me in hello when they saw I was heading towards them.

"Why, yes, we are the trophy-winning soccer players who will rock your damned world," Hank said.

Then I stepped into the light, and he was choking on his vape as Tim and Whistler both smacked him from either side.

"Shit. Mini Dev. Sorry."

I smirked and shook my head. "I'll give you a pass this once because of the occasion," I told him firmly.

He nodded. "Cheers. And, uh, let's not tell Jax, eh?" Hank looked between me, Tim and Whistler.

I thought that an interesting side note, but mimed locking my mouth. "Secret is safe with me, Hank."

He smiled, gratitude flooding his eyes. "Drinks on me, yeah?"

I wouldn't pass that up. "Deal."

The boys gave me another nod and I headed inside as Tom and Whistler gave Hank grief for flirting with me. I thought it was funny they were giving him so much flack for it when he hadn't even known who I was. As I barrelled into Dolce's, that thought made me pause for just a second.

There they all were, at a big round table in the middle of the restaurant the way Greta always put them up after a Hornets game. They were all in what they considered suitably 'suited up'. And whether that matched my definition highly depended on the individual.

River was in dark maroon trousers, a white shirt, grey striped blazer and his maroon tie with the little gold circles. I definitely counted it as dressed up. Drool-worthy was also a very good description of the whole package. But then, everything about the package of River Torres was drool-worthy.

He was standing up, leading them in a rousing rendition of 'We Are the Champions' while Greta tried to tell them to keep their voices down. But most of the people in here were regulars and they knew who the loud table on a Saturday night was. Being part of the university town, no one made a reservation at Dolce's on a Saturday without checking if it was a Hornets match or not. Not unless they didn't mind a bunch of guys being loud and overly happy, or utterly despondent and bringing down the whole damned place.

But the usual shenanigans of the Chester Chasers wasn't what gave me pause.

The idea that Tim and Whistler were giving Hank enough shit about flirting with me by accident, and there was River, actively hooking up with me behind everyone's back. Which was why we were hiding it. I didn't want that reaction to tarnish what might be growing between us. I needed time to work out what it was and could be before we dealt with everyone else's shit.

I took a deep breath and headed over to the table, noticing the empty chair between Taylor and River and knew they'd saved it for me. I plastered on the warm, friendly face I reserved for all the Chasers, because they were really more like extended family than a sport team at this point.

"Skye, you look really nice," Jax said as I stopped beside the table, as though it was unfathomable to him that I'd look nice for dinner at Dolce's.

I tried not to take offence, telling myself he wasn't surprised I was capable of looking nice but at how much he thought I looked nice. Or some nonsense that wasn't as bad as it had sounded.

"She always looks nice for Dolce's," Taylor said happily as he pulled the chair out for me.

"She always looks nice," River added.

Taylor scoffed. "Can you not give it a rest for one night?" he laughed. "We get it, you want my sister."

He looked around the table like it was all one big joke. Except it wasn't all one big joke and my insides fizzled unpleasantly. Then I caught River smiling at me, that cheeky shit-stirring grin that made everything okay. The same way we used to joke and tease each other mostly in private even if everyone knew it was there. It was normal and natural for us, and I didn't have to over think it.

"I wish I could say the same about you lot," I teased as River helped me into my seat. "Honestly, the least you could have done was make an effort and not leave a girl feeling overdressed."

They all laughed at my tension diffuser. Except Ajax. Of course. Ajax didn't laugh. The most you got was a slight twitch in the corner of his lips that could have been mistaken for him plotting murder.

True to his word, Hank bought three rounds of drinks and none but Tim, Whistler, Hank and I were any the wiser as to why.

And it was a good night out. Sitting at a table of guys I considered more family than friends, between my blood brother and a guy I couldn't imagine life without – for good or bad. We ate way too much, reminisced about old times, sang too many songs, and laughed so hard I was regretting my eye makeup – of course, I didn't have any decent shit that was actually waterproof despite what it claimed on the label.

But it didn't matter because we had such a good time together.

When we got to Mad Kitty, the boys all shucked their jackets and blazers. Within very little time, ties were loose, top buttons were undone and sleeves were rolled up. The whole team had gone from sophisticated gentlemen to rugged rogues in a matter of minutes, and I didn't hate it. I so didn't hate it.

River, in particular, just exuded the whole charming rogue vibe and I was jonesing hard for every small touch he thought he could get away with. And, boy, was he bold.

It helped that most of the guys were all drunk by the time we got to Mad Kitty. The hype of beating the Hornets that had taken them to Dolce's, was even more insane at Mad Kitty. They were basically bouncing off the walls and excuses were made for doing things in the height of the moment.

River danced with me. Only me. When I was talking to Taylor

or Frankie D or Robbie, River was with Taylor, and River and I were pretending we weren't constantly looking at each other. Tansy and Forbsy joined us at some point and the rest of the team were incredibly excited that they were all together for celebrating, even if they didn't really begrudge Forbsy an actual date.

It was past midnight when River and I were on the dance floor, and I leant up to his ear. "Want to come back to mine tonight?"

His arm tightened around me, and he groaned, low and sexy, in my ear. "I don't think that's a good idea, Calypso."

"Why not?"

"Because I am way too high to control myself tonight. It's all I can do not to kiss you right here."

Warmth spread through me, and I smiled. "Who says you have to control yourself?"

"Whoever's in charge of us not fucking this up. I don't want to make any decisions while we're drunk that we might not be ready for."

God, I hated it when he made sense. Even if I knew I'd been wanting to take things to the next level before having a few drinks, he didn't and me trying to assure him while drunk wasn't proof of anything. Likewise, how did I know that he wasn't just drunk and horny, and that was overriding his gut instincts? No, better to wait until we were both sober to tell him.

But, of course, without the buzz of alcohol in my veins, I didn't have the guts to just come out and say it. Which was ridiculous, because it was on the tip of my tongue the next day while we were lying in his bed, and I was so about to say something. I just…couldn't get the words out. Something was holding me back and I didn't really know what it was except I knew it was an illogical concern. Knowing *that* didn't help at all.

So, when he was between my legs – my bottom half naked and him in his boxer-briefs – and he pulled his dick out, I bucked my hips so he rubbed at my entrance. He froze as he was kissing me, tucked himself back in and rolled us over so I was straddling him. I tried not to feel confused or rejected. I told myself there was a reasonable explanation for it. But I still couldn't bring myself to just say the goddamned words.

I was just going to have to try to keep hinting and hope it all worked out. Like that ever happened.

And the rest of the week was just the same.

We were making out on my bed and, as soon as I even hinted at lining us up, River's hand was there, and he'd pulled his crotch away from mine. And look, I wasn't complaining about how willing – and so very capable – he was to give the pleasure, but I didn't know why he wasn't getting or taking the hint.

As much as I appreciated that River was taking my request for no actual sex seriously, I was definitely regretting the request in the first place. And every time I tried to hint that I wanted to take it to the next level, he pulled away like he thought he was about to take advantage of me. It wasn't like I wasn't a confidant woman who went after what I wanted, but the speed with which he pulled away made me hesitate all over again. Like it was reinforcing that weird feeling that was stopping me from just telling him what I wanted.

Logically, I knew he was just sticking to our agreement. He probably thought he was getting too sexual and making sure he stopped before he did something I didn't want. But emotionally, I felt like he was telling me he didn't want to take that next step. It made me uncertain about how much he wanted me, and I didn't want to bring it up anymore.

Stupid brain.

I determined I was going to tell him I wanted to go all the way with him. I wasn't sure how yet, but I was going to do it. I'd pull up my big girl pants and be as assertive as I'd been that first night I'd slept in his bed.

As I was putting away my clean clothes, the answer hit me.

I had one – singular – pair of lacy underwear. A bra and panty set I'd bought over the holidays because Tansy had insisted that I would want a pair one day, and I'd kick myself if we were stuck at school and I didn't have one. She was right, because it was the perfect thing to show River there was change afoot, without having to have a massive conversation about it. Because, apparently, I was too chicken shit for a proper conversation about it.

River

I know I said I'd take Skye however she wanted to be with me, and I was standing by that, but fuck's sake. The sexual frustration was real.

It had felt, all week, like I was coming closer and closer to fucking it up with Skye. Too many times that week I'd almost stuck it in her. We kept lining up perfectly, like fate was having a right old laugh at me and teasing me something shocking. My libido and my restraint were hanging by a very fine thread. I wanted her so badly I was doing absolutely everything I could to take my mind off it; I might not be a good guy, but I could pretend to be for Skye.

And, unfortunately, I was taking that out on the pitch and whoever else happened to be on it at the time. But as far as the team were concerned, I was focussed and taking all the chances. My shots were on target, my tackles were clean, I stayed on my man at all times I didn't have the ball. It was perfect.

I just wished that me coming too close to ruining things with Skye wasn't the cause of it, otherwise I'd be happy to walk this line for fucking ever. But even absolutely caining on the pitch wasn't worth the risk to me and Skye.

"Oh, I think I need an ice bath," Robbie groaned as he pulled off his kit after practice.

I shot a grimace at him. "Sorry about that."

He shook his head. "No. No. Had I not been on the receiving end, I'd have zero complaints. That was a tidy bit of play."

Robbie was our second keeper, and I may have been taking a run at goal when he slid out to stop me. I managed to jump over him, but Whistler was attempting to defend against me – if he could catch up – and they'd collided. Whistler's whole body had landed pretty heavily on Robbie's and they were both stiffening up.

"You coming out?" Taylor asked the room at large.

Forbsy shook his head. "I've got a date with Tanz."

Which meant I could have a date of my own.

Taylor nodded and turned to me. I shrugged.

"I'm wiped, man," I told him. "And I've got that paper due on Monday."

If Taylor had any idea as to why I was suddenly staying home more, he didn't make a mention of it. He didn't even raise an eyebrow. He acted like it was the most normal thing in the world.

"No stress. More girls for me."

I grinned at him. "Of course. You'll look damn fine without me to compare to."

Taylor flicked his towel at me. "Shut up. Just because you're losing your touch."

I wasn't even going to be mad about him saying it. He could think that all he liked. He didn't need to know that I hadn't lost my touch, it was just that I was only using it on one girl.

"Maybe I'm just maturing," I suggested with a wry smirk, and we all had a good laugh.

Riv.Torn
I hear Forbsy's heading to

yours after practice.

Sky'mDevestated

Can confirm.
Tansy actually decided to give me a head's up this time.

Riv.Torn

... do you have plans?

Sky'mDevestated

... I don't *not* have plans.

Riv.Torn

Colour me intrigued. Care to share?

Sky'mDevestated

Maybe you'll just have to wait and find out 😊

Colour me very intrigued indeed. I was going to head back to my room to get changed before I went looking for her.

Riv.Torn

If I must.

Sky'mDevestated

I promise it'll be worth it.

Fucking hell. Yes, please.

As I walked into my room after practice, I found Skye in my bed again, just as I'd hoped. Suddenly, I didn't give a shit about how sexually frustrated I was. Just seeing her, everything was fine. My heart relaxed. My muscles relaxed. My mind settled. It made me wonder if it wasn't sexual frustration after all, but just Skye withdrawals.

"How was practice?" she asked as she closed her book.

She looked cold, rugged right up. Something about the idea

that she was getting comfort or warmth or something good from my bed, of all places, made this bubble of warmth radiate in my chest and I didn't give a shit about frustration so long as I could see her face and talk to her.

"You know, you're going to get me addicted to this," I told her as I got undressed.

She made herself totally at home among the pillows and duvet, stretching out under the blankets, fully covered. "Addicted to what?" she asked, feigning innocence.

"To coming home to you in my bed."

She rolled over onto her side with a wide smile. "And you spent all those years keeping girls *out* of your room."

I climbed onto the bed next to her and touched my nose to hers. "Maybe I was just waiting for the right girl?"

She bit her lip and flopped onto the bed, holding the blankets around her neck. "Coming in?" she asked.

I wasn't going to read into her tone or her words. We'd agreed on no sex, and I was fine with that. I was. Even if my libido tried to make me a jerk a lot of the time. I didn't need to penetrate her to bring both of us satisfaction. I wasn't going to pretend to anyone that I didn't think of it numerous times a day; I was a virile young man entering my prime. When I wasn't thinking about soccer or my grades or when I could sneak Skye time again, I thought about sex. Sex had been a big part of me and my life, and my attraction to Skye manifested in desire, even as I was more than happy with where we stood.

I still felt guilty, like I was letting her down by not being able to control my head, but I smiled and nodded as I pulled the covers back, and suddenly realised maybe I wasn't the only one.

Skye was lying there in very raunchy lingerie. At least, for her. If I didn't know Skye so well, I wouldn't have given it a second thought. But she wasn't the kind of girl to wear lingerie like that, waiting for me in my bed, without it meaning something. Except, I wasn't going to make any moves without her confirming that it did actually mean something.

"Are you going to just stare at it? Or do you want to touch it?" she asked me, and my eyes flew to her face.

"I, uh… I thought we said…?" My brain clearly wasn't working at all because that was very close to her confirming it, and I was still standing there like a stunned mullet.

She leaned forward and patted the empty side of the bed. "I know we said," she answered. "But I don't think either of us are…fully satisfied about it."

"Have you been trying to hint this all week and I've been a bit dim?"

She shrugged uncertainly. "You've been dim, or I've just been chicken shit and not just come out and said it."

At least it hadn't been fate messing with me. I swallowed hard. "You're not worried it's going to complicate things more?"

Her smile was pure temptation. "No. I am. But I feel like denying us is definitely complicating it more. We both want it, River." A flash of uncertainty lit her eyes. "Don't we?"

Shit.

I didn't want her second-guessing anything.

I climbed into bed with her and touched my face to hers. "If you're saying you do, then yeah, we both want it." I smiled at her.

Her relief was visible. "Then we can work out the complications. Can't we?"

Honestly, I wasn't sure what the answer to any of the complications was. We had to get around the Code, around Taylor, and around my past, which she knew very little about. Without any of that, what we were was perfect and I could see myself spending the rest of my life with this girl. As much as we wanted each other physically, everything else was so damned easy as well and it wasn't just about physicality or sexual gratification.

With the demons in my past, I couldn't believe how I'd got so lucky. I certainly hadn't done anything to deserve her. Yet, here she was, telling me she wanted to have sex.

So, I did the only thing I could. I nodded and nudged her nose with mine. "Sure, we can."

Because we would somehow. Maybe not to the point that we could date in public, and everything would be okay. But we'd work out this situation we'd found ourselves in and it would eventually have to come to an end. I just had to hope I had the sense and strength to let her go when she found someone else.

She dragged a finger down my chest, and I looked up to see her eyes on my face.

"What are you thinking?" she asked me.

"Just wondering how I got so lucky."

She smiled softly. "You haven't…yet."

All my trepidation left me. She had the unfailing ability to just make everything okay. Make me believe that everything could be okay.

I pressed my lips to hers, as my hand slid over her hip.

"I didn't think you even owned anything like this," I told her.

She shrugged, all cheeky and coy. "This is it."

"You know you didn't have to…?"

She nodded. "I know. But just because your boner rages for me in anything, doesn't mean I don't want to make an effort sometimes. And I wanted there to be no question about what I wanted anymore."

I liked that visual. I shook my head. "Nope. Definitely no question."

She bit her lip. It was all at once nervous and expectant and anticipatory, but she was confident in whatever she was thinking. And I smiled.

"What are *you* thinking?" I asked.

"I know settling down and monogamy aren't–"

I huffed. "Nothing about you is settling, Skye. You're not a consolation or a compromise. You're fucking endgame, baby."

"You're really going to break all your rules for me?"

"I'm really going to break all my rules for you." I paused. "Are you sure about this?"

She nodded and I believed her. She was all in on this, but I was still at risk of thinking without my bigger head over her and I wanted to make sure we were both considering all the consequences.

"Even if it crosses that line we can't take back?" I checked.

She nodded again as she put her hand on my chest. "In the spirit of being open and honest with each other, I'm not sure that this is still just casual, Riv. Not for me. I don't know how we go public without running the risk of everyone else's shit getting in the way, but I don't think I want to be just friends with benefits anymore."

"Do you want to be my girlfriend, Calypso?"

"Do you want to be my boyfriend, Pond Scum?"

I snorted at her – and loved her for – using my less than complimentary nickname at a time like this, and nodded. "Yeah. Yes, I'd like – love – to be your boyfriend, Skye."

"Even if we still keep it between us for a bit?"

I gave her a knowing look. "I mean, I'm assuming Tansy knows."

She grinned and had the decency to be a little sheepish about it. "She does."

I nodded. "I'm not going to pretend we don't have baggage, that there's not external factors that are going to make this messy and awkward as soon as they find out. So, yeah, I'm okay keeping it between us – and Tansy – for a bit longer."

"We'll need to tell them at some point."

I nodded. "I know. And I want to work out a way to do that."

She smiled widely and I knew she felt the same. "Even if you have to wear a G-string and forfeit game time?"

I smirked. "Look, I'm not looking forward to it, but I'm not breaking code without thinking about the consequences here. I know what's waiting for us…"

"But kind of just want to enjoy us guilt-free for just a little bit longer," she said as though she was finishing my sentence.

"Yeah. Yes. That."

"Did I just totally ruin the mood?" she asked.

I smiled. "You're lying there, in my bed, in nothing but skimpy lingerie, telling me you want to have sex with me, we've just put very definite labels on this, and you think you've killed the mood?" I teased and she nodded, even as she bit her lip against a full-blown smile. "Baby, your brother could walk in here and catch us together and I'd still want to have you."

She wrapped her arms around my shoulders. "Then why don't you?"

"Oh, I will. I just want to bask in the whole 'you're my girlfriend' thing for a minute longer."

Warm happiness smouldered in her eyes, and it gave me this floaty bubble in my chest. She was my first real girlfriend and, with any luck, maybe she'd be my last. I just had to not fuck this up.

She snorted and nudged my nose with hers. "I thought I knew you so well, and yet I never knew just how goddamn cheesy you were."

"Is it embarrassing?" Then I opened my mouth like I'd just thought of something. "Is that why you don't want to go public yet?"

She laughed. "If your cheesiness was embarrassing, I don't think we'd have got to girlfriend stage."

I nuzzled into her neck. "So, you don't just want me for my banging bod?"

I felt her smile against my temple. "I'll reserve comment until I know if it is actually banging or not," she chuckled.

I gasped sarcastically as I pulled back to look at her. "You mean, you don't just *believe* the rumours? Don't tell me you have a mind of your own."

She grinned as she pushed against my chest and sat us both up. "Maybe I know you're not above making up rumours that paint you in a very well-endowed light."

I brought out all the cocky smoulder I possessed. "You've seen it. You've had your hand around it. What's your opinion?"

She leant her lips up to my ear. "It's not the size, River, it's the way you use it."

Oh, she wanted me to use it? All right.

I took hold of her hips and pulled her down the bed. She gasped as her mouth dropped into an 'o' of surprise, with humour shining in her eyes. I ran my hands slowly up over her hips and waist, gripping her tight. She bit her lip as she ran her hand up my chest.

"You ready for me to use it, baby?"

She nodded as she bit her lip and heat pooled in her eyes. Fuck but she was the sexiest thing ever. I honestly couldn't get enough of her. And she was going to be all mine.

I trailed my hand down and into her panties. She was slick and moist and warm. Her hips bucked to meet my hand as she took my face in her hands and kissed me hard. My fingers danced over her clit, teasing and playing.

She bit my lip. "Practicalities, River," she said.

I opened my eyes and found her staring into mine pointedly.

"I want your dick inside me. Do not draw this out longer than you have to."

I grinned then started kissing down her body. "And what if I *have* to draw it out a *real* long way?"

My lips were at the top of her panties when she grabbed a fistful of my hair and coaxed me to look up at her. She was frowning, but there was humour in her eyes.

"Do I need to say it any more clearly?" she asked.

I shrugged, not taking my eyes off hers as my fingers found her clit again through the material. "It couldn't hurt, surely. I'm known for being a bit dim."

She smirked and leant towards my face. "Fuck me, River."

Yeah, all right. I could play with her as much as I liked. I could act like I was in charge here and she was at my mercy. But she comes out with something like that, and all pretend went out the window. All control went out the window. I wasn't going to deny my goddess anything she wanted when she phrased it so eloquently.

I gave her a nod to show I understood, then wasted no time in getting her panties off and then getting her off. It wasn't my finest performance, but that wasn't the point. It got the job done.

When I emerged again to go looking for a condom, I found she'd buried her head under both of the pillows and had her arm quite heavily over the top.

I laughed and slid my hand over her stomach. She wriggled and shied away from it before pulling her head back out.

"I'm taking that as two," I told her as I grabbed a condom from my beside table.

She glared at me, a smile playing at her lips. "Convenience only. Hardly required."

I nodded. "Sure. Whatever you need to tell yourself to sleep at night."

That smile broke through, and she reached for me. I finished pulling on the condom and went to her. She positioned me between her legs and kissed me. It was deep and slow and left me with absolutely no doubt about what she wanted. What we both wanted. Still, didn't hurt when she dropped her hand between us and guided me into her.

Fuck, that was the height of sexy.

Then I just kind of stopped thinking as I slid into her and holy shit, it felt fucking fantastic.

♡ 13 ♡
Skye

"Fuck, Skye…" River breathed against my shoulder, and I felt it, too.

I ran my hands over his back, holding him tightly, as my knee rose to hug his hip and he slid in deeper. Everything was still tingly and sensitive, so every thrust just rewound the coil of pleasure in me.

He pushed himself up onto his arm and looked down at me. His hair was getting long on top and hung over his forehead. There was something very sexy about that, and the fact that he was finally inside me, stretching me. I could feel him throbbing already and figured that was probably on me. It had been a while since he'd had sex and he was used to getting it with almost alarming regularity.

Like he realised I knew, he chuckled. "Sorry. My stamina is usually much better than this. I might be just a *little* overexcited."

I wrapped my arms around his neck and nuzzled my nose over his. "You do know that you can just…let go and there's always round two?" I know he heard the laugh I was trying to school.

Humour shone brightly in his eyes. "That feels like a cop out."

"Or it's strategic. Be excited now and we can both savour it later."

"Are you sure you're not mature *and* wise?" he asked.

I shrugged. "You're attracted to me for a reason."

"Oh, there's way more than one reason." He sighed, but the humour was still in his eyes. "This is not the first time I've been imagining."

I kissed him, my lips lingering as I said, "Imperfect is far better than perfect because it's real."

"Fuck," he breathed. "That's almost as beautiful as you."

I laughed as I hugged him and buried my face in his shoulder. "The cheese, River!" I cried. "So much cheese!"

"You love it," he growled playfully.

I nodded as I looked up into his eyes. "Yeah. I really do."

I took his face in my hands and he kissed me as he thrust into me hard. He felt so good as our bodies moved together, finding our unique rhythm. He kept himself propped on one arm while his other hand roamed my body. My fingers skimmed over his scar. And we kissed.

Considering he'd seemed about to blow his load almost as soon as he got in, he hung on admirably. But our breathing both intensified and I knew he was close again. He slid his hand between us and found my clit, making sure I came a moment after him. His lips captured my moans as he thrust into me lazily and I felt the smile on them.

"Still not everything you hoped for and more?" I asked him.

He chuckled roughly as he slid out of me and dealt with the condom. "Definitely everything I'd hoped for and more," he answered easily.

"Even if it didn't showcase your excellent stamina?" I teased.

He laughed as he came to lie back in bed with me. "Any complaints on your end?"

I shook my head. "I've definitely had worse."

He snorted. "Stellar review."

I nodded. "Oh, yeah. 'I've had worse. Four stars'."

"Four stars?" he asked, sarcastically indignant.

I shrugged. "I can't give you full marks now, you might get complacent."

He wrapped me in his arms as he peppered kisses on my neck. "Smart plan. You deserve nothing but the best, baby."

Warmth spread through me, but we'd had enough cheese for one night. "Oh, well then. What am I doing with you again?"

He huffed a rough laugh then started tickling me. "Yeah, I dunno," he said casually, not letting up. "I mean, I don't get it personally. I'm sure – what was his name? – was much better."

I finally batted his hands away from my most ticklish spots and grinned. "I wouldn't know. We didn't get that far."

His eyebrows rose. "Oh, really?"

I nodded. "Really."

He leant his elbow on the pillow next to me and his head on his hand. "Out of *very* casual curiosity…?" he started, sounding anything but casually curious. "Why not?"

I walked my fingers up his chest and booped his nose. "Because I'd just had you between my legs, even jokingly, and Tansy would *not* stop going on about the Seven Minutes in Heaven hypothetical."

"Hypothetical? But it happened."

I nodded, feeling my cheeks heat. "Yeah… But you know how Tanz and I do those hypotheticals with each other?" I paused and he nodded. "Yeah, well, she'd given me you and me in Seven Minutes in Heaven and…I honestly couldn't stop thinking about it so…I may have taken my moment when I could."

His smile was warm and wonderous. "Seriously?"

I nodded again. "Seriously. Literally all I could think of on that date was you, and he wasn't really doing anything to change my mind."

"I honestly only have Tansy to thank for us, don't I?" he teased.

"Uh, yes. Meddling best friend is like the *only* way to get together anymore, didn't you know?"

"I did not know. What else don't I know about dating?"

I looked at him. "How long have you got?" I sassed.

"All damn night, baby. To start with."

We lay in his bed for a while, just chatting and laughing. There were lazy kisses but nothing heating up too much until his fingers found their way between my legs again and I felt his dick getting hard against my hip.

I smiled against his lips and felt him return it.

"You're fucking addictive," he said against my lips.

My fingers played with his hair as his fingers played with my clit like he'd been perfecting all my favourite spots his whole life. My body arched into his and he kissed me hard as he slipped a finger into me and his thumb circled my clit.

"You are way too good at that," I breathed against him.

"Oh, would you like me to stop?" he joked.

I nipped his lip playfully. "Don't you dare."

I didn't think I'd ever seen River smile as much as I had that night. I'd certainly never seen him smile so hard the corners of his eyes crinkled. It transformed him from merely sexy and gorgeous and smouldering to so utterly lovable in a way I'd never felt before.

His finger pumped me as he worked my clit, and I felt the pleasure growing again. As my orgasm started washing over me gently, he shifted his hand slightly and totally broke the cycle. My eyes flew open, and I saw his were wide in mock-surprise.

"You–" I started, but then he was done with slow and steady and, dare I say it, romantic.

He unleashed orgasm after orgasm on me. Not big ones. The kind that just keep going, both nowhere near enough and also just far too much at the same time. I writhed and moaned under him, but he wouldn't let me smother myself with a pillow. Every time I went to grab it, he held my wrist above my head and shook his.

By the time I felt nearly spent and he did it again, I bucked under him. "If you're going to deny me a muffler, the least you could do was get a condom."

"Mm…right now?" he asked, teasing in his voice.

I nodded. "Right now."

He chuckled. "You don't want me to take my time?"

I shook my head. "I don't."

"All right, then."

As River pressed one last kiss to my neck, I looked at the clock and smirked when I saw it was two minutes past midnight. "What happened to the no sex after midnight rule?"

He pulled back to look at me with an adorably quizzical frown on his face. "What?" he laughed.

"You told Grant no sex after midnight because my vag grows teeth and I'd never let go."

"Did I say that?" he asked.

I nodded. "Yelled it, more like."

"Hm. That does sound like me."

"You still breaking all those rules for me?" I teased.

He grinned, then started kissing down my cheek to my neck. "Maybe I don't want you to let me go, baby."

Butterflies erupted in my chest, and I couldn't have wiped the goofy grin off my face if I'd wanted to. I wrapped my body around his and he hugged me back tightly, echoing the sentiment I hoped he'd understand. Then he peppered me with kisses as he rolled us over.

His lips found mine as his arm searched his bedside table and I smiled against him.

"Need help?" I asked.

He shook his head. "No. I'm trying to be suave and sexy."

I laughed, gave him another peck, then pushed myself up on his chest to give myself more reach to his bedside.

"Top drawer," he mumbled as he took my nipple in his mouth. In his defence, it was dangling right in front of his face.

I paused as tingles zinged around my whole body.

"You forget what a drawer is, baby?" he teased as he angled his head to be seen under my arm.

I shot him a look that told him to shut up and finished reaching over to get the condom.

As I hauled his drawer open, he reached around my arse and ran his fingers through my folds. My body came alive under his touch. Again. It was like I'd become hyper aware of him, and I was just waiting for that next touch. My nerve endings tingled in anticipation, like they were just waiting to be the next one to feel it.

"Mm," he said as he dragged his lips across my collar bone. "No teeth that I can feel."

I smirked as picked up the condom and settled at the top of his legs. "Maybe they're in *real* deep?" I teased.

Heat burned in his eyes as he sat up and wrapped am arm around my back. "Then I'd better get in real deep to check."

I nodded. "You'd best."

"It could be a serious medical issue you've got here, Calypso."

I bit my lip against a full smile. "It could be. But are you willing to risk your manhood for the sake of my health?"

The smile was deep in his eyes, and I felt it against my lips as he nodded. "Yeah."

"Yeah?"

He nodded again, mumbling against my lips. "Yeah. I'm willing to risk my manhood for your health, baby."

"It's like you're falling in love with me or something," I sassed.

He pressed a kiss to my lips as he took the condom from me. "Yeah," he said as he opened the packet. "It's like that, huh?"

Then he'd grabbed me firmly and was flipping us over. My laughter became a squeal of surprise until I caught his eyes and saw everything in them. God, but he was just the right combination of domineering and sweet. Able to do quite literally whatever he wanted to me, but only exercising that power for the things I'd enjoy. Jesus, that was sexy.

He sat up, took up position between my legs and rolled the condom on, his eyes on mine the whole time. He bit his lip as he shook his head, and I had never felt so desired, so needed, so sexy. As he leant back over me and captured my lips again, he did that low groan and I almost shattered right there.

Then his lips were trailing down over my jaw and his fingers were heading decidedly lower. I arched into him. His hand trailed over my clit, but then was guiding him into me and I breathed out heavily as I relaxed around him.

River's thrusts were strong and hard and deep as he coaxed my leg further up. He said nothing, clearly taking this time very seriously, and I felt it, too. There was something different about this, only in all the good ways.

This was what all the fuss was about.

And I was there for it.

River took full control, his body a high-precision machine

designed purely to bring me pleasure after pleasure after pleasure. I lost track of the positions and the number of times I cried out his name.

His hands on my skin were strong and sure and firm. Always touching, caressing, loving. Wrapped around my breast. Splayed on my stomach to hold me to him. Lifting my leg higher. Flipping me over. Sliding over me in the most sensual of ways. It was like his hands alone were worshipping me, to say nothing of the rest of him.

His lips were hot. And sure.

He pressed me gently into the bed, bending me over to enter me from behind and tingles ran through me over the sheer domination. He gripped my arse hard with both hands as he thrust into me over and over again.

"Shit," I breathed heavily, my hand fisting his sheets tightly. "River…"

He leant over me, and I felt the smile at his lips as they kissed my shoulder.

My whole body shook as I came again, but he wasn't going to give me any respite. Not that I was complaining.

River flipped me over effortlessly and pulled me up to drag me into his lap. He plunged into me again in one strong thrust and kissed me hungrily. It was messy and passionate and made my toes curl all by itself.

As I felt my orgasm growing again, I pushed against his chest and he fell back onto the bed, his eyes telling me 'all right, let's see what you can do'. And, boy, was I going to show him.

Just as I'd hoped, he lay back and let me ride him. It wasn't long before I could see his carefully crafted control wavering. I could feel it in the way he squeezed my breast just a little harder. Hear it in the way he groaned my name under his breath.

"Fuck, baby," he sighed as he nodded to me. "Yes."

I couldn't help smiling in victory as I rode him harder and faster. He matched my thrusts, and I felt the pleasure rush through my whole body. Then he started to tense. He sat up abruptly, wrapping one arm around me while he used the other as an anchor behind him for more thrust leverage.

My head dropped to his shoulder as he fucked me hard. My orgasm crashed over me just as hard and just as fast. As my body shivered, he fully tensed and moaned my name as he came equally as hard.

We both stayed there for a few heartbeats, both breathing heavily and holding each other tightly. As his breath was finally returning to normal, River chuckled and pressed a kiss to my shoulder before sitting up to look at me. He brushed a piece of hair from my face and gave me a quick kiss on the lips.

"That," he said, still a little breathless. "That was much more what I had in mind for our first time."

I looked at the clock and saw it was almost two. "If we'd done that first, I think I'd have been horrified and absolutely ruined."

He smiled. "In what way?"

"Well, did you really want that to be the standard we'd have to keep up? That would be exhausting, and I'd think quickies were completely off the table."

"Okay," he laughed. "Good point. Good to know quickies aren't off the table just because I couldn't control myself."

I ran my fingers through his hair and tugged on it a little. "You got the job done more than satisfactorily. Both times."

He nodded once, a shit-stirring humour in his eyes. "I'm glad. I should deal with this."

"If I let you go," I teased.

I climbed off him and we shared a 'what do you know' look, smiling warmly.

"Seems you were wrong, Pond Scum," I told him.

He shrugged. "There's a first time for everything. Maybe I was just hoping to get you to myself and just destroying the competition."

"I'm not entirely sure you weren't."

He huffed a small laugh as he got up. "No. Me either."

I settled back again his pillows and his eyebrow rose as he watched me.

"I thought you didn't do sleepovers on school nights?" he said carefully.

I played coy. "Boyfriends get different rules, don't they?"

"Do they?" he asked with a smirk.

I nodded. "They do."

He sighed sarcastically as he climbed back into bed with me. "If you'd told me that earlier, I would have sealed this deal much sooner."

I laughed. "Really?"

He gave me a very noncommittal head waggle. "Wouldn't you like to know?" Then bounced his eyebrows at me again before kissing me hard.

♥14♥
River

Like it was some unspoken agreement, Skye and I seemed to have decided that acting like we hated each other more than usual was going to hide the fact we weren't just hooking up but also now dating in secret.

Part of me liked the sneaking around purely because the thought that we could get caught was kind of exciting. It added that next level of taboo we hadn't quite reached before there was so much at stake. Because there was now. So much at stake. We hadn't just crossed a line we couldn't take back, but we were fully emotionally invested and committed to this. To each other. To us.

And, after we'd spent a few hours saving face and acting like we still hated each other, the sex was basically just always make up sex. Phenomenal make up sex. Not that I was complaining. It was spicy and a fucking big turn on. And based on how hard we both tried selling the whole 'we still hate each other' thing to everyone else, I was pretty certain she felt the same.

"You haven't had a date pick you up for while…" Taylor started while we were having lunch in the plaza, and she looked at him expectantly.

"That's because she's a square who'd rather have her nose in a book than a cock up in her," I said easily and threw her glare a cheeky grin in return.

Taylor grimaced. "Too visual, man." Then he looked back at his sister. "Seriously, I'm starting to get concerned. I know study's important and shit, but this is a whole new level of…" He indicated her entire person and that spoke volumes about what he'd left unsaid.

I snorted, still finding the humour in that regardless of what she meant to me.

Skye shared a look with Tansy. "Since when does my dating life shadow my mental state?" she asked.

"Besides, Skye's dating," Tansy added with a shrug.

"She is?" Taylor asked, and I only just managed to stop myself asking as well, as though I'd forgotten that Tansy was on our side and – hopefully – just placating Taylor. "When?"

"When are *you*?" Skye asked him pointedly, reminding him they didn't know each other's' whereabouts every second of the day.

Taylor gave her a knowing look. "I'm perfectly fine not dating."

"Then why can't I also be fine not dating?"

Taylor shrugged. "I dunno. You're a dater. Or, try to be."

"So, you have an obligation not to be?" she fired back at him.

"It's how you cope," was Taylor's answer and we all knew what he meant.

Skye's glare softened slightly. "And you fuck around?"

Taylor grinned. "We've each got our strengths. You and Tansy date. Riv and I fuck around. It's who we are."

"Couldn't possibly riff off your thing, Calypso," I added, mock-apologetically.

Skye rolled her eyes at me. "Couldn't possibly be a decent human being, Pond Scum," she corrected me, and I grinned.

I leant towards her over our table. "I promise I'm *more* than satisfactory." Like she didn't know. "Four-star rating, don't you know."

I saw the heat in her eyes, but she kept her face neutral. Tansy, on the other hand, snorted into her coffee. Clearly, Skye had been talking. I kicked my eyebrows at her to show her I knew she'd been talking, even if Taylor wouldn't see anything more in the interaction as a whole.

"Who did you pay to give you a four-star rating?" Whistler asked as he, Forbsy and Frankie D joined us.

"Oh," Skye answered before I had a chance. "He doesn't pay for the *review*, only for the advertising of his 'skills'."

The boys laughed and Tansy smiled. I stuck my tongue out at Skye and she did likewise.

"Funny," I said sarcastically.

She nodded. "Funnier because it's true."

I frowned at her. "Maybe you should advertise," I suggested. "Might get you *some* action."

"Unlike you, I don't need to advertise," she shot back.

"All the advertisement I need is word of mouth, Calypso," I told her with a wink. "The ladies sure can't get enough of mine."

I could see she bristled, annoyed as much by the fact I'd had a decent comeback and she was clearly struggling to find one. My smirk grew and I felt the old rivalry between us rising.

"It's probably just because it's biggest thing about you," she said and the whole table went 'ooo' and waited impatiently for my rebuttal.

I felt my eyes narrow at her. "It's not the size that matters, Calypso, it's the way you use it."

She huffed and I knew I had her. Or was at least incredibly close to winning this.

The others at the table looked between us like they were watching a particularly engrossing and fast-paced tennis match. I popped a chip into my mouth around a cocky grin while we all waited to see what she'd come up with next.

"You know what they say, River. There're guys who believe that…and then there're guys who don't have to lie to themselves to feel good."

"Okay!" Taylor said loudly, actually standing up and holding his hands between us. "Fucking hell, you two." He shook his head as he rearranged his crotch like he was suddenly feeling as inadequate as any talk about size was wont to make a guy.

"Low blow, Mini Dev," Frankie D said, looking like he felt it, too.

Whistler shifted in his seat, and Tansy put her hand on Forbsy's arm like she was assuring him he was fine. As self-conscious as I was suddenly feeling, I still had to smirk.

Skye rolled her eyes. "Honestly, I don't know why you guys get so hung up on dick size. It doesn't matter!"

I huffed a rough laugh and sat back in my chair victoriously. "Too nice to stick to your guns, eh, Calypso?"

She bristled all over again. "What?"

I shrugged as I leant forwards again. "You're too fucking nice. If you weren't so worried about making the boys feel better about themselves, that might have been a real nice zinger." I gave her an arrogant nod and sat back again, crossing my arms over my chest.

I saw her jaw clench tight and knew I was in deep shit. It wasn't like before where, when I was in deep shit, I'd just give her more shit until she had no choice but to forgive me because I was just plain fucking awesome. This was better. Because I knew she still thought I was awesome, even if she was proper annoyed at me. There was no more uncertainty about whether she'd still be giving me shit later because there was no way in hell she wouldn't.

"I'm not at all surprised that that's a foreign concept to you, Pond Scum," was her retort, victory of her own shining in those beautiful blue eyes.

I was going to let her have that one. "Much like dating and manners, one doesn't need to experience it to grasp it."

Oh, she'd been impressed with that. I felt well chuffed. She remembered that conversation and she was impressed I'd used it again.

Taylor snorted. "I understood that reference," he said, pointing at Skye.

I laughed. "Nice work, Steve."

Skye dropped her fork to her tray and looked to Tansy. "I've got to get to class. Dinner?"

Tansy looked to Forbsy like they were a real proper couple.

Another 'Oo' spread around the table and both Forbsy and Tansy went a delicious shade of pink as they smiled sheepishly.

"Burgers?" Forbsy suggested to her, and she nodded before looking to Skye.

"Want to do burgers with the boys?" Tansy asked her, like we hadn't all just witnessed their exchange.

Skye bit her lip like she though smiling too hard would make them feel bad about what had just happened, and nodded. "Sounds perfect." She looked to the table at large. "See you degenerates later?"

We all nodded and made murmurs of approval.

Before she left, Skye picked up a stray chip from her tray and threw it at me for good measure. I couldn't help smiling and watching her arse avidly as she walked away.

A few seconds after she disappeared from view, a text came through on my phone.

Sky'mDevestated
I finish in an hour. Tansy's
got lab until five.

Riv.Torn
That a hint, baby?

Sky'mDevestated
You playing dim?

Riv.Torn
nodding GIF
Pretend I'm stupid.

Sky'mDevestated
I'm not convinced you're
not.
I'm inviting you over.
For movies.
Or ice creams.
Maybe sex.
If you're a good boy.

Riv.Torn
I'm never a good boy.

Sky'mDevestated
lip biting GIF
I can work with that.

Riv.Torn
See you in an hour.

And, yeah, I was in her room before her.

This time, I was the one lying in bed waiting for them to come home. I felt like a proper little seductress and loved every minute of it.

"I almost forgot I don't actually hate you as much anymore," she laughed as she climbed into my lap.

I smirked. "If it makes you take charge like this, baby, you won't see me complaining."

She rubbed against my cock. "Oh, I think you prefer it when I like you, River." She did it again. "Don't you?"

Yeah, all right. I totally did. Because I knew, logically, that this wouldn't be happening if she still hated me. Seven Minutes in Heaven was one thing. The kind of intimacy and relationship we enjoyed now was something totally different. I wasn't against the idea of a hate-fuck, but being with her like this was a hundred times better. Being with her at all was a million times better. And we wouldn't be together if we'd just succumbed to our chemistry when it would still have been a hate-fuck.

"Yeah, all right, I do."

"You seem more relaxed," she said suddenly, like it had just occurred to her.

"Than what?"

She shrugged, all coy. "Than before we…"

I grinned. "Sex will do that to a guy."

"Was it *just* the sex, though?"

I ran my nose over her face, knowing there was a time and a place for shit-stirring and another for cheese. This was one of those cheese moments. "Of course, it's not just the sex. It's you."

"Me?"

I nodded. "You."

"You're not so uncomfortable about hiding this anymore?"

I shook my head. "No really, no. You?"

She smiled. "Not as much. Why do you think that is?"

I wrapped my arm around her. "I think it's because we know what this is now. What we are. We're more settled. It's just *all* enjoyment now."

Her smile widened. "That's a good way of putting it."

"You just like sneaking around for sex," I teased.

She waggled her head noncommittally. "I might. Like you don't, though."

I smirked. "I love it. I mean, yeah, we can't do it forever, but it's fucking fun for now."

She laughed as I rolled us over to be above her. "It is a lot more fun than I thought it would be."

"Oh, you mean lying to all our nearest and dearest?" I joked.

The humour in her eyes softened as I ran my hand up her side and pressed my erection against her centre. "Yeah, that. It's kinda worth it."

I dropped my lips to her neck. "Worth three years of foreplay?"

She nodded as her body arched into mine and her arms went around my neck. "So worth it. You really rose to the challenge, Pond Scum."

I nipped her neck playfully. "I always rise when it comes to you, Calypso."

Her knee hugged my hip. "Cheesy," she said, humour in her voice. "So cheesy."

"Sexy," I corrected her with a teasing growl that was more a flamboyant drawl combined with a bit of a lisp. "So sexy."

I felt her nod. "I don't want to agree with you and inflate your ego even more."

"No, you'd rather inflate something else, wouldn't you, baby?"

She snorted. "Oh, I'm pretty sure I don't even have to try, baby."

"Cocky, aren't you?"

Her hand trailed down my body and wrapped around my shaft.

"Could be cockier."

I shook my head as I smiled down at her. "Fuck, you're perfect."

She ran her hand back up my body to slip it back around my neck. "*We're* perfect, River. I always thought we could be amazing together, but I thought it would just be sex. If it ever happened. But it's not. Is it?"

I looked into her eyes and, fuck, but I was so completely gone over her. Everything about her called to me. It always had, but we'd never had *that* relationship before. We'd always antagonised each other and teased each other and behaved like we hated each other. People always said there was a fine line between love and hate, but I hadn't realised just how much you could feel them at the same time.

And nothing was going to change that now.

"Now, who's cheesy?" I teased.

She bit her lip as the corner tugged insistently. "Sometimes the truth is cheesy," she said with an unapologetic shrug.

I nodded. "Sometimes, it is."

"I'm sorry I insinuated you had a small dick," she said, the apology deep in her eyes.

I smiled at her. "I would forgive you anything…but that." I was mostly teasing.

She ran her hand firmly against my cock. "Can I make it up to you?"

I rolled us again, so she was on top. "You are certainly *more* than welcome to try," I said, all shit-stirring.

And, like the fucking fantastic woman I knew she was, she didn't just ride – Freudian slip? – rise to the challenge, but far exceeded any of my wildest dreams.

♡15♡
Skye

Things weren't just good with River, they were fun. More fun than I'd had dating in my whole life. Not that we really went on 'proper' dates. Dates like dinner and dancing also involved my brother and whoever of the team and Tansy felt like joining. But we still stayed home and vegged on the couch to watch TV or a movie. Usually accompanied by, as promised, River eating all the food.

Just at that moment, he wasn't stealing my food. He was kissing my neck and he froze when he heard the damning revelation.

"Hold on," he said, and I heard the humour in his voice as he pulled away from me. "Hold right on. You got your nickname for me from *Doctor Who*?"

I mean, not consciously. I didn't think.

I shrugged nonchalantly. "Your point being?"

"My point being that you wouldn't dare besmirch your favourite show with anything to do with me unless you secretly liked me."

"Who even said I did? Besmirch my favourite show, I mean."

"Uh…" He pointed at the TV. "Her name is River because her parents' name is Pond. You call me Pond Scum because of River, because THAT'S what *Doctor Who* did!"

My cheeks heated. "Maybe."

He nudged me playfully. "No. No 'maybe'. You like me!"

I rolled my eyes. "I think the fact I like you is well-established at this point, *boyfriend*."

"You *like* me," he teased. "You think I'm *sexy*. You wanna *hold* me. You wanna *love* me."

I bit my lip as I looked at him, acting shy. "Maybe I do."

The teasing humour in his eyes turned into stunned amazement. "You do?"

I nodded and gave him a shrug. "Yeah. Maybe I do."

"I fucking love you, too," he said quickly and my heart thudded in my chest. Then he blinked and looked almost sheepish. "I mean… Shit."

I laughed as I rolled over and moved to straddle his lap. "You love me?"

He wrapped his arms around me. "I think so."

"You don't sound sure," I teased him.

"Because I'm not," he answered honestly. "Because I've always loved you, I think. You've been an integral part of my life for years. I always thought it was platonic, like the way you love anyone close to you, and now I'm not so sure. Maybe it has just been platonic. Or maybe I just know that, very soon, it definitely won't be *just* platonic."

"So, you're falling in love with me?" I was teasing a little, but I also appreciated the moment we were having.

He rubbed his nose over mine. "I'm definitely, one hundred percent falling in love with you, Skye Devereux."

I smiled at him, feeling like my whole heart had turned into over-excited butterflies. "I'm falling in love with you, too, River

Torres."

He did that groan I loved so much as he held me tightly. "I don't deserve you."

"Why not?"

He shook his head. "Because I don't."

I sighed, both because I wasn't feeding into his insecurities and because something hit me. "If we're…" I started.

He smirked knowingly. "Falling in love?" he suggested.

I nodded, fighting a goofy smile. "That. Should we think about taking this public?"

"You mean telling the team?" he said.

I nodded. "That."

His groan was less sexy and more resignedly frustrated as he leant his forehead to mine. "Yes. We definitely should."

"How?"

He shrugged. "I don't know. Any ideas?"

"When are you playing the Hornets next?"

He huffed a surprised laughed. "Why?"

"Well, I figure, we can skate off the back of the win. Everyone will be so happy that they'll be like 'hooray' instead of all 'argh, breaking code, grumble, grumble'."

He laughed at my impersonation. "Yeah, sure. Next game's in three maybe four weeks."

I nodded. "That gives us enough time to prepare."

"Exactly how do we prepare to rain a mountain of shit upon ourselves?"

"Buy a lot of umbrellas?" I suggested uncertainly and he laughed again.

"Sure. Maybe some gumboots as well?"

"Sensible," I agreed.

He nudged my nose with his. "I've got some other ideas as well. Very sensible."

I grinned. "Oh, yeah?" I asked and he nodded. "Does it have anything to do with using the condom I know is in your pocket?"

He nodded again. "Yes. Definitely."

I smirked. "That's also very sensible."

"Isn't it?" he agreed.e

He kissed me as he reached into his pocket awkwardly and pulled the condom out. Our lips barely left each other as we even more awkwardly arranged ourselves so we could get the condom on him, and he could slide into me in our position on the couch.

But, shit, was all the awkwardness worth it.

We were both breathing hard in a very short amount of time, and I was so very close, until…

"Ohmigod!" Tansy cried as she walked in, dousing a freezing cold bucket over my building orgasm.

I bit my lip apologetically at her over River's shoulder as he laughed into mine.

"Sorry," Tansy said, clearly flustered. "No. Wait. Sock, people! Come on." But she was smiling. "I'll go and be somewhere else for ten to fifteen minutes."

Her grin widened for a second and she paused, then she pressed her lips together and hurried out again.

River thrust up into me hard as we laughed together.

"First?" he asked.

"First time Tanz has walked in on me fucking you on our couch?" I clarified.

He nudged my nose with his. "Or anyone."

"Was it *your* first?"

"On the couch," he answered honestly with a nod.

I grinned again. "Same."

He thrust again, his arms tight around my waist. "Where's she caught you before?"

I rolled my hips over him slowly. "Her room."

The smile made his eyes crinkle. "Seriously?"

I nodded. "Drunken accident. I thought we were in my room."

He shook his head as we rocked together.

"You?" I asked.

"Where's Tanz caught me?" he sassed, then nodded and proceeded to punctuate every sentence with deliciously deep thrusts. "No. Uh. Mansion main bathroom. Lounge. Mad Kitty bathroom. Bathroom at your parents' place. And…" He nodded to himself. "Taylor's room at your parents' place."

I could have felt shit about that. He was either incredibly good at getting caught, or it went to show just how many girls he'd been with. But I wouldn't feel shit about how many girls he'd been with because it wasn't anything I hadn't already known, and a reminder while he was inside me wasn't going to change how I felt about him. I was falling in love with him as he was, not with some rose-tinted version of him who'd only let me down. He might still let me down, but I knew who he was.

We moved together, his hand sliding between us to my clit like he wasn't going to hold on much longer. As soon as he brushed over me, I knew I wouldn't either. We both came hard and fast, within seconds of each other.

And we just managed to make ourselves presentable again before Tansy walked back in, very loudly announcing herself in case we weren't done.

"Calypso," I heard River whisper a few days later while I was walking through the library.

I looked around for him, couldn't see him, and went back to finding the right row for my book. If River wanted to play funny buggers, that was just a normal Tuesday. I wasn't going to let it stop me going about my day.

River appeared up the aisle, acting like he hadn't seen me or didn't care I was there. Conspicuously so. The only thing to do was pretend he wasn't there either and wait to see if he'd let me in on whatever was going on.

As we passed each other, he caught my hand casual as you please, spun us 180 and looked around for potential witnesses before pulling me down the closest row and into an out of the way corner of the library. I didn't have time to ask him what he was doing because then he was pressing me against the conveniently placed column. His hand went to my cheek, and he looked down at me with this really warm, bright smile that made his rich brown eyes look like decadent ganache.

Then he was kissing me. His hand seared my hip, his touch tantalising even through the layers of clothing. My hands went to the bottom of his tee at his sides and pulled him closer.

The hand on my cheek slid to the back of my neck as our kiss deepened. Usually, this was the point at which one of us started the battle for supremacy. This time, neither of us did. Everything heated enough that I wondered if I'd finally join the ranks of the Franklin Reed Library shelf bunny club.

"Oh, sorry," came a vaguely recognisable chuckle.

River and I both looked at the interloper, who looked as

sheepish at finding us in such a compromising situation as I felt at being found in it. They looked familiar, but so did many of the people I saw on a daily basis.

"I'll, uh, leave you to…it." They nodded and hurried off.

River leant into me, his lips grazing my forehead with a smile as we both exhaled a quiet laugh. Then he bent his head until he was looking at me askance. Humour lit his face, and I wasn't just horny for him, but in danger of being totally smitten with him as well. Fall*ing* in love with him? I was close to fall*en* in love with him.

"Hi," he said simply.

I fought to keep my smile from blossoming into a full-blown cheesy grin. "Hi."

"How are things?"

I nodded. "Fine. How are your things?"

Both of us were fighting hard to avoid breaking out into proper laughter in the middle of the library. And both of us were getting closer and closer to failing the longer we looked at each other. I didn't know about him, but I was utterly incapable of looking away from him.

"I should really let you get back to…whatever it was you were doing," he said.

I nodded. "No. Sure. Kiss me like the world is ending, then just disappear again." I shrugged. "Cool."

His lips brushed over my temple as he said, "Where's Tanz?"

"Probably being railed by Forbsy. Why?"

He more firmly kissed the side of my head. "I'll meet you in your room in fifteen?"

I nodded. "Okay."

Because, at this point, the likelihood that Forbsy knew about me and River was high. I couldn't imagine Tansy spending that much time with him and being able to keep that secret. She was horrible with secrets, really, and I was surprised she hadn't let it slip to the whole team by now. I was also surprised River and I hadn't messed up and let it slip yet.

When I got home, Forbsy was definitely over but he and Tanz were in her room with the door closed. She'd even put a sock on the door, and I smirked as I headed for my room.

As he'd said, River was sliding in my door fifteen minutes after he'd left me in the library and throwing himself on my bed next to me.

"How long have they been at it?"

"Long enough."

"Maybe your place was a bad idea?" he said with a grin.

Clearly Forbsy was getting the job done to a high level of satisfaction as Tansy moaned and groaned and panted in pleasure.

"Jesus, but your walls really are thin," he laughed.

I nodded. "Do you see why I invade your room when he's here?"

He nodded, then nuzzled under my ear. "You want to stay over tonight?"

I pushed against his chest gently and he pulled away to look at me.

"Are you asking me to wake up in your bed tomorrow morning?"

He shrugged. "It would *not* be the first time." He was clearly confused as to where I was going with this.

"No, but that was me commandeering it and just not leaving. This is you actively asking me. Planning it. Wanting it."

His dragged his teeth over the skin of my neck. "Baby, I'd

have you in my bed every night if that was an option."

I knew why it wasn't. There were many reasons why it wasn't. Chief among them was the fact we were putting off telling anyone. Then there was the Chasers bro Code which he was seriously breaking just thinking about me, let alone dating me behind their backs. And also the fact that my brother would no doubt disapprove of me and River.

Taylor would never throw down with River if he found out we'd been hooking up. He wouldn't get into a fight or an argument over River not being good enough to touch his little sister, or berate my life choices. But I knew he doubted that River could treat me right, no matter what River's intentions were. I was still getting my head around my heart's willingness to risk the chance that River might break it. But I had to take the chance. I knew I would regret it for the rest of my life if I didn't.

"I'm not saying yes, but I'm not saying no," I told him.

The humour danced in his eyes. "Then what are you saying?"

"That you can sneak me into the McMansion and I'll get in your bed, then we'll see what happens."

He groaned appreciatively as his hand ran up my side. "I love not making plans with you, Calypso."

I threaded my fingers on his hair and smiled at him. "I love not making plans with you, too."

16
River

It wasn't unusual for me to be the first one in the locker room before practice, but it was unusual for the rest of the team to all walk in together looking like they were about to murder me. It had happened, maybe once before.

"Fellas?" I asked, aiming for calm and casual.

The looks of thunder on their faces, I wasn't delusional as to what this was all about.

Somehow, they'd found out, and I had answering to do.

Fuck.

Ajax pushed me onto the bench, and they all crowded me.

"What the fuck is this I hear about you and Mini Dev?" he growled, but then Ajax never said anything without growling it. Had I heard him speak any other way, I'd have thought it must be a bitch on his throat to sound that grumpy all the time. Turned out, that was just him.

I shrugged, but my heart pounded. "I dunno. You'll have to be more specific," I tried.

"Some prat saw you two hooking up in the library. You looked mighty cosy. Not likely the first time you'd done it."

The coward in me didn't want to look at Taylor or Jax, but my eyes still darted to them anyway. Jesus, but that was a bad choice.

Taylor looked ready to kill me and Jax was just obviously hurt, which was possibly even worse.

"It's not like it means anything," was my instant reaction.

I knew as soon as it left my lips that it was the wrong thing to say, but Taylor's backhand didn't hurt either.

"That's worse, arsehole," he growled at me, almost giving Ajax a run for his money.

"I'm not even going to get *started* on the fucking hypocrisy, Torres," Ajax seethed. "This team is built on trust. We have each other's back, on and off the field. We're a fraternity, a brotherhood, and that is more important than wetting your dick in some pussy."

I stood up violently, feeling the old anger burning in me. The anger that had been my friend far too often. I saw Ajax's eye widen and the rest of the team took a noticeable step back in case I lunged. I felt like it.

"You call her that one more time," I snarled, my fists balling at my sides.

"Oh, yeah," Forbsy huffed half-sarcastic, half-teasing. "Didn't mean anything."

I shot him a glare. Knowing Tansy, Forbsy had known this whole fucking time and kept his girl's confidentiality. Well, good for bloody him. Would that we were all such good blokes.

I was seething myself now. "Fine!" I yelled and they all took another step back, even Ajax this time. "Fine. It didn't mean nothing. It meant fucking everything. All right? That true love clause? Yeah, well, I've fucking fallen. It's goddamn true love. At least, for me."

I deflated and, they were still angry, but they were at least willing to hear me out.

I dragged a tired hand over my face. "She's the only girl for me. She's my fucking person. It sucks as a Chaser, but I tried not wanting her long before I *was* a Chaser and look where that got me."

"You are *not* trying to pull that I broke Code over her," Jax hissed, and I forgave him his fury.

I shook my head. "No. Fuck, no, mate. Not at all." I sighed. "I just... I'm fucking sorry, but I love her. I've loved her for years and there's finally a chance she feels the same and I don't fucking know what I'm doing." I ended on a humourless chuckle and dropped back onto the bench.

Taylor shouldered his way over, grabbed a fistful of my jersey and dragged me back to my feet. "You have some explaining to do."

I grabbed a fistful of his tee and pressed my forehead to his. "I'm sorry, man."

"You fucking better be."

"I tried not to."

"Yeah? How hard?"

I looked into his eyes and mentally begged him to rethink that question because he knew the answer. The darkness of my past wasn't the only reason I lost myself in girl after girl or bottle after bottle.

He breathed heavily. "You love her?"

I nodded against him. "I love her."

"If you fucking hurt her..."

"I know, mate. I know."

"I will make your past look like a fucking walk in the park." And that was a heavy threat.

"I know," I assured him.

"You're fucked up, mate. And I say that as someone who loves you."

"She knows."

He shook his head. "Not everything."

I searched his eyes. "I know."

"You going to tell her?"

I shrugged. "I don't know. This whole falling in love with each other thing is still new. We've been taking it kinda slow. We didn't want to fuck anything up."

"And how'd that go?" Jax asked and Taylor held a hand up for him to shut up.

"You damage her..." Taylor warned me, poking me none too gently in the chest.

"And you'll damage me," I acknowledged.

"She'll do worse," he corrected me, and I knew he was right.

"I know you think I'm not good enough–"

"You're good enough, mate. You just have to realise it. You just have to *be* good enough."

I nodded as I breathed out. "Okay."

"Can you do that?"

"I think so."

"You have to know so."

I nodded. "Okay. I know so. I can do it. I will be good enough."

Taylor put his hand on the back of my head, pressing our foreheads even closer, then nodded and stepped away.

"I don't like it," he pronounced. "But she's *my* blood and I'm going to allow it."

"What?" Jax and Lachy asked.

Taylor shrugged. "I'm gonna allow it. If he thinks Skye's worth breaking Code for, then that's his right. He's still gonna suffer for it, though."

I inclined my head. "I expected no less."

"That why you tried to hide it for so long?" Ajax asked and I knew why he was so pissed with me.

It wasn't just the hypocrisy. I was supposed to take over from him when he graduated. I was Captain in Waiting. I was supposed to lead by example. Be a shining model of admirable Chaser behaviour so the new kids that came through would adhere to years of tradition.

And I'd done my job fucking well…until I let him down.

I shook my head. "We were trying to figure out what it all meant. Was it just sex and so no one needed to know? Was it more and how did we go from what we were to what we are? It was fucking complicated enough without bringing the Code and my relationship with Taylor or my shit into it."

"And now?"

I shrugged. "Now, I see forever with this girl and, no matter what she feels, I'm willing to risk it." I scoffed humourlessly. "We were going to tell you after the next Hornets game."

Ajax frowned. "What?"

I nodded. "Skye figured you'd all be so high on another win that you'd forgive us."

"And if we lost?" Ajax asked.

I shrugged. "I was just going to have to make sure we won."

He sniffed, clearly not happy about it, but willing to give me a pass. I knew it was the only one I was getting.

"What size are you?"

Ah, fuck. We all knew what he was referring to. I couldn't help making a little light of the situation. "Last I checked, large."

Taylor snorted. "You wish."

I tried not to laugh in the face of our captain's utter apathy, and smacked Taylor. "Medium, Cap."

Ajax gave a single nod. "Enjoy your last practice with feeling in your extremities," he said dryly. Then again, his tone was always dry.

"That's it?" Jax exploded like he couldn't keep it in any longer.

Ajax shrugged. "What the fuck else you want me to do? You're not all fucking five anymore. I'm not going to tell him he can't fucking see her. Now, let's go!"

"Yes, Cap," we all chorused and nodded.

I knew I was in Shitsville with the team in theory, but I felt lighter than I had in a long time. Being with Skye had lightened me, but having the rest of the team know made it even better. I didn't have to hide the fact I loved her anymore. I wasn't going to rub it in their – Jax's – faces, but I didn't have to hide it. I didn't have to worry that they were going to find out at a moment's notice, counting down the days until we told them while trying to work out how to tell them and sort of not wanting to either.

I felt like I'd got off pretty easy. They'd found out. I'd fucked it up. Then we'd all come to an understanding and were going about our business like nothing had changed.

But I needed to tell Skye we weren't a secret anymore, and that filled me with the steady fluttering of a thousand nerves through the whole of practice.

"I know a girlfriend is a novelty for you, Torres, but get your head out of your arse!" Ajax snapped as he jogged past me to get into position.

I nodded. "Yeah, sorry."

"Don't be sorry. Be less shit."

I mean, I tried.

To say I succeeded would have been a bit of an exaggeration. But, other than some heavy glaring from Jax when he thought I wasn't looking, no one begrudged me being a little off my game.

As soon as coach blew the whistle for the end of practice, I was gone. I was out of the locker room before most of the team was even back in it. Not showering saved a buttload of time.

I raced to Tansy and Skye's place, and knocked on the door. Tansy answered it and her smile dropped as her eyes went from my face to my mud-streaked kit.

"Is not showering some kind of kink you're exploring?" she asked.

I shook my head, a little breathless after my run. "She in?" I asked, and Tansy nodded.

"Yeah, in her room. Everything okay?"

I shrugged. "I don't know." Then, "The team knows," I said to Skye as I burst into her room.

Skye looked up at me from her desk and I saw the wariness on her face.

"Okay, and that's me finding anything else to do right now. Bye, guys!" Tansy said and we heard the front door shut behind her.

Skye licked her lip. "They know?"

I nodded. "They know. It's… I guess we're public?"

"*How* do they know?"

"I dunno," I told her. "Ajax mentioned that kid who saw us hooking up in the library? I think he has classes with Tim and Jax."

Fucking Jax. Like he wouldn't have jumped on that rumour the second he heard it. I mean, I got it dude – she was a catch – but it was over a year ago! Then, I had to give him a break, because I was pretty sure that if Skye and I broke up now then I'd die still not over her.

"What?" she asked, and I blinked.

"What, what?" I asked.

"You just got this look." She shook her head. "Is that…? How did they take it?"

"As expected. Officially done my last practice in my kit."

"And games?"

I shrugged. "Ajax didn't mention it. I suspect he's thinking it over."

"Shit," she murmured. "Taylor? Jax?"

Because she knew, as well as anyone with a passing understanding of humanity as a whole, that Jax still carried a torch.

"Yeah… Your brother backhanded me, and I think Jax might kill me in my sleep."

She grimaced. "Ouch. Well… I guess it's good. Overall?"

I nodded. "I think so. Maybe not the way we wanted to do it, but it could have been worse."

"Maybe kind of easier?" she hedged, and I smiled.

"Says the one who wasn't confronted by a murderous team."

She waved away my point. "They'd never hurt me."

"No. But they will not hesitate to hurt me if they think I deserve it."

"Are you planning to do anything to deserve it?"

We both knew what would deserve it; hurting her. The Chasers might have joked about the fact that we'd go to war for Skye, but it was true. She was like a sister to all of them and, if I hurt her, I may as well quit the team and go and live as a hermit because they would not let me get away with it.

"You know I'm not," I said slowly. "I'm still scared shitless that I will anyway."

She stood up and came over to me. She went to put her arms around me, then her nose wrinkled. "Wow. You really didn't shower, didn't you?"

"What gave it away?"

Humour shone in her eyes. "The smell."

"Oh, the smell?" I teased and she nodded.

"Yeah, the smell."

I tackled her onto her bed, and she laughed. "You don't like the smell of *man*?" I asked her as I nuzzled into her.

She laughed as she half-heartedly tried getting me off her. "Man? More like beast!"

I growled playfully. "In the sheets, definitely."

She snorted and wrapped her arms around me as she looked into my eyes. "Cheese," she reinforced.

"Sexy," I corrected her.

She bit her lip and, fuck, but I loved that look in her eyes. It was all humour and love and teasing and fun. "*Por que no los dos*," she said.

I actually swooned a little over this girl. "Damn, woman. I'm falling hard for you."

"I'm falling pretty hard for you, too."

I kicked my eyebrows at her. "Wanna know what else is hard?"

She spluttered a laugh and shook her head. "No. Not until you've showered."

I licked my lip and poured on all my charming smoulder. "Want to join me?"

Oh, that changed the mood, and it was awesome.

She ran her hand up my chest slowly until she took my chin between her fingers and made me look at her. "I could be persuaded," she answered. Her voice was low and sultry and holy shit.

I dropped off her bed and pulled her to the edge of it. "Then let me persuade you, baby."

♡ 17 ♡
Skye

So, River and I were public. It was both better and worse than keeping it secret.

It was easier that I didn't have to sneak in or out of the mansion to see him, and he didn't have to make sure Forbsy didn't see him at mine. But when I walked into the mansion to see him, there would always be that awkward moment where Taylor thought I was there to hang out and I'd basically have to say, 'Oh, no. I'm here to fuck your best friend'. Though, obviously, not in so many words, and I wasn't always there for a booty call but that was how Taylor saw it every time.

It created friction between me and my brother. Friction that wasn't like any kind of friction we'd ever experienced. We'd been pissy with each other before – we were siblings, we'd shared a goddamn bedroom for a while, of course we'd had arguments. But this wasn't like that. This was the first time I could really remember when it was weird and awkward, and we weren't talking about it. I felt like I understood why, at least partly, but it didn't make it any easier.

So, I did totally just explode at him one afternoon in the mansion.

"Why are you so pissy?" I huffed.

"Because you've been fucking my best mate and you didn't say anything!" he yelled. "You fucking hid it from me."

"I thought you wouldn't approve!" I yelled back. I mean, there were a lot of reasons we hid it, but that one was the forefront just then.

The whole McMansion could probably hear us, but it wouldn't be the first time Taylor and I had shouted the place down.

"I'm not sure I do! But only because, forgetting River's personal issues, I don't want to have to choose between you two in the divorce. If you're happy and safe, then I'm okay with it!" Despite the niceness of the sentiment, we were still yelling at each other.

"What do you mean, in the divorce?"

"I love you both, but you're not always the easiest people to get along with. Two massively strong personalities? You're either going to fucking soar, or crash and burn."

My heart hitched and I think he saw it on my face. We were both pretending that the rest of the team wasn't listening in.

"Hey," he said more gently. "Hey, you know I'll pick you."

I shook my head. "You can't, though."

"Why not?"

"Because I'm your sister and you'll always love me."

He looked at me quizzically. "Exactly, so I'll pick you."

"And leave Riv with no one?" I snapped and Taylor took an amused step back.

"Are we going to fight about who I pick in the divorce?"

"*If* there's a divorce!" I yelled.

Taylor smirked. "Okay. Fine. You wanna throw down. Let's throw down. Why do I have to pick River?"

"Because he needs you."

"You need me."

"I'll have you anyway."

"And you think he won't?"

"You have a good point, but I'm still annoyed with you!"

"You're annoyed with me? You're the one hooking up with River behind my back!"

"Well, I knew this is how you'd react."

"You didn't know how I was going to react!"

"Of course I did. You've made no secret of the fact that you think River's not good enough for me."

"In my defence, no one's good enough for you, Muster."

My heart thudded. Taylor hadn't called me my old nickname in years. Dad had shown us the Terminator films years ago, and Taylor had started calling me Muster after SkyMuster, thinking he was hilariously original.

"Why not? What's so good about me?"

"You're my little sister! Everything's so good about you! You're smart and funny and beautiful and so goddamn kind and loving, and there isn't a single person alive who's good enough for you. Everyone's a potential threat to your happiness and I would protect your heart at all costs! Why do you think you're the first sibling to be an honorary Chaser? Because everyone loves you. You're one of us. The whole fucking team would go to war for you regardless of who you're fucking."

"Why is this always about who I'm fucking?"

"It's not! I don't want to know about it, but I don't give a shit as long as you're sensible. You can see as many or as few people as you want. You're ten times smarter and more mature than I'll ever be. If one of us is going to make stupid mistakes, it's me."

"You're not stupid!"

"Why are we still yelling at each other?"

"Because we love each other."

"Because your love language is fucking yelling!" Ajax joined in. "Are you two fucking done yet, or shall we tiptoe around you for another half a fucking hour?"

Taylor and I shared a smile.

Ajax was a grumpy sod. Like, so grumpy. A guy in his early twenties should not be that grumpy, and no one in the team knew why. But he also had a heart of gold. He liked to pretend he didn't, but Tansy and I had been drunk around him enough that he'd let it slip once or twice when he thought we'd forget.

"Give us another half an hour!" Taylor called to him.

"Fuck's sake," we heard him grumble, then we both laughed.

"We good?" Taylor asked me.

I nodded. "As long as you don't hate me."

"Of course, I don't hate you. I could never hate you. You've just spent the better part of the last ten minutes yelling at me that I could never hate you."

"And you don't hate River?"

Taylor smirked. "River had some very compelling things to say in his defence. And, as you pointed out, I'd never hate him either."

"What did he say?"

"If he hasn't told you, then I'm not saying it first. But as nice as they were, nothing could save him from punishment."

"How many months is he down for?"

"Ajax was…lenient. The team's not stupid enough to bench him for the rest of the season, so we compromised. He has to do the G-string for the rest of the season, and he's on cleaning duty for the rest of the year."

I shook my head. "I don't know why you act like G-strings are bad."

"Oh, there's nothing wrong with a G-sting."

"Isn't it a punishment because it's 'emasculating'?"

Taylor laughed. "No! Because it's the least amount of clothes they can wear while training in the middle of winter. We checked the Chester code of conduct. They don't like it, but it's technically allowed. The G-string's a temperature punishment, not an emasculation."

"Huh," I mused.

"What? Did you really think we were being sexist about it?"

I shrugged. "Yeah, kinda actually."

"That's bullshit."

I nodded. "It is bullshit."

"Yeah, it is. That's why that's not what it means."

I sort of deflated. "Oh. Okay. Cool, I guess."

He smiled. "Are we done now?"

I shrugged. "I dunno. Are we? Are you going to keep being weird about me and River?"

"I won't if you won't."

"How am I being weird about it?"

"I dunno, you just are. It's a two-sided weirdness. I'll cut it out if you do."

I shook my head. "Okay. Fine. I'll stop doing the thing I already wasn't doing."

"You totally were doing it!" Taylor said, his voice rising.

"No," Ajax growled as he stepped into the room. "You're not fucking starting this shit again. Give each other a fucking hug and we can all go about our *lovely* days."

Taylor and I shared a failed-hidden snigger, like Mum and

Dad were telling us both off for doing something naughty. Then we pressed our lips together and nodded, then gave Ajax a nod to show him we were going to do what we were told. As one, Taylor and I took a step forward and then hugged each other tightly.

"I love you," I told him.

"I love you, too," he answered.

"I might be fucking sick," Ajax muttered as he shook his head and walked out.

Taylor squeezed me harder. "I'm sorry I was weird."

"I'm sorry I was weird, too. And I'm sorry that it is weird."

I felt him shrug as he pulled away. "It was kind of inevitable, really."

I blinked. "What?"

"I dunno," he said, scrubbing a hand over his jaw. "I guess it just doesn't really surprise me. Like, I didn't see it coming but, now it's happened, it makes sense."

"Are you really worried about who to pick if we break up?"

"Not really. Like you said, you'll always be my sister so I'd pick River."

I chewed my lip uncertainly. "That's one reason we didn't say anything."

"What is?"

Now I was shrugging. "Well, we wanted to see what it was before we went public. What if it was just a couple of hook ups? It didn't seem worth getting everyone's knickers in knots for a couple of hook ups. And, with everyone's knickers in knots, I was worried that was all it would be."

"If you're not sure about him—" Taylor started, and I shook my head.

"No, it's not that. I wasn't sure about both of us. River and I spent so long hating each other, or at least acting like it, that I thought it would be way too easy for us both to fall back into that shallow, flippant relationship if it got too hard."

"And now?"

"Now I know it's worth it, no matter how hard it gets. We gave ourselves time to realise we were worth it. We were always going to tell you, we just hadn't found the right time yet."

"Fuck," he muttered.

"What?" I asked with a smile.

"Well, I can't really be mad at that, can I? You guys took a mature and actually kind of reasonable view of it and did what your relationship needed. I mean, I'm still pissed you didn't tell me, but I feel ever so less self-righteous about it now."

I laughed. "I'm sorry."

He waved a dismissive hand. "Just don't go full-on romance on us, okay? That's all I ask."

I nodded. "We'll do our best. I'm not really sure we're full-on romance people, anyway." I paused. "Although, River is so fucking cheesy."

Taylor snorted. "Seriously?"

"Yeah. It's pretty funny."

"Well, maybe I could deal with a bit of full-on romance if I got to laugh at how cheesy he is."

"Thanks, Tay."

"For what?"

"For not, like, beating him up, or me, or something."

"I'd never. You know that. You guys get to make your own mistakes. I just hope that, if it ends, it doesn't rip through the entire fabric of reality and ruin everything."

"Why are you boys so dramatic?" I whispered.

"Can't let you girls have all the fun."

"Touché," I said with a nod, then checked my phone for the time. "Shit. Late for Richard again."

Taylor's snort this time suggested he'd done his best not to laugh out of sympathy and just plain old failed. The force of it sounded like it hurt.

"You'd best get going, then."

I nodded. "I'll see you later?"

"Sounds good. I might let you beat me at three-point shoot off again."

I scoffed. "Yeah, 'let'," I chuckled, complete with air quotes as I started backing out.

I waved to him, then cursed my timing. I still had to go past my apartment and get my bag. No way was I going to Richard's lecture looking as unprepared as I was. I was just heading into my apartment as I saw River coming from the other direction.

"Hey," he said, kicking his head to me.

I nodded shortly. "Hey. Richard. Lecture. Late. Sorry."

That was all the explanation he needed. He shook his head. "Totally understand."

I smiled then hurried upstairs. Once I had my bag and was back downstairs, I found River still hanging around by the front door.

"I'm serious, River," I told him as I hurried by.

He fell into step with me. "And I seriously understand, baby."

I smiled. "I don't have time, River."

He gave me a nod, his long legs more than capable of keeping up with my short ones at any speed. "I know."

"Then what are you doing?"

"I have something for you. I don't want to have to wait any

longer than necessary, so I'm coming to your lecture."

I snorted. "You know Richard will totally give you shit."

"He will, but I'm prepared. And it's important."

I tried to hide my smile and knew I failed. "Okay, then. Don't say I didn't warn you."

"You say that like I didn't have Richard for two years of my own," he said, humouredly.

I just smirked at him as I led the way into the lecture theatre.

"Mr Torres," was out of Richard's mouth as soon as he saw us. "To what do we owe the grace of your presence today? Does your ego so need the boost that you're returning to high school Literature?"

River grinned. "Maybe I thought your class could do with the opportunity to feel intelligent for once."

Richard actually paused for a second, then there was a slight upturn of one corner of his lips. The smallest, softest smile I had ever seen on his face, but also the most genuine. Then he gave River a nod.

Then, he was back to his perfunctory business. "Do not speak unless spoken to, Mr Torres. I will not have you distracting my class. Without my permission."

River mimed locking his lips and nodded as we took our seats.

There was no pretending that the whole class was watching avidly as River Torres, the soccer king of Chester University, sat beside me in my lecture when he'd moved on years earlier. There was no pretending that it wasn't going to spread through the University College like wildfire, at a much faster pace than it was spreading through the uni.

The main distinction being of course that there was a vast difference between him being seen kissing me in the library and him being seen at one of my lectures. He was seen hooking up with girls all the time. He'd never once been seen at any lecture he wasn't required – for the sake of his semester grade – to attend. Just because he was required to attend for the sake of his grades didn't even always mean he'd be there.

For all Richard's talk about not wanting River to distract the class, River distracted the class. But there was very little that Richard could do about it, because it was just glances. No one was stupid enough to talk in Richard's class outside of answering a direct question. But they were just curious enough to sneak looks back at us like they thought we'd be hooking up in the back rows.

By the end of the lecture, I felt like I was about to slide off my seat and into a puddle on the floor. Richard gave me this knowing look, like he knew I'd only brought it on myself and it was all the punishment I deserved for whatever situation had made River come to the lecture. It was quite possibly the nicest thing Richard had ever done. Or not done, as the case may be.

I kept my head ducked as the rest of the class filed out, but I knew River was grinning and nodding to every single one of them. He even said 'hello' to a few of them, which had them scurrying out faster.

Finally, I felt him sit back and laugh. "That was the most entertaining shit I've been involved in for a long time."

"I'm so glad you got something out of it," I muttered as I zipped up my bag and stood up.

I shook my head as I started out of the lecture theatre.

"Oh, come on, Calypso," he called, humour in his voice as he followed me.

"*Is* it worth it?" I muttered to myself as I pushed out of the building and headed across the quad.

"Calypso! Skye!" he called again, then I felt his hand on my arm and he gently tugged me to face him. "I'm sorry."

I shrugged, refusing to look at him. "Whatever, River. It'll be fine."

He put his finger under my chin and tipped my face to his. "I'm sorry, baby. I won't go to any more of your lectures."

River held out a box for me and I looked at it quizzically, instantly forgetting the preceding hour's shenanigans.

"What's that?" I asked.

"Can I call it a belated birthday present?"

"My birthday was months ago."

"Very, very belated?"

I smirked. "You've never got me a birthday present."

"I know," he said with a cheeky grimace. "But if it's not a birthday present, then it strays into romantic territory…"

I nodded as I took the box from him. "Ah. Well, we can't have that."

He smirked. "No, we can't."

I opened the box and found a little… "What even is that?" I asked him.

He looked unreasonably pleased with himself. "It's a jar of dirt," he said.

So, it was. A little jar of dirt about the same size as a fifty-cent piece with a rose gold lid and chain.

But… "A jar of dirt?"

"For my Calypso."

It all fell into place, and I realised what was going on. He had every reason to be relatively pleased with himself.

"Am I meant to put your heart in it so you can't get it back?" I teased.

His cavalier, "If you want. It's your jar of dirt," suggested, without the need to say it directly, that that was exactly the kind of the message he was giving.

"It is at least clean dirt?"

"Probably not. I got it from the goal line after we won our last home match last year, and I did take a ball to the face at that exact position. Blood went everywhere."

I remembered that match. His face had saved the penalty that stopped the opposition equalising. The bruise on that face had him scoring pity sex for a whole week. But I remembered something else about that match. Something I'd forgotten until now.

"You nearly kissed me at that match," I accused him, and he smiled.

"I was hopped up on some fantastic painkillers and had absolutely zero control over myself."

Illogical panic gripped me, and I couldn't stop myself saying, "So that's what I am? I'm the thing you do when you have no inhibitions and then…what? Regret?"

He shook his head, smirking like he knew I knew I was just having a temporary moment. "No. Never regret." He cupped my cheek. "You're the thing that can implode my whole world. You're the Surtur to my apocalypse. But I'd burn the whole world to be with you, baby."

"That's why you call me Calypso," I said softly.

"Why?"

"Apocalypse."

He smirked. "You were always the smart one."

"Why do I have the power to implode your world, River?" I whispered.

"It doesn't matter anymore."

"Why not?"

"Because, out of the ashes of the old world, rises a new and better one." His nuzzled my nose with his. "And that better world is waiting for us," he said before sweeping me off my feet like some old-time movie and kissing the daylights out of me.

A great chorus of 'woo' surrounded us, because of course it did. Very little was sacred in this place, much less a private moment like we were having.

When we finally pulled apart, I was gratified to find that people at least hadn't lingered. I shoved him away playfully and got my feet back under me.

"Why do you insist on having these moments in the quad?" I huffed, trying not to laugh.

He shrugged with the casual ease that was River at his most arrogant and relaxed. "I dunno. Maybe it's our spot? Fuck, am I going to have to propose to you here?"

My heart skipped. "You're already planning the proposal?"

"Planning's a very strong word. I like to think of it as fantasising," he said, his tone totally shit-stirring, but I suspected the sentiment was sincere regardless.

Not knowing what to say, I chewed my lip for a few moments. Then I shook myself out of my head and picked the jar of dirt out of the box.

"Will you do the honours?" I asked.

He took it from me with a cheeky bounce of his eyebrows. "I'm used to taking stuff off you, baby, not putting it on."

I snorted as I turned my back to him. "Consider it practise for your proposal," I teased.

He put the chain around my neck and did up the clasp before untucking my hair from under it. Then he kissed my cheek.

"Consider me practised," he said softly, and I leant back into him.

I took his hand and we continued on our way.

"You wanna hang out?" he asked me.

I shrugged. "Tay said he'd let me beat him at three-pointer."

River scoffed. "Yeah, *let*," he chuckled.

"That," I told him as I swung our hands, "is exactly what I said, too."

River laughed as he put his arm around my shoulder, and we headed to the mansion.

Things were still kind of weird, but we were making it through it together. It did feel easier now that everyone knew. The fact that River and I both knew this was worth fighting for made it even easier.

♥ 18 ♥
River

As we jogged back to the centre for kick off in the next training, Jax's shoulder smacked into mine.

"Sorry, man," he said, sounding the opposite of sorry.

I gave him a nod to show that it was okay, but honestly, it kind of wasn't anymore.

I wasn't going to pretend I hadn't noticed that Jax was feeling something about Skye and me dating. I mean, the whole fucking team felt something about us dating, but Jax's feelings were way more complicated than the rest of the team. And I didn't blame him.

Just because I didn't blame him, didn't mean I was okay with him being shit about it.

But then, being cold as fuck would do that to a guy. Because I was a man of my word, so I was in nothing but a G-string, my socks and cleats. Ajax had done me a solid and bought a leopard print one and, honestly, as much as it suited me, it was clashing with my socks.

Not that it stopped a fuck tonne of people from coming to practice to see me in very nearly all my glory. If I hadn't been so cold, I'd have been putting on more of a show. Unsurprisingly, a G-string wasn't that great protection from the sleeting rain. But then, that was the whole fucking point of the exercise, wasn't it?

And, fuck, I sound just like Ajax.

"Just give it time," Taylor said as he passed me.

I kicked my head in acknowledgement. "Sure. Time."

I didn't know how long it was going to take, but I wasn't going to let Jax's issue get between me and Skye. We'd been about to tell everyone about us, to deal with all the bullshit, so we were ready. We just had to remember that we were ready.

And, for the most part, the majority of the team were satisfied that I was serving my punishment and any further punishment was unnecessary. So, things were largely the same as always.

Even still, Skye and I spent more time at her place than the mansion. It just seemed easier, and I was all for not looking like we were shoving our relationship in anyone's face – namely Jax.

And it wasn't all hooking up. It couldn't be, or she wouldn't have let me see her as often. Because, even though we were basking in our new relationship, she was still taking her studies seriously, and it was a reminder that I needed to as well.

When we weren't in her room or the library, we could be seen wandering around the campus, holding hands or our arms around each other like any other bona fide couple. And, finally, people were starting to not care anymore. To start with, it seemed the talk of Chester that River Torres had settled down. Now, we were starting to be old news.

How interesting could we be if we just acted like a normal couple? Not very, apparently.

We were out for dinner with Forbsy, Tansy and Taylor and it felt the same way it always had. Except, I got to put my arm around Skye and kiss her and steal her food without just taking the piss. I could be sincere. Didn't mean I *didn't* take the piss, though, naturally.

"Okay, so if it's the end of season coming up, what does that mean for River and training in a G-string?" Tansy asked.

"We still train off season," Taylor said through a mouthful of food.

"And Riv will have to keep up the G-string."

Tansy's eyes widened as she took that in. "Guess it'll be comfier in summer."

I grinned. "That is an excellent point."

Taylor snorted and rolled his eyes. "You hope. Better you than me having that thing rub in your arse crack with sweat running through it."

Skye and Tansy shared a grimace. "Talk about visuals, man," Skye protested.

"What?" I teased. "You don't like my arse crack?"

Her nose wrinkled. "I don't like anyone's arse crack all sweaty and being rubbed raw. That just sounds painful."

I pressed a kiss to her neck. "Will you make it all better, baby?"

She laughed and shied away from me shyly, like I'd tickled her. "I am not rubbing lotion on your arse crack."

I smirked. "You don't want to take some of the blame here?"

She gave me a smile that shone in the depths of those beautiful blue eyes. "I guess that would only be fair," she sighed.

I nodded. "It takes two to tango, you know."

She rolled her eyes. "It's takes two for a lot of things, Pond Scum."

"Is this the cheese you warned me about?" Taylor snorted and I shot him a cheeky grin.

"You jealous, Dev?"

"Of you making goo-goo eyes at my sister and spouting absolute nonsense?" he clarified, and I nodded. "Yeah, no. Hard pass. Thanks."

"Aw, he's jealous," I teased, looking at Forbsy.

"Aw, jealous," Forbsy replied, shit-stirring in his eyes.

"I'm no jealous," Taylor laughed.

Tansy and Skye shared a look.

"I mean, he sounds jealous," Tansy said.

Skye nodded. "He kinda does."

Taylor huffed, a smile at his lips but resignation in his eyes. "I'm not jealous, I'm just not used to being the odd one out. Look at me. The very definition of a spare wheel here. You lot pairing up and I'm left to hold down the fort of bachelorhood alone. It's a lot of responsibility!"

We all shared a laugh, and I kicked him companionably under the table. He didn't need the reminder that we were just giving him shit, but a reminder never hurt anyone.

"I presume you're all planning to boring couple things after this?" he asked the table at large.

I shrugged. "Depends. What did you have in mind?"

"Dunno. Movie?"

I nodded. "I could do a movie."

Skye nodded as well. "Yeah. Sounds good. But I can't be late. We've got a test tomorrow."

"Oh, is that for Gale?" Tansy asked and Skye nodded. "Shit. I forgot all about it."

Skye huffed. "Like you won't pass it in your sleep. Your brain is a steel trap of knowledge."

"It never hurts to be prepared."

"Hence, not a late night."

"What chapter did she want?"

"Five."

Tansy smiled. "Oh, I did my assignment on five. Piece of

cake."

I watched as Skye forced a smile, but her eyes were more dull than I'd have liked to see them. "See? You'll be fine. I, stupidly, chose eight. So, I'm fucked."

I shook my head and aimed to lighten the mood. "Not tonight if you've got a test tomorrow," I said sagely.

The humour returned to Skye's eyes as she laughed. "Oh, no. What a pity," she teased.

Later that night, after the girls had gone home to study, Taylor pulled up in my doorway and leant on the frame. I looked up and kicked my chin to him in greeting. He returned it.

"Sup?" I asked. "Need something?"

He looked down at his shoes. "You and Skye..." he started, and I felt like nothing good was coming.

"Uh...?" I said. "Yeah?"

He sniffed. "You get her, huh?"

I blinked, now not sure where this was going at all. "I guess so?"

He shrugged, acting totally weird for him. "You don't guess so, you know so."

"Ye-es?" I agreed uncertainly.

"I saw you tonight."

"Mate, I love you. But I am very confused about where this is going," I told him outright.

He crossed his arms over his chest. "You and my sister. I saw what you did for her tonight."

Was he talking about the quickie between dinner and the movie? Because, as much as I loved him like he was my own brother, that wasn't the kind of shit I wanted to share, even with him. I think he guessed what I was thinking based on the look on my face.

"I don't want to know what kind of hanky panky you got up to. I'm talking about dinner."

"I paid?" I guessed.

He shook his head. "When she and Tanz were talking about their test tomorrow. You saw she was worried, you saw she felt…not enough, and you just made her smile."

I blinked. "Am I not meant to?" I asked.

"No. You are. You're dating her. I've just never seen you so in tune with anyone like that before. It looked so natural."

Now I was shrugging. "It is natural," I told him honestly. "I just want her to be happy, man. If I can make her happy, then that's fucking awesome."

A smile broke over Taylor's face. "You really care about her, huh?"

I nodded. "Yeah."

"No, I mean, like, more than just the whole proximity breeds familiarity care about her."

I smiled. "Yeah. I do. I meant it when I said I loved her, mate. Like, not platonically. Romantically. In love with her kind of love her."

He gave a single nod. "Yeah, nah. I get that now. I mean…" He shook his head noncommittally. "I didn't doubt you. But knowing it and seeing it are two different things."

I smirked knowingly. "This you being cheesy, mate?" I teased.

He grinned, but it looked unbidden. He ran his tongue over his teeth and, for a moment, couldn't look at me. Finally, he did look at me again and I saw the warmth in his eyes.

"Yeah, mate. This is me being cheesy. This is me with no more reservations. My blessing, if you will. Not just publicly defending you to the team, but actually fucking happy for you."

"Thanks, Dev. That means a lot."

He patted the door frame like he wasn't sure what to say next, or maybe he wasn't sure how to say it next.

"Out with it," I told him.

He pressed his lips together, then just went for it. "You thought any more about telling her?"

My heart constricted. "About what happened?" I clarified and he nodded. I shook my head. "I've been kind of avoiding it."

Taylor gave a nod. "I just don't want it to blow up in your face, Riv."

I nodded. "I know. I know. And she deserves to know." Fuck, but talking about it was difficult, even with my best friend who knew all the sordid details. "I just…"

He nodded. "No. I get that. I do. I just… Don't give yourself an out."

I frowned. "What's that supposed to mean?"

He flailed wildly. "I know that's not an overly popular standpoint. But just don't leave it as an out. Don't keep it from her because you know, if she finds out from someone else, it will fuck everything up and you'll be proven right about how shit you are and all that bull."

I nodded, feeling slightly less generous towards him than I had a few moments before. "And who's going to tell her? You?"

He frowned. "No. Of course, I'm not fucking going to tell her. You tell her when you're ready."

"Then who else is?"

He shrugged again. "I don't know, man. Just don't keep it from her for the wrong reasons."

I scrubbed a hand over my chin. "What exactly are the right reasons?"

"That's up to you, Riv." He patted the door frame again. "That's up to you." Then he walked away.

I was left feeling like the world was perfect and horrible all at the same time. I was surprised he'd commented on me and Skye, but glad that it was positive. On the other hand, I wished he hadn't brought up my past.

I knew I needed to tell her at some point but, much like us putting off telling the team about our relationship, I was taking the easy road. It all felt too new and fresh to come in with a fucking life-changing secret. I didn't want to make her feel like I'd trapped her into loving me before telling her, but I also wanted to shed the doubt that she wouldn't be able to love me when she found out.

And, in the meantime, I had to hope that it didn't completely backfire on me.

♡19♡
Skye

"Killer! Killer! Killer!" vibrated across the stadium.

There had been a lot more fans at the games since River had started his punishment. Ajax had given up trying to keep the riffraff out of their practices and more and more people went each day. The team – minus Jax – had voted to let him keep playing matches. They all knew they needed River, especially with their last Hornets game coming up. If they beat the Hornets, then the Chasers would secure their lead on the ladder and win the season. Another trophy meant far more to them than who River was dating.

The Hornets went down two-nil and River had been responsible for one goal, and assisted on the second. The Hornets' captain was pissed, to say the least. For some reason, Jax was also pissed.

I bumped into him after the game while I was looking for River and my brother.

"Looking for Torres?" he asked me, and I was surprised by the venom in his tone.

I nodded. "Yeah. They're still chanting his name out there." I huffed a laugh. "I guess they'll have to come up with something else now he's taken."

"What?"

I looked at him. "His nickname. Killer."

Jax scoffed. "Skye, why *do* you think we call him 'killer'?"

I frowned in confusion. "What do you mean?"

"'Killer' has nothing to do with how good he is on the field."

I swallowed. "I thought it was about how quickly he moved on after hooking up with a girl?"

Jax's face said, 'oh, isn't that cute?' and I didn't care for it. "A convenient coincidence."

Something ugly swirled inside me. I was feeling a little sick, actually. "What does it have to do with, Jax?"

"He killed someone," he said, like it was supposed to be obvious.

I scoffed. "No, he didn't."

Jax's smug smirk told me he knew something I didn't. Or, at least, he thought he did.

"Did you *not* know?" he asked, full of self-righteous humour, as though he hadn't known I was ignorant of the real reason but was still laughing at me for it.

I felt like I'd been hit by a sledgehammer, or a semi-trailer. My head actually felt a little dizzy. I shook it as though that was going to clear it.

"No. I mean, he can't have." I was pulling myself together. Slowly. "I assumed you'd have feelings about me being with River, but I didn't think you'd stoop to *lying* about him."

How did he get even more smug? "Oh, I'm not lying. Go on. Ask him yourself."

I blinked at Jax. He was so very sure of himself. He was so sure that, if I went to ask River, then I'd finally know the truth. Well, fine. I'd go and find River and I'd ask him, proving to Jax that he didn't know shit after all.

I pushed out of the locker room and back out to the pitch. River was talking to the coach. When he saw me, he touched Coach's arm and jogged over, all smiles and happy to see me.

"Hey," he said warmly.

"Is it true?" I blurted out quickly before I lost the nerve.

He was giving me his usual lazy smile. "Is what true, baby?" he asked, unsurprisingly not knowing what I was talking about when I just word-vomited everywhere like that, as he stepped towards me.

Instinctively, I took a step back then scolded myself for being ridiculous. At least until I had my answer. "Did you…?" I could hardly say the words. "Did you kill someone?"

River's face completely shut down. "What?" he breathed.

"Did you…?" I took a steadying breath. "Is it true?"

I couldn't read his mind. I didn't know what he was thinking. I couldn't tell if he was on damage control, or wondering why I'd ask him such a preposterous thing.

Please let him be wondering why I'd ask him something so preposterous…

Finally, after what felt like forever, he ran his tongue over his bottom lip and nodded. "It's true."

My heart cracked and my stomach roiled as I suddenly felt like I didn't know the guy standing in front of me after all. "Wha–? What?" I stammered.

"It's true," he said again, and I realised that I was starting to back away from him and he wasn't trying to stop me.

He wasn't giving me any explanation. Nothing. No reasonable excuse. Nothing that would stop me from thinking the worst about him. And I couldn't help it; I thought the absolute worst. I fully believed it was something River could do. I'd seen the darkness in him. I knew he was troubled. The idea that he'd killed someone didn't surprise me in the slightest. Like I'd always known there was something so much darker in him than he'd allowed people to see.

The next thing I knew, I'd turned, and I was running.

Jax was ahead, like he was making sure he'd well and truly ruined everything. And he looked pleased about it. God, but I'd thought he was one of the good ones.

Tansy was coming out of the locker rooms and saw me, being understandably confused that I – of all people – was running.

"Skye?"

But I didn't stop until the rolling heat in my stomach made its way up my throat. I came to a pause against one of the random statues dotted around the campus and threw up all over its base.

"Fucking hell," I heard Tansy say, then felt her hands on my arm and brushing my hair back. "Fuck, you're not pregnant, are you?"

I scoffed, but it was all humourless. When the words didn't want to come out, I just shook my head instead.

"What's wrong? You haven't had anything to drink. Have you eaten today? Are you getting sick? What can I do?"

I shook my head again, leaning back on her in case my legs gave out. They did and she made my descent to the floor slightly more dignified, sitting down with me.

"What's wrong?" she asked, running her hand over my hair comfortingly.

"He killed someone," I finally rasped.

I felt Tansy tense for a second, then she was all dismissive reassurance. "Did Jax tell you that? I'm sure he's just jealous. River wouldn't kill someone. He couldn't."

I shook my head and my stomach roiled again. "I asked him. He said it was true."

"Well, fuck…" Tansy muttered. "I'm sure he had a good reason. He's not in prison, is he?"

"It must have been when he was underage. Taylor mentioned court once."

My mind was racing with nothing helpful, trying to fit pieces together that I'd picked up over the years. The only conclusion I could come to was that it made total sense. That it fit in with this idea of River I had in my head. I couldn't shake it. I was sure I could remember snippets of conversations, overheard whispers when they thought I was asleep, that made more sense with the information I now had.

I nodded, convincing myself. "It must have been. They probably let him out when he turned eighteen and—"

"Are you listening to yourself?" Tansy laughed. "You've known him since he was like thirteen."

I shook my head. "Maybe *that's* when he got out. What do I know about his life before he and Taylor became inseparable?"

"That it sucked. Come on. Take a breath and calm down. I don't want to lessen your feelings, but you are actually sounding ridiculous right now. Let's not jump to conclusions. Conclusions bite us in the arse. Why don't we go back and ask him what happened? Ask him to explain?"

"I can't. Not tonight. I need…" I took a deep breath. "I need to… You're right. Calm down first."

She nodded. "Okay. Sure. Not a problem. Shall we go home and snuggle under the blankets and watch Disney movies until we fall asleep?"

"Yes, please." God, but my voice was so damned small.

She hugged me tight. "I'll even make chai for you."

I smiled, despite the utter turmoil in me. "Thanks. I love you."

She hopped up and helped me up as well. "I love you, too.

We'll work it out."

I nodded, knowing she was right. I just had to calm down and do what River and I always did; talk.

Tansy and I walked home, her with her arm around my shoulders as best as her shorter frame could manage, and talking absolute nonsense to keep my mind on light and fluffy things to give it time to calm and refocus. She made me chai and bundled me up on the couch. I fell asleep against her before the first movie finished and we both woke up there the next morning, stiff but feeling a million times better already.

All that was left to do was talk to River. Except River didn't want to talk to me.

I texted him all day. I went by the mansion where all the boys just looked between each other like they weren't sure what to tell me. I felt everything in me plummet as I, for the second time in twenty-four hours, thought the worst about him.

"Just be honest with me," I told Whistler. "Is he…? Has he been with someone else?"

Whistler licked his lip. "Not unless you count a few bottles of Jack as someone else."

"He disappeared in the bottom of a bottle at Mad Kitty last night, then came home and locked himself in his room," Robbie added.

"The amount he drank, he's probably not even awake yet," Tim said, as though that was reassuring.

I nodded. "Oh, okay."

"He could very easily be dead," Frankie D said.

That did not fill me with butterflies. They were more like angry moths that felt furry and suffocating in my throat.

"Don't say that!" Hank snapped. "I'm sure he's fine. We'll get him to message you when he surfaces."

"Okay. Uh, thanks."

"Everything okay?" Forbsy asked.

I shrugged. "Sure, why?"

"Just, Tanz…said you needed girls' night last night." He gave me an adorably uncertain shrug of his own. "You've just never missed a celebration. We worried."

I knew they'd worried. All of them had messaged me through the night saying they missed me and was I sure I didn't want to come out. Even Ajax had said;

> **Aj_ax**
> It's just not a fucking celebration without you, Little Dev. Hope you're all right.

"Fuck's sake!" Frankie D suddenly blurted. "We know!"

Everyone groaned and chastised him for saying anything.

I looked around and felt a small smile that these great big men were all jumping to my defence. Even Frankie D in his own way.

Because he wasn't taking what the others were dishing out. "No! You want to support her? Fucking support her. You want to pretend Torres didn't come in and deck Jax for what he did?"

I blinked. "He did?"

They all nodded.

"It was fucking brutal," Whistler said. "Both of them."

I wasn't sure how I felt about the team always knowing my shit. But then, I realised it made it easier when you didn't have to explain the uncomfortable stuff to people who cared about you but they were still there for you. It was invasive and kind of nice at the same time.

I cleared my throat. "Well, I guess… I just wanted to talk to him about it."

They all exchanged glances again, and I felt like someone was about to crack.

"Don't you fucking dare," Ajax growled as he walked in. "We don't know the details and I don't want any of you fuckers even pretending to yourselves you do. Torres is a fucking good guy. You've lived with him for five fucking years. That's all you need to know."

I got the message loud and clear; whatever the truth was, Ajax wasn't having me think badly about River. And, after talking it over with Tansy and giving myself time to calm down, I knew Ajax was right. I just needed to talk to River about it to stop my imagination running away with me. To stop a rising panic that tried to tell me he wasn't in fear of the actual feelings that threatened.

But he didn't. For over a week, he didn't talk to me. As far as I knew, he didn't really talk to anyone. Even Taylor. The rejection made my imagination go into hyperdrive. It told me what I needed to think to not completely fall apart after everything River and I had gone through.

If I didn't think the worst of him, my heart wouldn't just break, it would implode.

River

To be honest, I didn't think the little twat had it in him. He totally blindsided me. Both by his knowledge and the fact he'd used it against me.

But, of course, he had.

It was Skye.

I'd have killed to keep her.

And I'm well fucking aware how in poor taste that hyperbole is. But I wasn't a guy who'd ever dealt well with his anger. Not since that night.

It had been stupid of me to think I could leave it behind. Stupid not to heed Taylor's warning. Stupid to think that it wouldn't rear its ugly head and… Fuck, the way she'd looked at me. I knew I deserved it. I'd lulled myself into a false sense of security, told myself that I could have nice things, that I was good enough for her when I could never be good enough for her.

"Is it true?" she'd asked.

Sure, she'd looked panicked and worried and like she'd heard something horrible about me. But I'd been faithful and never in a million years expected anyone to tell her the deep, dark secret that lurked in my past.

So, "Is what true, baby?" I'd asked, full of confidence that whatever it was, we'd get through it the same way we'd got through to this amazing point.

But then she stepped back when I stepped towards her, and warning bells were trying to leech through my unbridled confidence.

"Did you...?" She paused and licked her lip, but it was nervous. "Did you kill someone?"

Well, fuck.

"What?" I asked, my voice a mere tiny breath of desolate surprise.

"Did you...? Is it true?"

I might not have been able to read her mind, but I knew nothing good was going through it. I knew her too well. This wasn't partying until I forgot my own name. This wasn't drowning my shit in any other shit for a moment of solace. This wasn't making some stupid but relatively harmless decisions. This was, in her mind, murder. I'd ended someone's life. The circumstances were irrelevant; we couldn't come back from this. I didn't deserve for us to come back from this.

When it was way past time for me to give her an answer, I couldn't lie to her. I had to tell her the truth. If my secret had got out, then I wasn't going to try to hide it. She deserved the truth, just as I deserved the repercussions and cold hard reality of her finding out. And the look on her face as she searched mine, practically begging me to tell her it was a lie, destroyed me.

I licked my bottom lip and nodded. "It's true."

I saw the fear and denial play across her features. She'd always hated me, but there had been a love buried under that. There was none of that now. "Wha–? What?" she stammered as she started backing away from me and my heart fucking broke.

"It's true," I'd said again, knowing it was nothing less than I deserved.

Who was I to think I could have a good life after everything that had happened? They'd made me this person, and he would never be good enough to be loved, not the way Skye had been starting to love me. Everything I touched turned to shit. Everything but a soccer ball. It was all I was good for and, even then, I had a shelf life. Provided I didn't get injured and cut that shelf life even shorter.

So, I'd said nothing as she kept backing away. Knowing it was better this way. Better for her. Better away from the shit stain I'd be on her life given enough time to fuck us both up. I'd let her walk away. I'd confirmed her worst fears and then watched the only ending I was worthy of while my heart crumpled to the fucking floor in resigned acceptance.

It didn't stop me ploughing my fist into Jax's face at the first opportunity. Because I knew who was to blame. He was standing there watching everything I loved fall apart. Jax who somehow, inexplicably knew everything and was still carrying a fucking flaming torch for my girl.

After she'd left, he turned and walked back inside. Even from that distance, I'd been able to feel the smugness radiating from him.

So, I followed him into the locker room and straight up to him. No hesitation. A satisfying crunch in my knuckles as his head recoiled. The team were on us in seconds. Those closest to Jax grabbed him. Those closest to me grabbed me. Ajax stepped between us with his fiercest glare.

But I didn't feel anything except that gaping darkness swallowing me whole.

A bottle wasn't going to solve my problems today.

I needed to bleed. I needed to break. Preferably taking the

other arsehole down with me. I was chomping at the bit and full of restless energy I was more than happy to direct straight at Jax. But our captain stood in our way and even I wasn't stupid enough to take a swing at him.

"Get out," Ajax growled at me.

I blinked. "Excuse me?"

Ajax took a step back and was so thunderous that the guys holding me let go and stepped back. I didn't, but neither was I throwing my fists at him. Yet.

"You heard me," he said in that gravelly voice we all knew him for. "Get the fuck out."

I pointed at Jax. "And what about backstabbing shitheads?"

Ajax snarled. "He'll be dealt with." Then he looked around at the team proper. "This! This is why we have a fucking code! So stupid shit like this doesn't come between us."

"We were fine until little Jackson over there decided to open his great big mouth!" I snapped and took a threatening step towards Jax. "How the fuck did you even know?"

"We all know, Torres," Ajax said. "We all know, and we don't fucking care." He rolled his eyes. "We fucking care, but we fucking love you anyway. Shit happens. You got more shit than most and that was fucking unfair, but it doesn't give you the right to come in here and deck Jax."

My mouth opened in shock. "Seriously? The fucker told Skye the *one* secret he knew would ruin us, and he's getting no blame here?"

Ajax nodded. "He'll get what his jealousy brings on him."

Jax scoffed, all bluster. "Jealousy?"

The whole team, even Frankie D and Lachy, looked at him like that argument wasn't going to fly and he lost his bluster.

He held his hands up. "Fine. Fine. I was jealous. Why does

Torres get to fuck around for years, on and off the field, and he gets the girl when I did nothing but love her this whole time?"

Even in the pit of my despair, I felt for him. It sucked, loving someone and them not feeling the same. I knew that viscerally. He might have been the reason I knew that, but I could still, unfortunately, recognise that it was a shitty position for him to be in.

My answer to it had been to fight whoever was responsible and put my whole life on the line for revenge. His revenge had come differently, but it was at least the truth. A truth I should have told Skye a long time ago.

I took a step forward and the whole team was on high alert, but I just slumped down on the bench and dropped my head in my hands.

"I should have fucking told her," I muttered.

"Yeah, you should have," Ajax said.

I sighed. "Thanks. I'll just hop in my time machine and fix that, will I?" Fuck, I'd spent to much time watching Skye's shows.

"You could talk to her?" Taylor suggested.

I shrugged. "What good will it do? She's better off."

"What do you mean she's better off?" Jax asked.

I looked up at them all. "If this wasn't going to end us, then I'd do something to fuck it up eventually. Better she gets out, hating me again, than drag her into my fuckery."

The team all looked between each other like they were trying to decide who was going to say something. It was fifty-fifty who would step up and whether it would be supportive or call me out on my dramatic bullshit.

"You going to mope all day or we gonna celebrate our win?" Forbsy asked. "Hornets are now five points behind us on the table. With a game in hand, we're unlikely to lose now."

I spared him a small smile. "Yeah. All right. Let's get drunk." Because, let's be honest, it was one of the two things I was good for.

I hadn't forgiven Jax and, it turned out, I wasn't about to forget it anytime soon either.

Falling back into old patterns was easy. I fucking spiralled. I didn't leave my room unless it was for soccer or drinking and, even then, I was a liability more often than a help. The guys started avoiding me and even my best mate left me to stew in my own shit.

To a point.

Taylor walked into my room after practice ten days later, and I didn't give a single shit that he was clearly not impressed with me. It hadn't been my fault that Ajax sent me home early that time. Jax had been asking for it.

"Your captain tells you to take a break to cool down and you get through…" I assumed he was counting. "That your third bottle?"

I shrugged. "The first one was almost empty. Seems silly to waste it by not finishing it."

"It's not wine, Torres. It'll keep."

I scoffed humourlessly as I lifted the bottle to my lips again. "Not if I have anything to say about it."

"ENOUGH!" Taylor yelled and even I paid attention.

"Enough, Dev?" I huffed and shook my head as I stood up somewhat unsteadily. "No. No, not nearly enough." I held up the bottle to him. "I'm going to finish this one, then I'm fairly certain there's another one with my name on it, just begging for a taste of my lips."

"You're fucking miserable!" Taylor snapped at me. "And it's making *me* fucking miserable! It's making the whole team fucking miserable."

"Well, I'm sorry my heartbreak is inconvenient for you!" I snapped back.

Taylor deflated. "If you like her so much that you'd risk the Code, why are you letting anything come between you?"

"I don't *like* her, Taylor," I said sadly. "I love her. I've loved her for years."

"I know."

I looked at him quickly. "What?"

He shrugged. "I know. It's depressingly obvious."

"How?"

He scoffed, but there was little humour in it. "If you thought you were being subtle, you're a bigger idiot than I thought you were."

Fuck, I was drunk. I scrubbed a hand over my face. "Fuck."

"We all saw it. She's good for you. The last few weeks, I've barely seen you drink, you've been hyper focussed, and there's been something ever so less sarcastic about you."

My laugh was anything but humoured. "She's not some magic cure for my problems, Dev."

He nodded. "I know. I know it's more complicated than that. But that doesn't mean she doesn't help you want to do better."

I sighed. "Well, as nice as that is, it's irrelevant now."

"It's not irrelevant," Taylor said.

"It is. She hates me. I mean actually hates me, not just says she hates me. How do you even come back from a revelation like this?"

"You explain it to her."

I shook my head. "It's better this way. Now, I can't let her down any more than I already have."

"You're making a mistake, Riv."

I nodded, feeling the sarcastic self-defence kicking in. "Well, gotta be a first time for everything," I told him before draining my bottle pointedly.

"Mate, I love you, but this self-deprecating shit is gonna get real old."

And because I clearly wasn't done pushing away everyone I cared about, I told him, "Perfect timing. Now you don't need to choose between me or your sister."

Taylor growled in annoyance. "I'm not picking sides, arsehole. It's not you *or* Skye, it's you *and* Skye. We're family. We get pissed off with each other and we get over it. If you're not going to fight for my sister, then get the fuck over it and we'll all move on with our lives!"

"She's not the kind of person you just get over, Dev."

"Then fucking fight for her! Explain it to her. Tell her what happened. Don't let her imagination run wild, picturing you as some guy they'll make a serial killer documentary about in a few years' time."

I glared at him. "Because you clearly haven't thought much about it."

"Mate, I've spent too much time thinking about it. I spent years watching you, trying to see if you were going to succumb to the darkness we both know is in your blood. You danced on the fucking precipice for years but, for all the times you gave it temporary control, you never let it completely take over. You always came back to us, and you never touched bottom. Of course, I said I was worried about you corrupting my sister, but I thought that was just bullshit ribbing, a stupid – and in hindsight poor-taste – joke. I didn't know you loved her. Not romantically anyway. I never actually thought it was a possibility."

"It's better this way," I told him again.

"Except it's not! Because you're using this as an excuse to succumb, Riv! You and your self-fulfilling prophecy bullshit. You're not proving anything right; you're doing this to yourself."

I looked at him, wondering about his word choices. "Fuck, but you're your sister's brother, aren't you?"

"What's that supposed to mean?" he asked.

I shook my head. "Nothing."

"Are you going to pull your finger out?"

"No. She's better off without me."

"Oh, my fucking Lord. You're so fucking dramatic!"

I pulled my arm back but stopped myself from throwing the bottle at him just in time. "Just fucking leave it."

He nodded and I saw the wariness in his eyes. Wariness and love. I ignored the second bit. "Fine. I'll leave you to your wallowing, but don't come crying to me when you bounce back from this dark patch, and you want to know how to make amends. You burnt the bridge, Riv, you can work out how to rebuild it."

"It's better burnt."

"It's better burnt," he mocked. "Who even are you?" He gave me a disgusted head shake, then stormed out, slamming my door behind him.

"Good fucking riddance," I muttered as I flopped back onto my bed.

I couldn't say I remembered anything after that as – while I was being fucking dramatic – the maw yawned out of the dark and swallowed me whole.

♡ **21** ♡
Skye

It had been two weeks and I wasn't proud that I'd just given up on River. But, in my defence, he'd given up on me – us – first. So, really, I'd given it our best shot.

And I was going to keep telling myself that until I believed it. Or I died, which was more likely to come first.

Annoyingly, my brother took it upon himself to check in on me ALL the goddamned time. Tansy said it was because River wasn't letting him check in on him, and I didn't want to say she was right…but she was probably not wrong.

"You're miserable without him," Taylor said, during a check in as we both sat on my couch and pretended that Wii on my smaller TV and tiny couch in my even smaller apartment was anything like playing in the Chaser's mansion.

But I wasn't going to set foot in there ever again if I didn't have to.

I frowned, knowing it was useless to lie to him. "Of course, I am."

"Then go and be with him."

"I want to, Taylor, but…"

"But what?" my brother asked.

"But he killed someone. How do I be with a murderer?" It was my standard defence, because if I was rejecting River then he wasn't rejecting me.

Taylor sighed and sat next to me. "Did you ask him about it?"

"I asked and he admitted it."

Another sigh. "But did you ask him what happened? How he killed someone and yet he got into one of the most prestigious schools in the country?"

"Someone paid a lot of money to make it go away?" I guessed.

Taylor was clearly losing patience for my wilful self-denial, and I didn't blame him. "You know what he comes from, Skye. His family had nothing. Who would have paid to make that go away?"

I shrugged and I was pretty sure my brother wanted to thump the idiocy out of me. So did I, but I was too deep in it by now. Only road to travel was further in.

"Ugh," he grunted. "It shouldn't be my story to tell, but I think this once he'll give me a pass," he muttered to himself, then looked at me. "River killed his uncle in self-defence," he explained slowly like he was worried I wouldn't be able to follow.

"What?" I asked.

"Riv's dad and uncle were bad guys, Skye. Like, fucking bad. They'd drink themselves into oblivion and beat on their wives and kids. At nine, he had to sit by his mum's hospital bed just waiting for her to die from wounds they'd inflicted on her. The scar on Riv's back?"

I nodded.

"River's never been rock climbing. His dad put it there. But he weaves the tale that will get him the least sympathy. Almost ten years ago now, Riv's uncle tried…assaulting him. Riv fought back," Taylor continued. "In the fight, his uncle fell, hit his head, and died. In the ensuing legal battles, River was cleared of charges, his dad was put in gaol for all kinds of shit, and River decided he had to get out by any means necessary. He found soccer and he found me." Taylor took my hand. "He found us."

I could guess what kind of assault Taylor was talking about and my heart broke for River. I didn't blame him for his vices or his darkness with a past like that. All I could think was how well he functioned considering. I could only hope to be that strong if our lives had been reversed.

"He never said," was all I could say.

"Of course, he didn't," Taylor said kindly. "He didn't want you to look at him differently. The way you can't help but look at him now."

But I shook my head. "I love him, Tay."

"Wait, what?"

I took a deep breath. "I love him. A part of me has always loved him. I think…" I stood up abruptly and Taylor joined me. "I need to tell him," I said, my mind running too fast. "If I can just talk to him. Get him to talk to me. It always works. It has to work this time."

"You…" Taylor was obviously confused. "Sorry, catch me up. You heard the story I just told you and now need to tell Riv that you love him?"

I started nodding then paused. "Is that bad?" I asked.

He shook his head. "No. I just… I expected sympathy and 'poor Senor Pond Scum'. I thought you'd put him in the too hard basket and move on."

"Gee, thanks," I grumbled sarcastically, thumping him. "You think that highly of me?"

"I just figured, when he didn't fight for you, then maybe that was it. He'd lost his chance. Like, great you had the full picture, but nah."

My brother had a point. It was a good point. Why should I fight for a guy who wouldn't fight for me?

I knew why.

"Maybe River's fought enough," I told him. "Maybe it's time someone fought for him."

Taylor blinked like a stunned mullet.

"Are you going to disagree with me or tell me where you last saw him?" I asked.

Taylor snapped his mouth shut. "Home. I left him at home."

He hadn't even finished the sentence and I was running for the door. I ran the whole way to the soccer team's manor, past a surprised Lachy at the front door who let me right on in with no words exchanged. And I didn't stop until I burst through River's bedroom door.

Fuck this him avoiding me bullshit. I was going to make him talk to me.

He didn't even move or look at me.

"I told you to fuck off, Devo," he sighed. He sounded so tired. Like he wasn't just physically exhausted, but mentally and emotionally as well.

"I love you," burst out of me much the same way I'd just burst into his room.

Except that got slightly more of a reaction.

River leant up on his elbows and looked at me.

"Skye?" he asked.

I'll admit, I was a little deflated that I'd told him I loved him, and his answer was to check it was me. Like any number of girls would bust into his room and proclaim their love for him.

Actually, now that I'd mentioned it…

"I don't care how many girls have–"

"Please don't be another hallucination…" he begged as he sat up slowly. I tried not to get distracted by the shifting of his stomach muscles as he did it.

I paused. "What?"

He stood up and came over to me, taking my hand in his and laying it on his cheek. He closed his eyes and breathed deeply.

"You're here."

I nodded. "I'm here."

"Why are you here?"

"Why didn't you tell me the truth?"

His whole body tensed. His eyes flew open, and he dropped my hand like I'd suddenly scolded him. "Taylor told you?" Figures he'd guessed.

I nodded. "The better question is why didn't *you*?"

His eyes narrowed. "You didn't exactly give me a chance."

That was on me. "Fair. But that was two weeks ago, River. You could have told me since."

"Would it have made a difference?"

"It would have made all the difference!" I cried. "I should have heard you out, waited for an explanation, that's my fault. But River…" I took a breath. "I shouldn't have jumped to conclusions. I'm sorry. I am so sorry. But there's a darkness in you that–"

"Why do you think I resisted you for so long?" he asked, his voice raspy and choked. "I couldn't bear it if I hurt you."

This.

It was this. This that had always scared him. This that he'd always worried about. This that had made him try to push me away after that first night we spent together. Had he dreamt about it, and the reminder had made him want to protect me by pushing me away?

"You won't hurt me, River."

"You don't know that."

"I do know that. I know you."

"It was stupid of me to think you could be falling in love with someone like me," he scoffed, and I was sure he'd been drinking and wasn't really listening to me anymore.

He was doing what I'd been doing all week; wilfully ignoring the truth the evidence pointed to and making up a truth that had less power to hurt him.

I went over to him and made him look at me.

"Not just fall*ing*, River. Fall*en*. Totally. Utterly. Completely. I love you."

"Even with my past?" he asked, like he still couldn't believe it.

I wrapped myself around him. "You protected yourself. No one can fault you for that."

"Clearly someone did, or they wouldn't have told you about it."

"Maybe you could have told me about it and then Jax's jealousy wouldn't have come between us."

He dropped his head to mine. "I'm sorry."

I shook my head and looked into his eyes. "Don't be sorry. I know it wasn't something that I *had* to know, and you are allowed to keep things to yourself. Unless they could hurt us. Please don't hide things from me anymore if they could hurt us. Honesty, River. We got this far on it; I'd say it's pretty good for us."

"Would you?"

"Without it, this might have just been a couple of heated

kisses. We wouldn't have admitted we wanted each other, and we wouldn't have taken the time to see what this could be."

"What do you think we would have done?"

"You know what we would have done," I told him ruefully.

He nodded. "We'd have fucked far too quickly and then the uncertainty would have gnawed away at anything good we could have had, and we'd hate each other even more."

I nodded as well. "Exactly."

He breathed out heavily. "No more omissions," he promised.

"How many more are there?" I asked.

He shook his head. "None. That I can think of. That was it. I mean, there's the whole fucking Childhood of Horrors, but I'm not sure either of us need to relive that."

I nodded. "I don't think the specifics are likely to hurt us, are they?"

He wrapped me in his arms more tightly. "I can't see how." He kissed my temple. "I'm sorry," he said. "I was a fucking idiot."

I shook my head. "I should have trusted you."

"I don't blame you for not. Manslaughter's kind of a big deal."

I shivered and I felt him tense. I hugged him closer. "Not having second thoughts, just a simple human reaction."

I felt him nod. "No, of course."

I pulled away only so I could look at him. "River, I love you. I'm not going anywhere. Okay?"

He nodded but didn't look convinced.

"When did you last sleep properly?" I asked.

He shrugged. "I don't know. The night before the Hornets' game?"

I smiled softly and took his hand to lead him to the bed. He let me tuck him in and I climbed in next to him, sitting up on his pillows a little so he could snuggle into me.

I kissed his hair. "I'm not going anywhere. Sleep, baby."

He nuzzled into me. "I love you, Skye," he murmured, already sounding half-asleep. "So, fucking much."

I ran my hand over his head. "I love you, too."

"Can–"

"Shh," I said softly. "We'll talk tomorrow. Just rest."

Once his breathing was even, I pulled my phone out of my pocket and texted Tansy to let her know I was in River's room.

I'd, unthinkingly, left the door open, but Ajax was the first one to come past and he paused. He looked as dour and grumpy as usual, but he gave me a single nod and closed the door for me. If I didn't know him any better, I'd have said that there was a moment of relief in his eyes, like he knew that River was going to be okay after all.

22
River

When I woke up the next morning, I was convinced that I was still drunk as fuck because Skye was in my bed. She was asleep on my arm, explaining why it had lost most of its feeling.

As I tried to extricate myself, she stirred and looked up at me.

My heart felt like it had stopped as I waited to see what the moment would bring. I remembered most of the night before, but it felt like a dream. A very real dream that I wouldn't have believed were she not currently smiling up at me like nothing had changed between us.

"Calypso?" I said softly, like I was afraid she might not be real after all.

She stretched against me, and my cock stirred despite my reservations.

"Morning," she said gently. "How are you feeling?"

I blinked. "Uh… Confused mainly."

She grinned and rolled over, bringing her even closer to me. "About what?"

"Kind of everything?" I offered.

"Were you too drunk to remember last night?" she teased.

I shook my head. "No. No. More like it's kind of fuzzy. Like a dream. But I think that has less to do with the booze and more to do with the fact I just don't believe it."

"Well, believe it, baby. You're not getting rid of me that easily."

I shook my head. "I don't deserve you," I said as I leant my head to hers.

She pressed a kiss to my lips. "Yes," she said pointedly. "You do."

I had nothing more to say to that, so I just kissed her. I'd been intending it to be soft and somewhat chaste; I didn't expect her to feel like jumping me just after we'd reunited. But it didn't stay that way for long, and I wasn't sure I was the only one to blame for that.

Her arms wound around my neck as she kissed me hungrily. Her knee hugged my hip, pulling my body close to hers as she rocked against me.

"Shit," I murmured.

"What?" she asked.

"I didn't mean–"

She shook her head. "Do you not want to?"

I scoffed. "Not want to? Baby, I always want to. I just feel it's a bit disingenuous."

"A bit disingenuous to have sex with your girlfriend when you both want it?" she teased.

I couldn't help smiling at her tone. "You're still my girlfriend, then?"

"I haven't decided if it's still or again, but yes."

"You forgive me."

She nodded. "I forgive you. I've missed you. I just want to be with you, River."

I tried to tell myself I wasn't happier than I had a right to be. I tried to believe I had a right to be that happy.

"Fuck, I love you."

I felt her smile against my lips. "I love you, too."

She kissed me to distraction, dispelling all my worries and my fears and my inadequacies until there was nothing left but her and me.

My stamina was for shit, but I held on until I felt her clamp around me in pleasure and she'd moaned my name like it was a fucking prayer.

As I kissed her lazily after, she chuckled. "I've really missed you."

I felt myself smirk. "Just wait until round two, baby."

Her arms tightened around my shoulders and the smile was so deep in her eyes. "Looking forward to it."

It took me very little time to be ready for round two and, this time, my stamina was much more impressive. It wasn't quite the two hour marathon of our first night, but she didn't seem to be complaining.

In fact, her exact words were, "That was, like, really good." She gave me a piss-taking grin. "Five stars, baby."

I laughed and couldn't help but kiss her again. And again. And again. She was mine now and I was hers and, in her words, I wasn't going to let my insecurities get in our way again.

A few days later, Skye and I were walking across the quad when my phone started ringing. I picked it up, frowning at the unknown number.

"Hello?" I said.

"Is this Mr River Torres?" came a voice on the line.

"Uh, yes, this is Mr River Torres. Who is this?"

"I'm Dr Natalie Floyd at the Royal Adelaide. You're down as the emergency contact for Mr Gabriel Kane."

It took me a second to realise why that name sounded familiar. Then my blood went cold. "Sorry? Ajax?"

"Ah, no…" She paused like she was checking notes. "I have Gabriel Kane."

I nodded. "Yes, sorry. Ajax is a nickname."

"So, you do know Mr Kane?"

I swallowed hard. "Yeah. Yes. He's a friend. My captain."

Skye frowned at me, wondering what was going on. I shrugged.

"Mr Kane is in emergency."

"What? What happened?" I asked, starting to pace like that was going to help anything.

"He was in a car accident. His leg's in pretty bad shape. You said he was your captain? Is that military-related? There wasn't anything in his file."

"Uh, no," I said through the confusion. "No. Soccer captain. We play for Chester University."

"The Chasers," she said warmly, and I nodded dumbly.

I was numb. Ajax had been in a car accident? His leg was messed up? What the hell did that mean for his future? And somehow the doctor knew about the Chasers.

"That's us," I said, equally as dumbly.

"He must be quite good to be captain."

I was clearly not thinking straight because I was just going along with the conversation like there weren't far more important things to worry about. "The best. He's going pro overseas next season."

"Ah." That was not the good kind of 'ah'. "Well, we'll know more in a few hours. They're taking him in for surgery now. Are there any family members you should notify?"

I liked how the onus was on me. But no. "None he'd want notified," I told her.

"Okay. Well, you're down as his contact so we'll let you know when we have an update. Is this number okay?"

I nodded again. "Yeah. Yes, this number's perfect. Thanks."

"Thank you, Mr Torres. I'll speak to you again soon."

"Does…?" I started quickly before she had a chance to hang up. "Does anyone need to come in to be with him?"

I felt her sympathy through the fucking phone. My inexperience, my age – or lack thereof – shone brightly.

"Not just at the moment, no. Unless you want to."

I knew how Ajax would feel about us leaving uni and sitting by his bedside while he was unconscious. We'd all end up in emergency right alongside him for our troubles.

"Okay. Uh, well I guess we'll wait and see what happens?" I suggested, like I wanted her to tell me that was okay.

"Perfect. If you change your mind, you can just come right in. Call the main switchboard for visiting hours."

"Sure. I will. Thanks, Doc."

"Bye, Mr Torres."

She hung up and I dropped my phone from my ear.

"What's happened? Is he all right?" Skye asked.

I blinked at her. "Uh. Car accident. His leg is… She didn't sound all that optimistic about it. They're taking him into surgery now."

Skye took my hand. "I'm sure it's just too early to tell."

I nodded, my eyes were hot and there was a lump forming in my throat. All I could do was bundle her up and take comfort in her presence. Ajax's accident was just proof of how quickly everything could be taken away from you. The doctor may not have said the words, but it sounded a hell of a lot like she didn't think Ajax was going pro next season after all.

Career.

Love.

Life.

It could all be gone in the blink of an eye, and I wasn't going to waste it or take it for granted anymore. I finally had Skye and there were no more secrets between us. It was time to stop worrying about whether I was worthy and just fucking be worthy already. For her. For taking on the captaincy with Ajax injured. For not just passing my degree but getting good enough grades to stay on as long as I goddamned wanted to.

Coming up with a project I wanted to sit with for four years was going to be my only hurdle. I wasn't getting in my own way again.

"I love you," I told her firmly.

She hugged me tighter. "I love you, too." She rubbed my back. "Do you want to see him?"

I shook my head where it hung over her shoulder. "Not really. Is that awful?"

"I don't think so. For starters, he would pretend to be *so* pissed if you went in that it's really not worth the bother. But I also think he'd understand."

"Understand what?" I asked her.

"That you hate hospitals."

"I hate hospitals?" I stood up straight to look at her.

Her head was cocked, and she was looking at me like I was adorable. "Don't you?"

I blinked. "I've never really thought about it."

She nodded. "I remember when you were…fifteen? And you and Taylor decided to do that knife throwing thing for the talent show?"

Oh, shit. I remembered that, too. It was both unbearably tragic and fucking hilarious.

"And Taylor sliced me good?" I lifted my sleeve and there was the scar.

She smiled. "And you refused to go to the hospital. You said you'd rather sew it up with that weird paper and wool practice toy sewing kit I had than go to the hospital and you were bleeding everywhere, so Mum had to run up and down the street trying to remember where that doctor lived and ask them if they'd stitch you up."

I snorted. "And Taylor passed out as soon as the anaesthetic needle went in."

"And Mum spent the next year trying so hard to make it up Carol, that they became best friends." She sobered somewhat as she trailed her fingers over my cheek. "I heard you telling Taylor you weren't going back. Something about your mum. You sounded really scared."

My heart hitched in my chest. Yeah, I remembered exactly what she was referring to. I'd freaked the fuck out as soon as Mrs Devereux had mentioned the hospital. All I could see was Mum. Bleeding. Broken. Dying. The noise of the machines. The dry, sterile smell. The weird air. That feeling of being alone but surrounded by people who had better things to worry about.

I shuddered, just thinking about it.

Skye was right. I hated hospitals, I'd just never really put it into cogency before.

But I wasn't going to dwell on a depressing past I couldn't change. "You've known this about me for like six years and never said anything?"

She shrugged. "Of course, not."

"You could have wiped the floor with me."

She shrugged again. "Yeah. I could have. But I didn't."

I shook my head as I wrapped my arms around her waist. "I always loved that about you."

"What?"

"That you were witty and sassy and never put up with my shit, but you were never mean."

She smirked. "Maybe I was scared of how mean you could get if I opened that can of worms."

I nodded, knowing who I was. "Fair. But I probably wouldn't have meant any of it."

"It's not always the truth that cuts deepest, River, but the intent."

I swallowed. "I know."

She lay her hand on my chest and stared at it. "Like not telling me about your uncle. It hurt that you didn't trust me, but I know it wasn't *just* self-preservation."

"It wasn't?"

She shook her head. "No. Well, yes. But you weren't just scared of how I'd react, or of it messing us up. You were scared of having to talk about it. You didn't know how to – the feelings are messy and muddled and confusing – so it was easier not to. And that's okay."

Yet again, I marvelled how she knew me so well. She knew me better than I wanted to know myself.

"It shouldn't be okay. I shouldn't have been scared of talking to you about it."

Her smile was full of love and support. "You shouldn't have to talk about it before you're ready."

"Do you…? I started, looking down. "Do you think it would help? To talk about it?"

"I don't know. I think it would help me, but we are thankfully not the same person."

I looked up at her through my hair and grinned. "Thankfully? You too good to be me?"

She pressed her body into mine. "No. It would just be a lot more difficult to hook up if we were the same person."

I nodded. "Sensible. Intelligent. Very goddess-like, Calypso."

She patted my chest. "As much as I'd like to go back to someone's bed and put that to the test… Do you need to tell the rest of the team about Ajax?"

Fuck. "Yes. Thanks, baby." I pressed a kiss to her lips and pulled up the team chat.

Torres
Team meeting in half an
hour. Red card.

"Red card?" Skye asked, looking over my shoulder.

I nodded. "Red card's our way of saying it's super fucking important. It apparently evolved from and old captain who used to threaten the players with being benched – so kind of like being carded – for the next game if they didn't turn up because it was *that* important. Over time, it just became known as a red card situation."

She nodded as the notifications started pouring in from the team. Most of them just 'liked' the message, but at least I knew they hadn't accidentally opened the app and not seen the message.

"That's kind of cool," she said.

I smiled. "It is kind of cool."

She came back to the mansion with me, Richard be damned, and held my hand while we waited for the team to arrive.

"If you tell us you're getting married, I might be ill," Taylor said when he saw us.

"That's not red card worthy," Forbsy said, having my back. "That's dinner at Dolce's and too many bottles of Sparkling worthy."

"We're not getting married." I smirked. "Yet."

Skye squeezed my hand. "Yeah, we'll talk about that later, Pond Scum."

"Gladly," I replied, squeezing her hand back.

When everyone was present, expect Ajax, I stepped forward.

"Wait, where's Ajax?" Hank asked and they all looked around as though sure they'd seen him.

I cleared my throat. "Yeah, that's the red card. I got a call from the hospital. Ajax is in Royal Adelaide after a car crash. It doesn't sound good."

"He's going to die?" Whistler cried.

I held up my hands. "No. Fuck. Sorry. No. For his career. Fuck! Sorry. Doc said his leg was messed up. She'll call when they know more, but she didn't sound optimistic about him going overseas next year."

The team were understandably all concerned.

"Let's collect up some cash and we'll get him something nice that he'll love to hate," I said over the hubbub.

The team nodded.

"Can we skive on training tonight then, Cap?" Frankie D asked.

I put on my best Ajax grumpy face. "Fuck, no."

The tension eased somewhat, and we hung out for a little while longer to come up with what we wanted to send Ajax before heading back to classes or whatever else we had going on for the rest of the day when we seemed to all naturally gravitate to each other's company.

♡ **23** ♡
Skye

I spent more time at the Chasers mansion in the next couple of days than I probably usually would have. I got no work done and knew a mild panic attack was waiting for me over how much work I had to do.

Once I knew Ajax was out of the woods.

He didn't wake up for what felt like years but, when he finally did, the doctor called River as promised.

A bunch of us were hanging out in one of the lounges, where we pretty much had been since the night we got the news, trying to take our minds off the worst case scenario and eating way too much pizza. There was comfort in being all together and we'd spent the previous few days basically having one big, unending sleepover.

River kissed me, slid out from under me and headed into the hallway when his phone rang. The rest of us pretended we were paying attention to the competition going on the console while we waited for him to return.

"Hospital?" Taylor asked when River walked back in.

River nodded. "That was the doctor. She said Ajax is going to be fine. I heard him in the background asking her to redefine 'fine' when he wasn't going to be able to go pro after all. He also wanted her to tell us that he 'fucking hates the flowers, you wankers'. He sounds his usual chipper self."

I grimaced. "It sounds bad."

He sighed. "It does sound bad. He's apparently got like a year of rehab to do, not to mention the fact he has to re-evaluate his whole fucking life now."

"What's he planning to do? Does he know?"

"We all have contingencies," Taylor said. "Some of us are planning on those being our future, the rest of us hope we won't have to deal with it until we're in our forties, or later."

"What's Ajax's contingency?" I asked.

River rubbed the back of his head. "Coaching the Chasers while he gets his PhD."

"Coach'll die of excitement to have Ajax alongside him," Taylor said with a smile, but there was a hint of sadness to it, and I knew he was mourning Ajax's career ending before it began, possibly almost as much as Ajax himself.

"Yeah, but we'll just plain die from all the shit he'll put us through in training," Hank said.

"And we'll all be the better for it, yadda, yadda," my brother replied.

"Four years, Dev," River added. "A PhD goes for four fucking years."

"Like you're not planning on doing one so you can stay here with Skye," Frankie D laughed.

River shrugged, all cocky nonchalance. "I've got a plan. Drag it out. Work my way up. No shortcuts. Honours. Masters. Second Masters, why not. PhD. Post-grad."

"I'll be done before you," I said with a smile.

River grinned. "She should *always* finish first."

The other guys weren't the only ones groaning at his

innuendo. I shook my head.

"You want them to add more time to your sentence for bad behaviour?" I asked.

"A year," Taylor said with a nod. "You get a year of the G-sting."

River shrugged again. "Sure. It'll be an easy-breezy summer."

I closed my eyes, but all I could see was River in a G-sting, so I opened them again. "I don't need the whole school seeing practically every single part of my boyfriend for longer than necessary," I reminded him.

"Like they haven't already seen it," Taylor scoffed, and River thumped him.

I could smile and see the joke in it. Yeah, it was probably also pretty true. But River was mine now. I didn't care what was in his past. That past was what made him the person he was, the man I loved. The good bits, the bad bits, the annoying bits, the unsavoury bits, and the charming bits. I couldn't erase any of them and say with any surety that we'd be standing here together.

So, I wouldn't begrudge him his past. Not the drinking, the girls, the fights.

But I also wouldn't say no when he decided to try to make it up to me in the privacy of one of our bedrooms.

We went back to our games with more brevity than we'd had and there was a generally lighter mood to the whole Chasers' mansion from that moment on. Of course, it helped that River was only about half as grumpy a captain as Ajax was. He did try his damnedest to live up to Ajax's reputation, but he just didn't have it in him.

Still Ajax came back to campus before the end of the year and, while he was obviously not playing, he was back in the mansion where he belonged. And, despite being even quicker to anger and dropping even more f-bombs than he used to, he seemed genuinely happy to be back again.

And River and I kept taking things one day at a time.

He started therapy, claiming he just wanted to learn how to talk to me better. I didn't much care what he said his reasons were, if he thought that it would help – or just wanted to see if it would – then I was going to be supportive. I'm not sure how much help it was, because things always seemed better when we were together. We weren't a fix for each other, but we made getting through it less daunting.

We had what happily ever afters were made of, and I could see it happening. It was something we both, in the moment, wanted. But we were young, it was new, and only time would tell if we could stick it out for the long haul.

Of course, when River offered me a ring four years later and I accepted, we were older, more mature, wiser, smarter. Well, one out of four ain't bad.

He still annoyed me. He still teased me. He still got on my nerves, and I occasionally wanted to throttle him. We argued, over important and stupid things. But we talked. We were honest. And we got through everything.

River Torres would be the guy I would always love…'til death.

THE END

Read on if you want to know more about the future of the Chester University Chasers.

Chester University Chasers

If you enjoyed *Love to Hate You*, share the love and let me know! You might be just the voice the sequel needs to get off the ground. There's a whole team of players ready to explore and, if there's enough demand, I will supply.
(Tentative title ideas only, atm. And more.)

Prince of Thorns

If you liked *Love to Hate You*, you might also enjoy *Prince of Thorns*. A New Adult darker, enemies-to-lovers, academy, romance. Get it here: https://books2read.com/u/bryaD7

From Elizabeth Stevens, writing as E.J. Knox, comes...
The bad boy willing to risk everything – even his life – to get the girl.

People call them the V.I.C.E.S. because they'll wring you for everything you are and leave you ruined. They are the Princes of Rosewood Hall, and no one says no to them. Until now.

Vaughn Saint. The racer. He dubbed the Prince of Thorns. Pretty as a rose, but one touch and he'll leave you bleeding.

He chases death on two wheels at least twice a week. Used to controlling powerful things between his thighs, nothing is more powerful than the lure of the pleasures he promises.

And he wants to give them all to me. Only problem? I'm the daughter of the leader of the Blood Roses. His leader. I'm off-limits. Dad wants me to walk away from all that, not get dragged down deeper into their hell, but Vaughn Saint threatens to take me to the very depths and still have me begging for more. Loving me will kill him.

Not loving me will destroy the both of us.

Reign

If you liked *Love to Hate You*, you might also enjoy *Reign*. A New Adult darker, academy/high school, bully romance. Get it here: https://books2read.com/u/4D6Qa7

From Elizabeth Stevens, writing as E.J. Knox, comes…

A King. An Heir. And the unwilling pawn with the power to win or crush a Royal coup.

Beckett Maxwell reigns over Rivermont Academy with his loyal court: the Royals, their courtiers, their harem. He doesn't have time for a nobody like me: a scholarship student and daughter of faculty to boot. I'm the lowest of the low in a school full of highs.

One year everything's going fine. Enough. The next, I'm some pawn in a Royal power struggle. Well, I won't have it. They can bully me, they can torment me, they can make my life miserable. But I will not be used in one of their twisted games.

But when the fox is lurking at the door, sometimes the only safety is in the arms of the lion. Beckett might actually be the lesser evil in this case. And I can't deny there's something between us. Something I wish wasn't there.

The closer we get, the further he pushes me away, but something keeps pulling me back. When it comes to Beckett Maxwell, I'm a sucker for punishment.

But I'll only bear it so long. If Beckett wants his claim on me to stick, then he might need to choose between his crown and my heart.

Accidentally Perfect

If you liked *Love to Hate You*, you might also enjoy *Accidentally Perfect*. A Mature Young Adult enemies-to-lovers, high school, romance. Get it here: https://books2read.com/u/bxZaLP

Sometimes, you say everything when you say nothing at all.

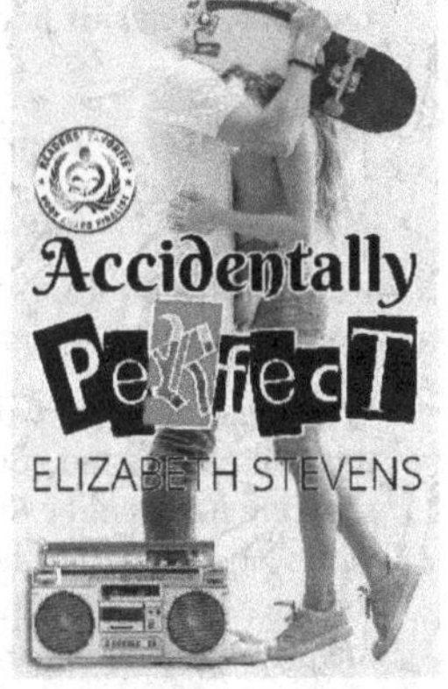

Everyone's convinced the hottest guy in school's going to ask me out – that Mason and I would be the perfect couple, that he's my John Cusack. Except, he hasn't.

One holidays, I find myself hanging out with the resident underachiever, and he surprises me. With Roman, I don't have to pretend that little Piper Barlow is perfect; even if we're both in a foul mood, just sitting in silence together is perfectly enough. Until it becomes more.

But, Roman doesn't do more. Does he…?

What do you do when you accidentally find perfection with the wrong guy?

You fight for it.

Being Not Good

If you liked *Love to Hate You*, you might also enjoy *Being Not Good*. A Mature Young Adult, opposites attract, high school, romance. Get it here: https://books2read.com/u/b5r9Pp

If you don't like a smattering of serious on a bed of satire, clichéd characters, and over the top situations that know exactly what they are, then this book is definitely not for you.

What do you get when you introduce Deadpool's personality to Giselle's? If you answered a love story for the ages, you wouldn't be totally wrong… But, you wouldn't be totally right, either.

With a heroine who won't let a stupid little thing like being too good get in the way of showing her stupid ex what's what and a hero who wants no part of being the male lead in a romance novel, these two opposites find themselves in an unconventional partnership.

When peppy-go-lucky Avery eventually wears down bad-to-the-bone Davin's defences, he agrees to help her trash her reputation. And if Davin can help her pass math while he's at it, all the better. So it's goodbye to Little Miss Goody-Two-Shoes and hello to a whole new Avery.

Davin was only supposed to be Avery's mistake – the guy that everyone would eventually call her 'little phase' – and he figured it would be good for a laugh when he looked back on it. But the more they're together, the less either of them feel it's a mistake.

Now if only one of them could mention that to the other and ease all that angst-ridden tension…

A laugh-out-loud modern-day fairy-tale told in dual POV for those who know life never quite goes according to plan.

Love to Hate You

Thank you so much for reading this story! Word of mouth is super valuable to authors. So, if you have a few moments to rate/review Skye and River's story – or, even just pass it on to a friend – I would be really appreciative.

Have you looked for my books in store, or at your local or school library and can't find them? Just let your friendly staff member or librarian know that they can order copies directly from LightningSource/Ingram.

If you want to keep up to date with my new releases, rambles and writing progress, sign up to my newsletter at https://landing.mailerlite.com/webforms/landing/y1n6q2.

Follow me:

Thanks

Like many of the books that came before it, this one is not at all what I expected. But, unlike many of those other books, this one is so much more.

To my newest penname to join the fray, welcome and thank you. I wasn't sure if this one was right for your first official book, or if you should co-write it with Elizabeth Stevens, or what, but we got there in the end, and I think we did a good job. We certainly did better than my first attempt at full-on New Adult. I hope.

A massive thank you to those of you brave enough to give this a try after the debacle that was my previous foray into New Adult. God, I hope it was worth it. I certainly had such an amazing time writing it and I love it.

I'd like to extend my gratitude to Finland's atomic brussel sprout. It's been stuck in my head all week. You were robbed. Robbed, I say. And I *will* die on that hill.

Thanks, as always, to Kaity and your invaluable help in wrangling my ideas into shape. Our chats are always a highlight, even if I forget to reply.

And to my friends, family and miscellaneous loved ones; thank you for letting me be me, and accepting and loving the chaos gremlin I am.

My Books

Pippa's list is just getting started, but you can find out about what I have planned at my website, as well as have a look at my older YA books; www.elizabethstevens.com.au.

About the Author

Pippa Langhorn is the New Adult/Adult Contemporary Romance penname of bestselling author Elizabeth Stevens. Pippa is the name to read if you want New Adult/Adult Contemporary Romance. Think university, workplace, and the general awkwardness life. Pippa brings my usual wit, banter, and repartee in good old rom-com fashion. There'll be fake-dating, enemies, friends, love triangles, weddings, second chances, and more.

Writer. Reader. Perpetual student. Nerd.

Born in New Zealand to a Brit and an Australian, I am a writer with a passion for all things storytelling. I love reading, writing, TV and movies, gaming, and spending time with family and friends. I am an avid fan of British comedy, superheroes, and SuperWhoLock. I have too many favourite books, but I fell in love with reading after Isobelle Carmody's *Obernewtyn*. I am obsessed with all things mythological – my current focus being old-style Irish faeries. I live in Adelaide (South Australia) with my long-suffering husband, delirious dog, mad cat, two chickens, and a lazy turtle.

<u>Contact me:</u>
Email: pippalanghorn@elizabethstevens.com.au
Website: www.elizabethstevens.com.au/pippa-lanhorn
Twitter: www.twitter.com/writer_iz
Instagram: www.instagram.com/writeriz
Facebook: https://www.facebook.com/elizabethstevens88/